Seducing Sensei

(Notice Me Senpai, Book 1)

By

S.N. McKibben

www.trollriverpub.com
Seducing Sensei
(Notice Me Senpai) Book 1
Copyright © 2017 S.N.McKibben
Artist: Zoe Coughlin
Editors: Estee Marie, Amy Nedrow
ISBN: 978-1-946454-19-5

Join the fun with Author S.N.McKibben for giveaways, updates and new release opportunities at: http://eepurl.com/bAfZR5

Dedication

This is where I call out all the awesome people that shaped this story into what it is today. This book would have been very different had it not been for a few precious beta readers and editors acting as beta readers. Rox, Rachel, Teresa, Marilyn, Mom, Dave, Tbird, Kec, Connor, RL and Madeline. You shaped this into what it is. I think you helped me make it better. You helped me be a better writer. Thank you.

Chapter 1

Of all the schools to substitute teach, coming back to my own high school was a surprise. Now, at twenty-three, it felt strange wearing my best Oxford shoes, Nordstrom slacks, and Calvin Klein button-up shirt and tie in the hallways of my old stomping ground.

What was freakier was my old shop teacher smiling at me from down the crowded hall. This time, I wasn't his student, but a fellow teacher. Mr. Goyas was a bear of a man. Height-wise my old shop teacher was larger than any of the students. His vertical stature only served to make him stand out even more.

Mr. Goyas waved me down from across the hall of passing students. Old habits overcame my sense. My cheeks warmed a little. Like a puppy, I wagged my proverbial tail and rushed right over to him. I'd liked him even way back, when I took his class. But I wouldn't dare tell him that.

"Hey, Mori," Mr. Goyas said. "Thanks for letting me borrow these." He returned the red-handled pair of wire cutters I'd given him. For a brief, fleeting moment his fingers brushed my palm. My heart gave a thump. *Oh, stop that. He's married.* Meaning, Mr. Goyas was straight. Not gonna happen.

"You're welcome," I said. "Didn't think I'd have to loan out my cutters. Especially to the mechanics specialist."

Mr. Goyas laughed. "Mine keep getting swiped. I had to pocket yours so they wouldn't get taken."

His deep, slow-cadent chuckle reverberated inside me down to my toes. "Oh, I see how it is," I said. "You just want to get to know my wire cutters better. You haven't changed." *Shit. Stop flirting.* I really must get a boyfriend. Chastity was a bitch I wanted to break up with in the worst way.

Mr. Goyas ruffled my brown hair. The ends of my strands tickled my thin chin-strap beard.

"Hey!" I combed fingers through my brown shoulder-length locks. "I'm not your student anymore. Give me some respect."

He shook his head and chuckled. "How are those seniors treating you?"

Ugh. He had to remind me. Most the students were fine. Only one gave me problems. "They're okay." I shrugged off the reminder of Itsuma.

"Don't let 'em get the better of you." Mr. Goyas patted my head. "It might be summer make-ups, but that's no reason to be soft on 'em."

"Riiight." I waved at him to stop touching my hair. Mr. Goyas, being a shop teacher, taught the fun classes. Every guy wanted to take wood-working or metal shop. His class was perfect for those who wanted a few extra points to make sure they graduated. On the other hand, teaching algebra to a bunch of kids who didn't want to be wasting their summer on math was a challenge.

"Maybe next time you can teach gym." He smirked.

"Not gonna happen." I'd only taken this gig as a favor to my dad, who was friends with Principal Ellis—the head of this fine school. "I'll be teaching as an assistant professor at CIT after the summer."

"Congratulations." The warning bell sounded and Mr. Goyas turned and waved. "Thanks again."

Like a dolt, I just stared at his backside mentally drooling while he walked away. *Snap out of it, Mori.*

Cerilia High School was going to kill me.

This place didn't have bad memories, just lonely ones. My old friends would be surprised if they knew that's how I felt, but it was true. When I was a pupil here, for all I knew, I was the only gay student on campus. At the time I was co-captain of the wrestling team and, with one exception, I didn't say a word about my attraction to men. Everyone blamed my virginity on the fact that I was a raving study freak.

I made up for lost time chasing boys in college. Didn't matter if they were gay, curious straights or dedicated bisexuals. Anything male was fair game. While experimenting, I found out I was a top, a bottom and everything in between. On the downside I could not get it up for girls in any way, shape or form. But that was okay. I'd already accepted it back in junior high and moved on. College was fun, and I was glad to have gotten the crazy sex out of my system, because I was teaching now. Time to settle down, find a good man and concentrate on work.

Sighing, I pocketed my wire cutters, turned down the hall and went to my classroom. Mr. Goyas brightened my dismay. I wasn't looking forward to homeroom. The reason—Itsuma Karter. My personal hellion and troublemaker, class clown, ring leader, jailbait agitator. Well, he was technically legal, but trouble all the same.

The bell rang and Itsuma strolled in like a tomcat who'd been laid the night before. *Jealous much?* I sighed.

Itsuma was wearing his infuriating iPod earplugs while in class. Again. For the past week I'd been asking him to leave the MP3 player in his bag. School rules dictated that any devices were to be shut off during school hours. I was within my rights to yell at him for breaking the policy, but I didn't care during homeroom, usually.

Smoothing down my imperial mustache, I started roll call.

"Lori Rogers," I said.

"Here."

"Jake Rayier."

"Present."

"Pierre Gaskal."

"Good morning."

I went down, concentrating on the list. Granted, I must have sounded like a bored baby sitter, but the difference between here and university was a world of difference. Especially in student attitude. College at least had some students with a semblance of paying attention.

"Itsuma Karter," I said.

Nothing.

I kept my eyes on the roster, trying not to lose my place on the list. I wasn't great at names and faces. Something I was trying to work on.

"Itsuma?"

No answer. I looked up. Itsuma's hand was propped under his chin while he stared out the window.

Damn it. Yes, I knew he was here. Yes, I should let it go. But the blatant disrespect made my shit flip. "Itsuma?" *Just fucking answer.*

Across the way, in the seat next to him, Scott Cooper waved at his classmate, trying to gain his attention. Itsuma even ignored his friend. That was it. Who did he think he was? Why the fuck was it so hard to just respond to a roll call? Hell, right now, I'd even take an *up yours* as an answer. And I hated losing my place on the roster.

"Itsuma!" Standing up, I rounded my desk, put my hands in my pockets and made my way towards my problem child. Students leaned away from me as I barreled down the aisle.

iPod in hand, Itsuma continued to stare outside, acting like he didn't see me. If he thought he could act like a prick and then turn innocent and gracious like he did yesterday, he was in for a surprise.

I pulled the wire cutters out of my pocket, snipped the cord and snatched the MP3 player out of his hand.

Itsuma jerked his head, and in that split-second I saw the molten hate within his pupils. I expected him to scream back, call me nasty names and threaten me with bodily harm. He did nothing but sit there. The darkness in his expression chilled. Fast as a flick he smiled like everything was okay.

"Itsuma Karter," I said. "At least respond to your name."

"Yes, Mr. Reis. Sorry about that." Itsuma batted his eyelashes.

Not buying it. His blasé faire attitude made me want to smack him. Was he just going to pretend everything was hunky-dory even though I'd annihilated his personal property? The school allowed confiscating electronic items. Destroying them—not so much.

I'd never yelled at a student before. Granted, I'd only been substituting for the last week, but I never raised my voice, even back when my wrestling teammates were screwing around and cost us a victory.

Itsuma was the first person that got under my skin. What was I doing? Trying to start a fight?

I walked back to my desk, dropped both the cutters and the iPod mess in my desk drawer and finished roll call. Other than responses of "present" or "here" the class was dead silent. No clicks. No sounds of fingers tapping on phones they shouldn't be on. No socializing. No scratching of pens on paper. No desperate attempts to finish last night's homework. I might even dare say some students were making a valiant effort not to breathe. Shit. I was so fired. Fucking Itsuma. Why did I snap like that?

When I was done with roll call I met those chilled, narrowed, dark eyes and said, "You can retrieve your things at the end of school."

"Thank you, Sensei." Itsuma smiled like a shark. His tone of voice implied anything except respect.

We would have a chat after school if he had the guts to get his stuff. Maybe by then I could pinpoint exactly what made me go ballistic on the kid.

Chapter 2

After homeroom, I calmed down. I felt like a heel. A part of me was angry at myself for losing it. That wasn't like me. Voted as most laid-back eight years ago, at this very school, there wasn't much that could get me to blow a cork.

To redeem myself I ran over to the nearest electronics store during break and bought a replacement for Itsuma's broken earphones. I got him a matching color for his iPod. Metallic blue. After lunch, I hadn't given the scene much thought until, at around three o'clock, both Itsuma and Scott Cooper walked into my classroom.

My little troublemaker owned the space when he walked in. One might have mistaken him for a Japanese prince of some small, unknown province. Only royalty of a tiny country would have that much self-admiration. *Don't hurt yourself squeezing your ego inside the room.*

Standing with feet firmly placed as if he were on the first-place winner's podium stand, Itsuma exuded energy and confidence. I glanced at him with what I hoped was my best disparaging look.

Behind him, Scott Cooper twirled a wrangler's rope with expert precision. The loop circled Scott in meticulous up-and-down motions. He danced a cowboy's jig with the rope as if he'd been born to raise cattle. With those boots, jeans, button shirt and cowboy hat he should be on the back of a horse, not in a classroom. Bringing in the rope was odd, but hell if I knew what high school kids liked these days.

Scott looked at me with those beautiful green eyes, effortlessly continuing his rope hopscotch. His eyes weren't those of a child, but of a man who'd seen a lifetime of evil and decided he was here to save everyone. It was heart shattering to look into his soul, and yet, Scott instilled hope in my heart. Like a survivor, he threw off an air that people could overcome the worst of times. As if he were living proof.

In contrast, Itsuma's inflated ego and Cheshire smile set off all my warning bells. I wasn't afraid. Inwardly, I was reprimanding the chubby that sprang as soon as the duo stepped across the threshold of my classroom. I'd waited way too long to find a partner. Maybe after this I'd go to the bar to relax. Find someone to help keep my head on around this jailbait of mine. That was it… I just needed to let out this frustration.

I stood, pulled out my drawer of no-no's and set out Itsuma's iPod on my desk. Then I placed the two pieces of his headphones next to the small chunk of metal.

"If I take this again," I said, "you're not getting it back." I pulled out the new package of earbuds and set them next to his equipment.

Itsuma picked up the unopened accessory, then laughed like I'd told the best joke he'd ever heard. "Sensei, you sly fox."

The sound of his mirth tickled my heart. Craptastic.

Itsuma wiped the amused tear under his eye and said, "I was wondering why a math teacher would have wire cutters in his pocket. You planned this from the start."

"What? No!" *Had I?* "I bought the new headphones at break." I thought the gesture would soothe any harsh words he might throw my way. "The wire cutters were just coincidence."

Scott stopped his deliberation, folded up the lasso and sat on one of the student desk tops. *Pull up a chair and some popcorn. This should be a fun show, cowboy.*

"Thank you for replacing my property, but I want something for my pride." Itsuma twirled the package and tossed it on my desk.

My mouth ran off before I could think. "Great. The high and mighty emperor gets ass-hurt for being called out for his lousy attitude."

"Scott," Itsuma said. Molten lava burned in The Prince's eyes. "Close the doors."

The cowboy stiffened and stood up. "Zuma, come on, man."

Something about Scott's plea heated my blood. He might have been speaking to his friend, but it was almost as if he were telling me to run.

"No," Itsuma said. "I won't be humiliated. I want a piece of my honor back."

Japanese and their honor. No *out* for me. That was fine. *Let's go.*

One moment Itsuma was grinning like an innocent fool, and the next battle-ready eyes pierced my soul. He spread his legs out like a mixed martial arts master and lowered himself to fighting stance.

This kid's capability to go from normal to death-con five was a bit unnerving. But if he thought I was his bitch, he was in for a surprise. I wasn't the co-captain of the wrestling team in my day because I waved pom-poms around.

From behind my desk I assessed the challenger. I may be a typical white-boy math geek, and I was, but I was not your average nerd that sat on my ass all day. His provocation pulled at my dignity. *Fine. I'll be your huckleberry.* I rolled up my sleeves and rounded the desk.

"Zuma!" Scott said.

"Stay out of it." Itsuma came at me with a power strike. He'd had training. His form remained balanced. He was also fast.

I dodged the strike, a side kick and a few flying fists.

My specialty was up close and personal. At the moment I was at a disadvantage. All I could do was block and dodge until I could find my opening. That was okay. Let him tire himself out. The kid was smart, though. He realized I was trying to get closer and he pushed me back with his flying feet. Just one more fancy spin and I'd have him. Oh, fuck yeah. This was as much fun as Nationals. Having Itsuma as a dancing partner freaking turned me on. He was awesome. His form beautiful. I could watch him for hours making these high flying, black-belt moves.

The Little Prince was energy incarnate. Still I smiled, dodged, blocked and watched his technique. Then it was my turn. I couldn't say he made a mistake, just that he must have thought I didn't have any offensive tactics. Maybe he thought I'd trained in Judo. I wasn't that passive.

Finally, I snuck in from behind when he went for a side kick. With a head lock I crumpled Itsuma like a piece of paper. My hands clasped together while he tried to finish his fancy spin.

"Give up," I said. "You won't win."

"Fuck you," Itsuma spat out.

"Do you yield?"

"Hell no." Itsuma struggled.

We grappled, but every move he made I anticipated. I kept him locked down. He wasn't going anywhere. "If you don't yield," I said, "you'll force me to choke you out." Not that I would. He might be legal, but he was still a kid.

"No," Scott said. "You won't." The rough leather of a lasso clenched down around my ankle. "You will not hurt my friend." He yanked my leg.

Standing wasn't an option. He'd pull my balance from under me. I went down on my right ass cheek. Itsuma gasped for air. Shit. That was a new one. I was going to get beat to hell.

Scott started pulling me towards him. With all my effort I scampered on my butt with flailing arms and legs, across the tile floor, past metal desk legs, and crammed myself against the closed door.

Gasping, Itsuma grabbed his neck. I expected him to be a raging ball of fury. But he wasn't so gung-ho on going after me anymore. The kid was proving that my expectations of him were backwards. He stared at me with a gleam of respect in his eyes.

Itsuma rounded behind Scott, putting me and the rope on his left side. Shit. I watched him come towards me, all the while thinking of defensive scenarios to execute.

I needn't have thought about fighting at all. Itsuma squatted five feet in front of me and raked a heated glance over my body. When his sights focused on my middle he smirked and leaned forward on his hands. My hard-on was undeniable.

"Aren't you going to scream, Sensei?" Itsuma planted a palm down on the tile floor and crawled toward me. Pft. As if going slow would prevent me from noticing his advance.

"Why would I?" My heart thumped faster. After six months of chastity my body was desperate enough to construe any attention into an invitation. *Damn it. This is not what I should be thinking about.*

When he grabbed my leg above the ankle my cock jumped. Ridiculous. Getting hard for such a jack-ass. But his grip wasn't threatening. On the contrary, he placed his other hand around the back of my knee, which made me very uncomfortable. "Um, Itsuma…"

"Check the hall," Itsuma said to his friend.

Scott gathered the rope as he walked toward the door, making sure the line to my leg was taut, and looked out the window. "It's clear."

Great. I didn't expect much traffic, but there were still people around.

"Go ahead, Sensei," Itsuma said. "Scream as loud as you can. There's no one around."

"Let me go before you both regret it." It wasn't a threat. I was more concerned about how this looked if someone came in and saw us. Although—a teacher strung up by two students—the blame would probably still be on me.

Itsuma laughed. Scott didn't. I was worried for the cowboy's sanity. The kid's wounded eyes carried the look of a tormented soul. He reminded me of the delicate type who'd bear all kinds of atrocities but sob at any tenderness shown him. I wanted to hug him all the more. Tell him I was alright. That Itsuma wasn't scaring me in the least.

These thoughts were funny, considering my predicament. But the snot-nosed Japanese Prince didn't frighten me. For all of his big talk and huge pride, Itsuma wasn't the type to really want to hurt anyone. I'd known his kind. It was all bluster covering insecurities. In Itsuma's case, unnecessary self-doubt. The five-foot-eight-inch inferno of sexuality could get any girl he wanted. He was smart as a whip, and even I was affected by his charm and presence.

No, Itsuma only wanted to have fun and get his "Sensei" bewildered so he wouldn't lose face. Scott was only covering for his friend. Neither one of them was malicious, despite what it looked like.

Scott wrapped the rope around the push bar of the door and kept a connection between my leg, the metal bar and him so that I was comfortable, but pinned. Itsuma jumped on me like a playful Akita ready to test a new toy. He knocked the wind out of my lungs as he straddled me. I tried sucking in breaths and got a mouthful of Itsuma.

Stunned, I didn't react right away. As I gasped for air, his tongue rolled inside my mouth. My mind went blank for a moment. He was an amazing kisser. How could I not react? This was exactly what I needed, and exactly not the person to give it to me. *What the fuck am I doing?* I bit down on his tongue.

"Ow!" Itsuma pulled back. "Fucker bit me."

"Itsuma, stop!" I said.

"Come on, man," Scott said. "That's enough."

Itsuma turned to Scott. "Jealous?"

Scott's face turned red.

Itsuma's winning smile emerged. "Sensei, why are you so hard?" He rotated his hips, crushing my cock between his thighs.

Because you're hot and on top of me. Shit. Don't say that. Don't react. I gritted my teeth and closed my eyes. That made it worse. "It's a natural reaction," I whimpered. Oh yeah, that was convincing. "It's the fighting getting my blood flowing."

"I could believe that if you weren't hard as a rock." Itsuma ground his hips, hitting me where I needed it most. For fuck's sake, I'd come if he didn't get off me.

Gasping, I blurted out, "Stop!" I managed to push him away. Every ounce of battle-ready instincts were brought forth. This situation was becoming too much like the one time with Kai.

"Sensei, are you gay?" Itsuma's annoying smile burned brighter.

"No way," Scott whispered. The kid holding me fast stared at my hard lump and swallowed. That's when I knew. They were both like me. Or at least they liked men. I was one hundred percent homosexual, and these two were fulfilling an ultimate fantasy. One I couldn't partake in. But a sexy cowboy and a hot martial artist? How could I keep from sprouting a kick-stand? Because this was wrong.

Being the best in my wrestling class meant there were not many who could get the better of me. Those who could held a special place in my heart. But I'd managed to always keep myself under control. Never showing amorous affection. It was that damn kiss that flipped my switch. *Damn it, Itsuma.* He made me lose my cool in every way possible.

My cock made it painfully aware that, no matter what noble reason, the six months of self-induced celibacy was not appreciated. My heart started pounding. I breathed hard. My hips were going to declare mutiny. I wanted to pull Itsuma down and start going at it. If I didn't do something soon, I'd go into rut. But there was no way that was going to happen.

My Prince set his palms on the door behind my head and leaned over me. His pupils dilated. "Look, he's completely into it." He lifted my blue-collar shirt out from under my pants. Buttons went flying as he forced the top open.

"Wait!" I grabbed his hands in a wrist lock.

"Damn, Sensei," Itsuma stared at my abs. "You're cut for an old man."

I had to laugh. "Did you think a soft nerd was beating your ass?"

Itsuma raised his head and our eyes met again. Amusement colored his eyes, and a hint of lust sparkled within those pools. Somehow, I'd earned his respect.

Out in the hallway, a door banged open. Chattering echoed off the walls outside the classroom. The girls' volleyball team was coming through as they usually did, making a ruckus getting to their lockers to make their way home.

We all froze. I blinked. Scott watched the door. Itsuma watched me. If he thought I was going to yell for help—well, there wasn't any help needed here. Itsuma smirked, as if daring me to call out.

The rope around my ankle loosened. Neither of my students spoke.

The girls' volleyball team left as noisily as they came, and then it was dead quiet. I was free from my bonds, yet I had no will to move. The whole ordeal was exhausting.

"Zuma, if anyone sees us…" Scott whispered. "This is bad. What the hell are you thinking?"

I watched Itsuma as his expression went from confident to confused. Ah, he finally realized what he was doing.

Scott pulled at Itsuma's shoulder. The Prince batted him off and ran out of the room.

"Mr. Reis?" Scott's soft voice caught my attention. He sat beside me, coiling up his rope. "Are you okay?"

"Yeah." I got up, grabbed the earbuds off my desk and tossed them over to Scott.

He caught the package. "You hit the ground a little hard." Scott examined the hip I'd landed on when he'd pulled me down.

"Don't worry," I groaned. "I'm tough."

"Why didn't you call out for help?"

I smiled. "Why do you think?"

His eyes searched mine.

"Go after him," I said. "Tell him I'm fine. He ran because he's embarrassed."

Scott gave me a dubious expression.

"Go," I said. "I don't want you two catching heat over this." No harm, no foul. Though someone else might interpret this situation differently.

"Okay," Scott said. He didn't sound sure, but he saluted me with the earbuds and ran after Itsuma.

Chapter 3

I was ready to forget all of it. I even taught my first class without any qualm. Then, Itsuma walked into my classroom. He acted like nothing had happened. No embarrassment. No *sorry* face. Not even the *I got you* expression when a guy gets the one-up on an opponent. I was used to guys getting macho or even feeling entitled towards me. I could handle that just fine. It was easier to push guys away. But this…

Itsuma strolled in without a second glance at me. Earbuds in and music cranked so high I could hear it as he passed my desk. He just strolled in and ignored me. Fucking little… who the hell did he think he was? His dismissal of me chapped my hide.

Scott, on the other hand, kept his face hidden under his cowboy hat. His neck and the exposed part of his chest flushed red. He didn't seem as unaffected as Itsuma. Scott's reaction was adorable. But Itsuma's nonchalance wiggled under my skin. His indifference pissed me off. *Damn it. Whatever. Getting involved like that with a student will only lead to complications.*

"Fucker," I said with a hand over my mouth so no one would hear. The last bell clamored like the start of a boxing match. I opened my book and started roll call. All my students claimed themselves present, including Scott, until, "Itsuma Karter…"

Nothing. Nada. Zilch. Crickets.

I sighed in frustration. Taking my nose out of the roll call book, I looked at Itsuma. His body faced forward, but his head was turned. Chin in hand, he gazed out the window, ignoring me. The earbuds I gave him yesterday sat in his ears. I don't normally have a short fuse, but this kid pushed all my buttons.

The last proverbial straw on my back snapped. Maybe because I was so good at getting away with shit, I didn't think twice about my actions. I pulled out a modified foam-bullet gun from my desk drawer. These toys were always breaking down, jamming and never had enough power, so me and some science buddies had gotten together to solve the problem. The result… a fully automated, battery powered Nerf-like Tommy gun that could fire three Styrofoam bullets a second.

"Today, I think I'm going to show you all what science and mathematics can achieve together," I said.

I looked at the blonde girl who sat in front of Itsuma and said, "Lori, I'm a fantastic shot, but you better duck and cover. These hurt when you get hit in the face."

Lori's eyes widened and she flattened herself on her desk. She had a look of *I don't blame you he's an ass* on her face.

Itsuma didn't even know what was coming. I aimed and fired.

Long, thin Styrofoam bullets zoomed through the class, over Lori, and hit Itsuma's cheek, neck, and chest. The Prince immediately overreacted and leaped out of his chair. "What the fuck, motherfucker!" Itsuma lashed out. By that time, I'd emptied the clip of fifteen projectiles.

"Ah, well, I guess that's the best acknowledgement for roll I'll get."

Whatever the cost, it was worth seeing Itsuma spitting mad. The entire class roared in laughter. I felt pretty smug with myself.

Itsuma looked around. His eyes landed on Scott. The Cowboy buried his laughter in the crook of his elbow while hanging off his desk. My insulted Prince turned a shade of red I'd never seen on anybody. He turned around and flew out the back door.

I sighed and flicked a checkmark in the box indicating Itsuma present.

♂♂♂

For the rest of the day, those fiery eyes never left my consciousness. Whether it was fortunate or not, I didn't have either Scott or Itsuma in any of my other classes, so I didn't see them for the rest of the day.

The more I thought about it, the more I scolded myself for letting him get to me. Again. Now the brat was in my head. Those slit eyes and taut lips haunted my thoughts and aroused my interest. Instead of appeasing my sexual frustration, last night's sexcapades fueled my fire. It was getting bad. But if I excused myself to the bathroom for quick release, I'd be even more up shit's creek. If I masturbated to those eyes, that look, thinking about what was underneath those loose pants and tight shirt, I'd never get him out of my head. Also, it was wrong. Damn it. Why wasn't my shame coming in and shutting these thoughts down? He was barely this side of legal.

I needed to get a boyfriend stat. But I had no time. This needed a fix right now. Tonight. I'd pick up a "date" fast enough at the bar, but I really didn't want that either.

Lately, casual relationships just made me feel that much more alone.

As I resolved to go home after this last paper and try to jerk off to porn, Itsuma walked into my classroom. The air around him smelled dangerous. His chest was puffed out, his shoulders tense, his strides clipped. He was spoiling for a fight. My cock was doing its best to peek over my belt and see Itsuma for himself.

If the Prince wanted to intimidate me, he'd find out once I stood up that I thought of him as dangerous in a completely different way. Shit. I wanted that energy. I wanted to take it and have him use it to ride my ass until cum poured out my ears. Thinking about it made me catch my breath.

"Are you afraid, Sensei?"

I smirked. "You've done nothing to make me afraid."

"Is that so?"

"Yep." I wasn't afraid. My knees were weak for a completely different reason. Perhaps it was the way Itsuma's jeans hung on his slim waist, or the way his shirt grabbed his biceps. But what captured my attention were those eyes. Smoldering. Dark. Exotic.

The kid was itching for a rematch. If he'd hint at any kind of sexual innuendo, it wouldn't be a fair fight. I'd cave for any kind of attention like yesterday afternoon.

"I need to teach you not to embarrass me, especially in class." Itsuma stalked closer.

"But you always show me a good time." I crossed my arms and leaned deeper in my chair. "Why would I stop?"

His thick lips curved. "You have spirit." Itsuma came within kicking distance and squared his body in a fighting stance.

"This again." I lifted an eyebrow and stayed in my chair. "I thought you learned yesterday you can't take me alone." Without Scott to help him, I'd take him down as I had yesterday.

"I can take care of myself," Itsuma growled.

Ho, ho. I'd hit a sore spot. I used to have his notions of pride. I'd rid myself of the nuisance ever since I realized having my ass pounded felt fantastic.

"You're such a big man, Itsuma."

"Get up."

"Make me." Oh, my god. Two five-year-olds in a sandbox.

I did not even see his feet, but my body reacted without fail. Itsuma tried to swing his legs for a head shot and I blocked. I refrained from punching him in the junk or twisting his knee and jabbed him in the gut.

His foot bounced off my desk as he staggered back. Wrapping his arms around his middle, he glared at me. I remained seated. "Don't they teach you every stance is a fighting stance? Or do you just go to some cookie-cutter kata class?"

Itsuma's smile twisted in vengeful spite. He didn't say a word.

As they say, a prowling cat on silent paws proves more lethal than a snarling wolf.

He glided around my desk. I followed, twisting my chair around.

Now that he was serious it was time I gave him proper respect. I stood and kicked my chair away. It rolled to the corner and I leveled my gaze at my opponent. This trick only worked once. Pretending to be unprepared, I balanced on the balls of my feet ready to strike.

In a flash of movement Itsuma attacked. Knees, legs, feet, strikes, and jabs, he threw everything at me. I dodged and blocked them all. He wasn't letting me get close.

"You did your research," I said. "Good for you."

He threw another heated glance at me. "Seems your name is still known in certain circles."

I blocked another flurry of attempts. My eyes couldn't keep up. Thank god my body could. Muscle memory and training flowed, protecting me from his fancy footwork.

"They say you gained a scholarship. You could have gone on to the 2008 Olympics but chose not to."

Shit. He really had done some research. It made me a little nervous about what else he might know.

"Why didn't you go, Sensei?" Itsuma poised for another strike. "Were you having a hard time keeping your dick in your pants around all your teammates?"

Ouch. If he only knew. But I didn't let his bait get to me. "What about you, Itsuma?"

Like a hothead, he went for a kick to the gut. He was slow, and I blocked. Damn. I'd gone for it, and he grabbed my wrist and bent it over. I went to one knee. In a flash he was behind me. I heard a metallic snap and clank. The bite of handcuffs around one wrist sent me into a panic. I jumped up, but Itsuma spun me towards my desk, pushed me forward and clamped the other handcuff around my other wrist. I jabbed my elbow and hit ribs. Itsuma grunted, but the kid stayed the course and pushed me over my desk. He'd done it.

Very few obtained a win over me. He had my utmost respect, and even if it was my loss I was rather pleased to find a suitable sparring partner. Itsuma rested his head against my back and huffed out air. I relaxed over my desk and caught my breath as well.

"Sensei didn't hold back." Itsuma's smile came through in his words.

"Well, I might have let you win."

Hands smoothed over my body. *Oh, yes, discipline me all you want.* Crap. My shame kicked in always too late. He ground his hard cock between the cheeks of my ass.

"Now to teach you humility." Itsuma slid his hands over my hips, reached around my waist and unbuckled my pants. Once the belt was free one hand slipped underneath my slacks and rubbed my ass. Oh fuck. I was done. That's all it took for need to take over my body. My desperate cock demanded attention.

"Itsuma, if you don't stop and let me go you're going to have a broken leg." I poised my stance to kick. Many a career was ruined by a permanent injury. I didn't want to, but if he took this too far I'd be forced to hurt him.

When I looked back, I didn't expect the startled, confused expression on Itsuma's face. He wasn't sure about what he was doing. I'd thought he had experience, but maybe…

"Are you a virgin?" I said, trying to dislodge him further.

The arrogant, ironic eighteen-year-old attitude returned. "No."

"Get off me."

"You're not the one giving the orders."

I laughed. "You really think I'm helpless here? Get a clue. I'm letting you do this." He really needed to learn rules and boundaries. "You really are an amateur."

"Fuck you."

I kicked his thigh and sent him back.

"Damn it," Itsuma shouted. "Stay still."

The classroom door handle clicked and I just about had a heart attack. Shit. It was too early for the janitors. Itsuma froze. Despite what it looked like, my Prince was just a confused teenager trying to find out what the world was to him. He didn't need his life tarnished by this. I certainly didn't need exposure either.

Scott stepped inside looking ready to commit murder. Holy… hell. He looked like a cowboy demon charging down the aisle of chairs.

"Itsuma!" Scott growled. "What the hell are you doing?"

"Seems to me like you're cheating on your lover." I looked back at Itsuma.

"Shut up."

Scott stomped forward, his anger feral and raw. He was going to rip Itsuma apart. "I said, what the fuck are you doing? Get off him!" The Cowboy grabbed Itsuma's arm and yanked him away from me. "Mr. Reiss, I apologize for this idiot's petty vengeance."

"He deserves it." Itsuma spat.

Yes, I deserved a bit of a release for putting up with the Prince's crap in homeroom. Could I dial up a rent-a-boyfriend?

Itsuma broke free from Scott's grasp and straightened his pants. "I thought you were at the ranch."

"Give me the key." Scott held out his hand to Itsuma.

My would-be top dug into his pants pocket, all the while glaring at Scott. Itsuma pulled out a silver key and deposited it in Scott's hand.

"Whatever." Itsuma walked out in a huff. If his pride was hurt, it didn't show in his stride.

Once Itsuma pushed the door open and left the room, Scott unlocked me and pocketed the cuffs in his leather jacket.

"So you are you two involved with each other?" I rubbed my wrists, getting rid of the discomfort.

He stood firm, eyes averted, hands in his pockets, and shook his head. "We're better friends than anything more."

I zipped my pants and straightened myself. "Ah, so you both top."

Scott's face flushed, making his tan a shade deeper. "Well, not exactly."

He wouldn't look me in the eye. Still, I scrutinized him, trying to figure out what he meant by *not exactly.* "Wait, are you straight?" Yesterday he'd seemed really affected by watching, so I'd just assumed.

That's when he looked directly at me. Scott raised his hand in denial. "No, no, I'm gay, alright."

Brave kid. He knew himself and wasn't ashamed. That meant there was another issue. "But Itsuma's not sure?"

"He… struggles with it sometimes." Scott's voice was soft and reassuring. "I'm surprised you didn't report us."

I grimaced, shaking my wrists out. "What's to report?"

Scott's standoffish stance relaxed. He was here to protect Itsuma. The young, rugged cowboy had a budding confidence that, if cultivated, would make him irresistible. On top of that, he retained a shyness that would make people want to paw at the guy. He triggered my protective instinct. Scott made me want to take him under my wing and teach him everything. He was the type I'd want to own someday. The world would be his. I didn't blame Itsuma for being confused. Scott was the kind of guy anyone would love.

"I appreciate your discreetness." Scott shifted his stance. "But he's getting a little unbearable."

I shrugged. "He needs to be careful. Picking fights is a great way to get killed."

"Yeah." Scott nodded.

"Well, as long as it's me he goes after he'll be fine. He just needs some guidance." And a good beating.

Scott pulled back in astonishment. "You're a pretty different guy."

"Why?" I went across the room to retrieve my chair. "Because I understand what you're going through? There aren't many options or people to talk to. I understand the fear of everyone turning on you if they only knew who you were."

Scott lowered his head and hid his eyes. Poor kid. Everybody feels that way. But saying that to him probably sounded patronizing, especially since he was dealing with stigma along with puberty. Still, I wanted to hug him and tell him it would be okay.

"Sorry for everything. I didn't think he'd go that far yesterday. Then… I just kinda froze."

Oh, fuck me. This was not the time to get hard. But his apology was just so cute.

He stuck his thumbs in the pockets of his jeans. "I better go keep him out of trouble."

"Thank you, Scott." I didn't want him to leave, but there was no reason for him to stay. "If you need anyone to talk to, I'm here."

He nodded, turned and left.

Damn. I wanted to help those two. If I'd had someone like me in high school to clear up the uncertainty, the confusion, the pain, the loneliness—maybe I wouldn't be so fucked in the head. I mean, who wants to be pinned down and taken? By a student no less. Me, apparently. It felt good. From the last two days, I'd have enough spank material for the next year. That is, if masturbation did anything for me. Which it didn't. Only pure grade-A cock would suffice.

I gathered my brown, shoulder-length hair in a fist and pulled. Doing so helped relieve the frustration. As endorphins helped alleviate my dissatisfaction, I tried to stave off the memory of Itsuma pressing himself against my ass. I packed my things and left for the day. Tonight would be another long night of grading papers.

Chapter 4

How I travelled down the path of this inner war I couldn't remember. No. Not true. It was the moment Itsuma's lips met mine. If I were honest, that was the moment I'd gotten too involved with my students. Yet I couldn't help myself. I wanted to help those two. I wanted to punch something for getting involved. But I knew it was due to my ineptness at knowing how to help them that caused my distress. Who goes around picking fights and taking your teachers clothes off, anyway? Or was this my way of whining—Why me?

At the moment, I couldn't do anything. I'd thought about what to do all last night and still couldn't come up with anything. I was sitting at my desk waiting for homeroom to start when the chip on Itsuma's shoulder entered the room before my Prince even walked in. Scott was on his friend's heels giving me nervous glances, pleading with me to not do anything.

That wasn't the man I was, though. If he was nice, I'd be nice. Concentrating on the last of the papers to grade, I waited for the bell. When it rang, I started my usual routine. All my students answered until, once again…

"Itsuma Karter," I said.

Nothing. I waited… for nothing.

I pinched the bridge of my nose and looked up. Itsuma was in his usual chair, slouched. Looking out the window with his earbuds in. I heard a few of the students huff. Someone whispered, "Dumbass." Far as I was concerned, we both were.

All the pent up energy, the anxiety, the anticipation drained out my pores. Blast it. This was so tiring. I could ignore him, or…

As I stood up the chair screeched a warning. I walked over to Itsuma, grabbed his iPod and yanked. The earbuds probably hurt when I pulled them along with the MP3 player, but I turned and didn't look back.

Behind me, I felt Itsuma move. Ready for an attack, I whipped around only to watch him snatch his metallic blue earbuds and pull them out of their socket. He stuffed the cord in his jeans pocket and sat there, sullen.

"See me after class if you want this back." I flaunted the iPod.

"Keep it, I have ten more at home," Itsuma uttered under his breath.

And there was a clue. If I were a good judge of character, I'd say his problem was the wrong kind of attention. Spoiled. Great at everything. Life posed no challenge. Bored out of his mind. God, this was exhausting.

I turned back around and walked to my desk. After roll, announcements came on. The tension in homeroom felt like a prison cell. All the while Scott and Itsuma threw glances at each other. Their perfected silent communication couldn't be interpreted. Conspiring or conflicting with each other, I decided.

The bell rang for the students to leave homeroom and get to the next class, and all but Scott motioned to get up and go. Itsuma shot up and was the first to bolt out the door.

"Itsuma!" I yelled. Damn it. Too late. He'd slipped out.

After the hustle of students emptied the room of all but me and Scott, the cowboy got up, gingerly, as if protecting his chest. A wry grimace countered his usual soulful expression when he fully straightened. I saw right through his mask to the pain on his face. He was enduring physical discomfort. Before I could even ask if he was alright he held out a hand and said, "Give it to me and I'll make sure he doesn't come bothering you later."

I opened my drawer, ignored the metallic blue iPod and grabbed one of my business cards. "I want to see him." I handed Scott the card with my phone and home address. "Tell him I have chess club this afternoon but I'll be home by six-thirty."

Scott flipped the card around and stared at the number. "Chess club meets during summer school?"

I shrugged. "Nerds are nerds. Do you think he'll come?"

Deep blue eyes met my question with respectful awe. "Mr. Reis, he could have taken back his iPod, but the thing he cared most about were the useless headphones you gave him."

Scott set my card inside a folder and left for his next class. Guess we'd see if either one called.

♂♂♂

Lunch was the only chance I had to go to the offices for the files I wanted. The halls were empty, so I locked my room up and went to administration. Comparatively this campus was tiny. The buildings formed a horseshoe with the records facility at the middle of the "U."

I entered the offices and waved at Betty, the administrative assistant, who was helping a kid. I passed the front counter and went to the computers at the back. Three old green-and-black monitors sat at different desks. I scratched my beard and smoothed down my mustache. My god, these things were before even my time. I looked over at Betty. They probably weren't before hers. I'd have to wait till she was done to ask how to get to the files.

"Hey, Mori." Mr. Goyas strode in from the back.

"Hi!" I smiled.

"Did you pull the short straw?"

"Huh?" I blinked.

"Betty always wrangles the youngsters for data entry. I thought it was your turn."

Betty glanced back with predatory eyes while still talking to the student.

"Great, I think I've just been volunteered."

Mr. Goyas laughed and slapped me on the back.

"Omph." *Geez. Remind me not to try and wrestle with him.* "Does that mean you know how to work these things?" I gave him my best puppy dog eyes, pleading for help.

He laughed again. "You sure do know how to flatter a guy."

Oh, you have no idea. He leaned over and tapped at the keyboard. "Okay, who are you looking for?"

"Itsuma Karter and Scott Cooper."

Mr. Goyas paused. "Those two. What'd they do now?"

Oh crap. It had to be bad for Mr. Goyas to groan. "Nothing. I was just checking up on them. What do you know?"

He grimaced. "They've both had their troubles. It seems there was a mess between those boys and each other's parents."

I waited for more, but my old shop teacher was one of those types who didn't spread rumors. I wasn't going to get any more out of him.

"That's not the thing I was looking for, but knowing that might help. I just wanted to know about their academics." Anything to get to know them better.

"Well, here it is." Mr. Goyas pointed at the screen. "Good luck."

Mr. Goyas slapped me on the back, jostling my lungs, and headed out.

Itsuma Karter, top five of his class. Perfect attendance. He had technically graduated from high school but was taking college prep courses. Which didn't make much sense. He'd already taken all the college prep courses available in this school. Perfect SAT score. I read that twice and still couldn't believe it. Teachers' comments of "easy to teach" and "picks up things fast" made me grit my teeth. They obviously rolled over for the star student. Nothing like what I expected. On paper, he was a model citizen who respected his elders. Great. Was I the only one who knew the real Itsuma? Why was I so lucky?

Then I went to Scott's records. He was Mr. Hyde to Itsuma's Dr. Jekyll. His past seemed more checkered. He was barely passing at seventy-one percent. The summer courses were make-up classes so he could graduate. Detention for poor behavior. Twenty-one missed days. Fourteen of them legitimate as parental notes said he was in the hospital. Hmmm... Teachers comments were "inattentive," "sleeps in class," "tries hard but needs assistance."

Did I get the names wrong? Was I looking at the right files? Was there a switch between these two records? This was a mistake, right? Scott was smart. I mean, take away the hat and the cowboy swagger and I could see that boy's intelligence. Inattentive? More like bored with your stupid, droning lecture. Sleeps in class? Try using new material. Needs help? No. Scott could fool overworked high-school teachers, but not me. *Why? Were you covering for Itsuma?* It was as if Itsuma was attending summer school because of Scott. I skimmed through the stuff I already knew. Both were eighteen before the semester began. Home address. GPA. Something didn't add up.

Maybe I'd find the solution to this equation tonight.

Chapter 5

An hour before Itsuma would supposedly arrive gave me enough time to work out the stress from said kid. My home was a remodel of my perfect flow. At the entryway, to the left, the entertainment room sported an L-shaped leather couch that could fit seven.

To the immediate right was the dining room. Three chairs sat at a bar that was connected to the kitchen. A four-seater dining room table was right next to the bar. My dining room could comfortably seat eight, but I usually ate at the bar. After the kitchen, an entry into a long hall led to my master bed and bathroom, office, and the guest bedroom. Then there was my private dojo in the back. All I needed was a bag, padded floors and enough room to throw down or stretch. This was my thirty-six hundred square feet of bliss. My temple of pride. My comfort zone.

I started the hot water for a bath, stripped and got in. Soaping up, my hands wandered. Rosy Palm hadn't given me satisfaction since puberty. Too bad. I could have taken care of my nasty thoughts while in the tub. As the soak loosened my muscles I had a heart-to-heart talk with myself.

What the hell are you doing, Mori? Inviting them to your house? My cock answered with a bob. *Don't be desperate. Fuck. Yes.* Was that what I was planning? No, no, no. This prep work was for finding a "date" later tonight. It was embarrassing being a dirty bottom. I had more class than that. Crap. If I prepared, then it would just be license. I could hear it now. *Oh, Mr. Reis, were you expecting something?* Ugh. I wouldn't win this argument.

The desire to genuinely help them was the real reason I invited them here. If Itsuma pinned me down, I'd punch him off me. Just as I had before. This weekend was enough time to go out on the prowl.

Truth. You gave him your card because he was acting reckless. All it would take was a janitor or—fuck—Mr. Goyas coming in the room. No, let's not have that. If Itsuma just wanted to get back at his Sensei, then have at it. I've got a sparring room in the back just for sessions like these.

If we were going to fight, it should be done safely, and in an environment that didn't jeopardize anyone's future.

♂♂♂

After I got into my sweat pants and t-shirt I stopped and thought about my choice in clothes… and put on jeans and a baggy shirt. *Let's not tempt fate.* Or was it too late? I had twenty minutes left. If he, or they, were coming. We could eat together if I timed it right. Rice and chicken strips should be safe. Nothing extravagant. I downed a shot of whiskey that went to my head two minutes later. After prepping, bath time and the drink I was completely happy and relaxed.

At six-thirty-five the doorbell rang. Perfect timing. From the kitchen I walked to my entrance and opened up to my caller.

Itsuma sulked at my doorstep. Scott stood three feet behind him. I stepped back and waved for them to come in. But Itsuma stood there with his hands in his pockets for about ten seconds. That was my first clue that maybe he hadn't come here by choice.

Scott raised a leg, planted his foot on Itsuma's ass, and shoved my little delinquent forward. The Prince's surprise and flailing arms were comical. Scott tipped his hat to me and turned around.

"Oh, no you don't." Fast as a snake strike, I grabbed Scott's wrist and yanked him off his feet into my foyer. "You too."

"Asshole," Itsuma uttered to his friend. "You were going to leave me here to die."

Scott huffed. "This is your mess."

I closed the door and looked at Scott. "As I recall, it was your lasso that gave Itsuma the upper hand."

"The first time." Itsuma took off his shoes and left them at the front door. "I'd have had you if he didn't interfere the second time."

"As I said yesterday, I didn't want to hurt you." I expected a haughty comeback, but Itsuma never met my gaze as he stood uncomfortably with one hand holding his elbow like a nervous child. Perhaps he was ashamed of his actions. Good.

Scott dug his thumbs into the pockets of his jeans and stood with one leg relaxed. He seemed unconcerned, but his tight lips conveyed just the opposite.

"Have you two eaten?" I turned and went back to the kitchen.

"Yes," Itsuma snapped.

"No," Scott said at the same time.

Checking the rice was ready, I pulled the chicken strips out of the oven. "Too bad. Eat it anyway."

I scooped rice into three bowls, divvied up the chicken and set two bowls on the bar top. Two forks lay on napkins for them, and I grabbed my own bowl.

"Sit." I motioned to the chairs in front of the high counter and started eating. Scott, bless him, took to eating my food like he hadn't had anything this good in ever.

Itsuma walked over and sniffed at my offering. "What, no chopsticks?" He snickered. Like I was Japanese. What did he expect from a white boy?

From the other side of the bar, I pulled out a pair of my lacquer-finished chopsticks and, covering my annoyance with a saccharine inflection, said, "Koko masuta." *Here, master.*

No, it wasn't correct Japanese. No, I was not Japanese—it wasn't even correct Japanese—and no, I wasn't all that fluent, but it was fun to watch Itsuma's eyes bug out. Well, as much as his cat eyes could. Now he'd be wondering how much I understood whenever he whispered those derogatory insults at me in class. Without another word he sat down, picked up the chopsticks and started shoveling rice and chicken.

"If I'm the mediator, please speak English," Scott said.

Itsuma swallowed his mouthful and said, "He was being facetious."

Well, at least I got the point across. Of course, I could be inviting more insults in all sorts of languages. I took a deep breath, set my bowl down and looked at my troublemaking Prince. "Itsuma, I don't know how, but I think we got off on the wrong foot."

My mouthy student set down his bowl and crossed his arms. "You stole my shit."

"You mean your MP3 player?"

"Yes."

He was so cute. Trying to be macho with his pouty face. But I didn't dare smile. That would just obliterate his pride. When taming tigers, use flattery, not shame. Affection also worked. But as with predatory cats, flattery had to be on their terms.

"Any suggestions, then, on how I can get your attention during roll call?"

"What the fuck?" Itsuma jumped out of the chair, sending my stool to the ground. "You see me pass by. Why do I have to respond like some dog?"

"To high heaven with no manners, Zuma." Scott got out of his seat and righted my stool. "Please remember this is someone else's house."

Careful, Mori. Don't react. Just breathe. Ignore the tantrum. I moved out of the kitchen and leaned against the pillar separating the kitchen from the dining area. Itsuma stepped back. I'd gotten his hackles raised and in a defensive stance. I needed to take him seriously even if he was acting out. He was pissed over a simple question. Could this just be a simple case of angry attraction? Did he find me as alluring as I found him and Scott? Was he just confused? Hurt? Angry? I chose my next words carefully.

"I get it. You have a perfect attendance record and you don't want to lose that."

Itsuma stared at me, but a tiny inkling of recognition flitted over his tough expression.

Bingo. I had his attention. I continued. "You come in from the front door even though it would be more convenient to your seating arrangement to come through the back. I see you pass the far door just so you can pass by my desk."

Itsuma's emotions crossed over his face. Fear. Anxiety. Both under a spark of hope. I was dead on. It showed in his body language too.

"But I've always called roll by calling names and listening to your voices. I'm an audible learner." I shrugged. "So if I were to give you special treatment, then it would be noticeable." If anyone scrutinized me, they'd already know I was daydreaming about these two boys. "Do you understand what I'm saying?"

Itsuma's posture changed from fighting stance to completely relaxed. His hands limp by his sides. Eyes focused on my face. Shoulders slack. Yes. The message had gotten across. *I'm falling for you and I can't let anyone see that.*

"Sensei," Itsuma whispered.

"Yes, Senpai noticed you." I rolled my eyes. "Now that you have my attention, what do you want?"

Itsuma was on top of me, bending me backwards over the bar, his tongue so far down my throat I couldn't breathe. Shock prevented me from responding right away. He'd been so fast. My lack of action gave Itsuma time to break down my rationale. His kiss made me lose my mind. His body pushed me down and his arms clamped over my elbows so I couldn't fight him off. Or maybe that was just lust weakening my muscles.

Most embarrassing was my cock refusing to listen to reason. It was only a matter of minutes before I gave in and flipped my conscience the bird. I tried halfheartedly to push him back. The more I pushed, the more Itsuma clung. A hand clutched my long hair and pulled my head backwards. *I am in so much trouble.*

"Nauhhh…" Oh god. That cry was me.

Itsuma's lips were everywhere. My neck, sucking my ear, my lips. It was too late for me. Any resistance was met with excuses. He was legal age. It's consensual. I hadn't had a good fuck in six months. This was so bad. Self-control was out getting drunk on Itsuma's kisses.

A hand slipped under my boxers. Crap. My jeans were already unbuttoned and my shirt was halfway up my chest.

"Sensei, you smell nice. Did you bathe for me?"

"Wait, Itsuma." Shit. This kid pissed me off a little. He saw right through me. But it gave me strength enough to use a special trick I knew.

The body has pressure points that, when pushed, became a person's weak spot. Everyone has these. I'd learned in wrestling how to use them. One such pressure point was between the nose and upper lip. Lay a finger like a fake mustache and push. When I applied the Captain Morgan on him, his body bowed backwards. It didn't take much to get Itsuma off me.

"Bastard!" Itsuma slapped my arm.

"Itsuma…" I held up my hands. "Just wait a moment." My whole body shook. "Can we talk about this?"

"What should we talk about? Fucking?" Itsuma prowled towards me.

"Zuma," Scott voiced a warning.

"What?" Itsuma swung his glance to the cowboy.

"We talked about this."

"He's not saying no." Itsuma waved at me.

Thank god. I was given time to recuperate.

"You're a damn animal." Scott glared at his friend. "Look, you're scaring the crap out of him." The Cowboy pointed to me.

"Oh, bullshit." Itsuma spit. "You saw him the other day. Stop projecting."

"Itsuma!" Now that I had half my wits about me I could say what I wanted.

"What?" Itsuma crossed his arms and looked at me.

"Stop trying to bend me over. There are consequences." Crap. That didn't come out right. "I want to help you."

My Prince raked lascivious eyes up and down my body. "I bet you do." His eyes landed on my middle and he smirked.

I looked down. Holy shit. My cock was hanging out and waving a stiff salute. I quickly buried my eager weasel back into my jeans. The kid would have me undressed in a nanosecond if he hadn't stopped.

"No, I mean, what you do for fun… it's dangerous."

"So you think this is a gag?" Itsuma puffed out his chest.

Scott's eyes widened. "Mr. Reis, we don't do that. I mean, you're the first."

The first to pin down and kiss mindless? My heart went pitter-patter. So I was the only one they'd teased. Good.

Itsuma's face filled my vision. "You don't take me seriously at all, do you?"

I narrowed my eyes. "A little hard to when all you do is play games."

"Only because you're a snob."

"Excuse me?" I might be privileged, but I worked hard. How he could rile me up was annoying.

"You wouldn't lower yourself for someone like Scott, right?"

"He's a student. So are you."

Itsuma leaned a hand on the pillar behind me, blocking my escape. "Then we need to talk."

"We?" *Talk about what?*

"I want you." Itsuma flicked his eyes to Scott, then back to me. "He wants you. What do you say?"

"Excuse me?" My anger flared. "This isn't a booty call. Read my lips. No. Not ever."

"Really?" Itsuma quirked a smile. "Never?"

I compressed my lips and narrowed my eyes.

"Then why did you invite us here?" Itsuma challenged.

"Because we need to come to some kind of agreement. Taking your possesions isn't acceptable, neither is ignoring me in class. Fighting it out on school grounds is a liability."

Itsuma pulled back and raked a hand through his short, jet black hair. "You piss me off."

"You piss *me* off."

"You make me angry, but I can't wait to see you." Itsuma looked away. "I don't want to be *just* another student."

A soft chuckle pulled our attention towards Scott. "Yeah. I'd do anything to be near Mr. Reis too."

Oh. His words took my breath away. Scott's understanding and poetic explanation helped me realize our agitation was something other than anger towards the other. They were my students. Maybe I was angry at myself for finding them attractive.

"So what now?" Itsuma folded his arms. "How do we stay by your side?"

"What do you mean?" His question was suspicious.

"Tutoring." Scott's matter-of-fact tone made it sound like the logical answer. But I was still confused as to the question.

"Tutoring?" I parroted.

The Cowboy shrugged. "It makes sense."

Itsuma sniggered. "I could give Sensei lots of instruction."

"I'm not doing any kink you're thinking of." I set my hands on my hips. "And we're doing it in the classroom."

"What, sex?" Itsuma smiled.

"You're exhausting." I rolled my eyes. "Get your mind off your dick."

A phone chime halted the next round of perverted comments. Itsuma pulled an iPhone from his back pocket and answered, "Nani?"

Nice way to greet someone, by answering *what?* That was so Itsuma.

A deluge of Japanese spilled from the earpiece of Itsuma's phone. The woman on the other end spoke too fast for me to catch much. I wasn't fluent, I just knew phrases here and there. But it might be worth picking up the language. I did, however, ascertain enough to believe he was having an argument with family. Some words came through, like college, good-for-nothing friend, future, what time are you coming home... everything moms nagged their children about plus the kitchen sink.

Scott snuck shy glances at me. Cheeks aglow, his coy smile raised my confidence. He gave me the tiniest nod.

After another minute and a curt "*Jū ichi-ji*" that sounded more like a *fuck you* than the Japanese word for *eleven o'clock*, Itsuma hung up.

"Sounds like you have a curfew." I expected sparks to fly at my round-about question, but Itsuma only sighed.

"Yeah."

"Was that your mom?"

"Yeah."

"So... what university are you going to?"

This time Scott sighed.

"You heard that, huh?" Itsuma said. "I'm being shipped back to Japan for university."

Oh. That's why the long faces. Another piece of the puzzle came into place. But I still didn't have the full picture.

"Which one?"

Itsuma shrugged. "Don't know. I've been accepted to M and T."

"Not deciding isn't going to help you," Scott said. "They'll choose for you, if they haven't already."

I huffed. "Straight A student, no prospects? What do you want to do?"

"What is it to you?" Itsuma put up the defensive walls. I'd turned into a meddling adult. It would be easy to take the bait and become defensive, but that wasn't my style. Not in this kind of match.

Softly, I answered, "It matters. You matter." I looked between the two of them. "You both matter to me."

My Cowboy couldn't look me in the eye, but his face turned a beautiful shade of red.

Itsuma folded his arms. "My parents want me to be a doctor."

"So probably T University."

Itsuma nodded.

"A fine profession. But what do you want to do?"

He shrugged. "It's fine."

"That's an awfully hard road to go down with half-assed feelings."

"I said it's fine," Itsuma lashed out with his words.

"Playing the good son?"

"What the fuck do you know about anything?" Itsuma spat. "I bust my ass so I can follow in my ancestors' footsteps. Make them proud."

Ah. Itsuma was just a typical Japanese kid after all. He kept himself from having dreams because, why bother? Sons were to follow their father's footsteps. Japanese and their honor. Best of luck to any who wanted to go against the grain, against *tradition*. Where perfection was average. Dishonor meant suicide.

"Aerospace," Scott said.

I gave him a questioning look.

"He'd be really good in aerospace."

"Like engineering?" At least someone was answering my questions.

"Like anything." Scott smiled with the warmth of the type of knowing that comes with lovers. "Engineering, flying, testing, mechanical, defense, control systems, you name it."

"Well then…" My snark came out full force. "That requires math, doesn't it?" I stood proud. This was something I could help with. I looked at Itsuma.

"So, Mr. Hasn't-gone-past-algebra-two, you might need something a little more advanced. Luckily, you might know someone who's getting his PhD in math."

"Wouldn't you be in topology or abstract algebra by now?" Scott asked.

I stared with my mouth open at this unassuming cowboy. Scott peeked up from his lashes. "Or maybe real analysis?" He said it like he'd offended me and was trying to apologize.

"This is what I'm talking about." I pointed to Scott.

"What?"

"How does a high school student even know about topology?" Much less talk about it. "And why are you barely passing?"

"Yeah, Sensei, stop picking on me. He's the smart one."

I narrowed my eyes at Itsuma. "Both of you sit at the kitchen table."

Itsuma groaned, but he dragged his feet to the table and sat next to Scott. Thank god for the undisputable teacher's voice. The two were still lemmings to the system. College would cure that.

I went to my study and brought out two books. One pre-calculus workbook and a biography of George

Washington. I handed the workbook to Itsuma and said, "Read the intro. I'll be with you in two minutes."

He sighed, rubbed his face and took the book.

I handed Scott the biography. "It's not the standard history book they give you, but it tells a story. The language is a bit archaic, but I'll help you through it."

Hopefully Scott would ask when he was confused, but I knew Itsuma wouldn't bother. He'd power through the intro again and again until he got it. Before he got confused I'd help him out.

♂♂♂

Knowing Itsuma had a curfew, I kept an eye on the clock. A little after ten I asked, "What time do you have to leave?"

My question jarred Scott from another losing battle to remain awake. Poor kid was trying his best. He refused all my suggestions of resting on the couch.

Itsuma looked at his phone. "I should leave in thirty minutes."

"Alright then." I turned to Scott. "What time should you be leaving?"

Scott rubbed his eyes and winced. He protected his ribs like a beaten boxer after a fight.

"He should have been home at nine," Itsuma answered.

"I couldn't leave you here alone with Mr. Reis."

"You know I keep my promises." Itsuma read while talking to Scott.

"What promise?" My curiosity was piqued.

A red-faced Cowboy was sexy, but this promise between them had to be something perverted.

"He wanted to watch." Itsuma grinned. He glanced at me as if to say there was still a chance he'd have his way with me.

Scott hid his face behind a book.

"Is that so?"

"But I'd be curious as to the two of you." Itsuma's intensity turned to Scott.

I wanted to shake the Prince up just a bit. "I'm versatile, so…"

Scott looked at me in curiosity. Itsuma crept up, leaned over and grabbed Scott's arm. "You smell like a horse."

"Don't!" Scott pulled back and launched out of his chair.

The Cowboy's prominent hard-on impressed me. He filled out those jeans nicely. But something wasn't right. The conversation had turned and I wasn't sure what was going on.

"Hey, Sensei, let me ask you, would you normally wash before going out on a date?" Itsuma was deadly serious. The air in the room became somewhat unpleasant. The static charge between the two bounced between their locked gaze.

"I didn't have time," Scott spat.

Itsuma prowled around the table. "That's bullshit. You're hiding again."

"I'm not."

What was going on?

"Why do you keep wincing? Why are you holding your ribs? Why didn't you go home already?"

"Itsuma," I said. "Lay off."

"No, Sensei, you see, he wants you worse than I do. There's no way he'd just sit there without making a pass at you. Not unless he's hiding something."

"Huh?" I would not have guessed that. Scott seemed so devoted to Itsuma that I'd figured he had an unrequited love for him.

Itsuma leaped so fast he was a blur. He grabbed Scott's arms.

"Let me go, you gook!" Scott yelled and ran backwards towards my front door.

"Fuck you, trailer-trash." Itsuma ran with him, grabbed Scott's shirt and ripped the buttons off, exposing a white bandage over my Cowboy's ribs.

"What the fuck is this?" Itsuma pointed a finger up and down Scott's chest.

"I fell."

It was an obvious lie. Purple bruises peeked over the bandage. They were fist-sized.

"You're going to tell me you fell down the stairs of your one-story house again, motherfucker?"

"Itsuma!" I said. Oh, the language!

"I fell off a horse." Scott's face turned red. "I didn't tell you because I knew you'd react like this."

Itsuma shook. It was the type of violent tremoring of a man holding back his rage. "Who you been riding?"

Scott stuttered, "J—Jenks."

"Liar!" Itsuma grabbed Scott and pushed him against my bookshelf.

"Itsuma!" I yelled.

He paid me no mind.

"I checked the board," Itsuma said. "You've been on Sea Breeze since last week."

Scott was getting pushed into a corner both verbally and physically. Yelling would only fuel the fire. I slipped next to them and rested a hand over the purple bruise on Scott's stomach.

Both men stopped glaring at each other and turned to me. I'd seen bruises like this before. They weren't from training, competition or matches. They were battle scars of abuse. Their damage was more physiological than physical. The bruise would heal. The impact of it having been there would take significantly more time.

My hand caressed his stomach and Scott bowed his head. His gaze turned inward. His face crumbled in an attempt not to cry.

A protective streak coursed through my veins and the words were out before I could think. "If you like, you can stay here tonight." He was legal age, able to make his own decisions.

"Yeah, that's actually a good idea." Itsuma backed me up, though his anger was still palpable.

Scott didn't give me an answer. He furrowed his brow.

"You don't have to," I said.

"Don't let him say shit about needing to go home, Sensei. Nobody's going to miss him there."

In that one sentence Itsuma revealed more than he thought.

Scott jerked his head up. "That's not true."

As a teacher, I was bound to protect my students. If I suspected abuse, I'd have to tell the principal. But there was another complication. Scott was eighteen. Being of legal age probably didn't put him under childhood services. Deep down, Scott was like Itsuma. They both had a macho sense of pride. It sounded as if Scott's pride was his self-respect. Without a doubt I'd make this a refuge for Scott, at least for a night. If he wanted it.

It didn't look as if Scott would accept the offer. So, I did what any tutor with a student who didn't want to study would do. I appealed to his weakness—something he couldn't refuse. Since Scott's pride was on the line, I'd use pride to steer him around.

"Of course you wouldn't stay here for free." My words came out lecherous. I had to get his attention somehow. "You'll have to do something for me."

Scott's look of caution pulled a smile from my lips. Such a hopeful face.

"Don't worry," I said. "It's not sexual favors or anything like that."

The disappointment in his eyes puffed up my ego, but I had a more innocent request. "Your grades are an eyesore."

Scott frowned. "I'm just a hired hand, and that's all I'll be."

A hired hand, huh? I firmed my mouth. My words needed to be clear. "If all you want to be is a hired hand, that's fine. But you will have options. You won't continue to do something you don't want."

Itsuma stood back and smiled. From the satisfaction in his eyes he was enjoying this conversation.

"If you think this is trivial then it won't be difficult." My index finger made lazy circles on his chest.

Scott crossed his arms, preventing me from touching him. But he was a smart kid. If he wanted to spend time with me, he'd accept.

"What do I have to do?"

"This." I waved my hands to the books. "You are going to graduate high school."

Scott cast a dubious eye over me. I threw caution to the wind because if he needed a safe place to stay I wanted him here. By the teachers' comments on his records it seemed his needs had been ignored. "We'll continue your tutoring idea. You will come here after school. I will feed you. I will tutor you. And you will study."

"I have a part-time job."

"He leaves it at six," Itsuma volunteered.

"But I get up at four in the morning for work, too." Scott glared at Itsuma.

Got it. Don't let Scott stay up too late.

"You can get here at six-thirty, have dinner, and study for an hour." *Then maybe fall asleep in my arms.* Jesus. Four in the morning? I didn't wonder about the *sleeps in class* notation any more.

Scott tsked. "An hour? What's that going to do?"

"Oh, so pessimistic." I set my hands on my hips. "That's my offer. Be with me five times a week. Take it or leave it." Hopefully he'd take the bait. If he wanted to get to know me, he'd accept.

Itsuma chuckled.

"And you…" I pointed to my Prince. "You aren't off the hook either."

"What?"

"Your classes are crap."

"The hell you saying? I have a perfect record."

"Which means you haven't even tried."

"Oh, this is bullshit." Itsuma tossed a frustrated hand at me. "Sure, one night is fine, but every night?"

"If you're not struggling at something then you're not reaching your potential."

"Excuse me? I do everything—"

"The truth is you're bored. If you have time to screw around with me, then you have too much time on your hands."

Scott snorted, trying to laugh incognito.

Itsuma gave me his best stare-down. Those dark, cat-like eyes stared at me with bitter contempt. His lips pursed, making me want to have him again. I was weak to his whims, but this time I wouldn't stand down. Education happened to be important to me.

Chapter 6

"If you want to take a shower, I'll help rewrap your bandage."

"I can do it." Scott's stubborn side was like trying to open an MWRAP tank with a can opener. But I wasn't going to give up.

Funny thing was, he hadn't fought me on staying here for the night. Itsuma had loaned him his cell phone so Scott could call his mom. I couldn't hear any of the conversation because Scott didn't say all that much and kept his voice low.

"I'll be right back," I said to Itsuma.

He waved his hand in dismissive engrossment. I knew it. Itsuma relished the challenge. He'd been bored in his classes. Our one-on-one changed his indifference to math.

I took Scott by the hand and led him to the guest bathroom. It felt like pulling a reluctant child. I closed the bathroom door and lifted his shirt. Amazingly, he didn't hinder me and just let it happen. I stepped over to the tub, plugged the drain and turned on the water. Now for the bandage. I carefully unhooked the safety pin holding the wrap. He hadn't gone to a hospital. This was a homemade fix. I rolled the gauze around his midsection in a tight cylinder. Again Scott allowed it.

When I saw the complete whole of his torso, I stared. A torrent of anger swirled my insides raw. Bruises the size of fists covered his stomach. Some of them were bands along his side. Those were kicks. Scott had been in some sort of brawl. From Itsuma's reaction this had happened before.

When I looked up to Scott's face he averted his eyes. His jaw set and clenched. My Cowboy wasn't going to tell me jack shit. He'd avoided or ignored my probing about the bandage earlier. Stubborn Cowboy was thick as a mule. Ask no questions, tell no lies.

Breathe in. Breathe out. I kept quiet.

Underneath the bruises was one hell of a body. Hot shit on a bun. Was this the body of an eighteen-year-old? Those biceps could lift railroad ties. I was deemed a cruiserweight in wrestling and fought heavyweights as a matter of pride, but one look at Scott and I was impressed. Yet it was only a momentary awe. I placed a hand on his chest. Shit, I felt tiny.

I swallowed my intimidation. Scott exuded power, but he also was exceedingly gentle. I slipped my hand up his shoulder and down his arm, skimming over another lesion. I lifted his hand and traced a thumb over his knuckles. The soft tops of his hands were in contrast to the callouses on his palms. He hadn't fought back. No bruises. No scars. No roughness along his knuckles.

Maybe he had just fallen off a horse. I lifted his hands, exposing the underside of his forearms. In boxing it's common to get bruises while blocking. The underside of Scott's arms looked like a rainbow. All the colors of physical punishment were there. This told me the entire story. Scott had taken a beating. Literally taken it.

Shock prevented me from saying anything. I kissed his knuckles and shut the door on my way out of the bathroom. Once out of his sight I leaned up against the wall. My hand flew to my mouth to muffle sympathetic cries. My knees weakened. My head spun. I was sliding down the wall that no longer held me up.

Itsuma caught me. Our eyes met. His stern face held me from breaking into pieces. Once out in my living room he set me in his lap on the chair. My Prince stroked my hair while I held him and trembled. My fists had turned white from squeezing so hard they lost all blood flow.

"Breathe," Itsuma said. "Or you will after you pass out."

"Fuck." I couldn't get a handle on the torment whirling around inside. "Tell me that's all from riding horses." I clung to Itsuma as if he'd save me from the knowledge that Scott, the fairly timid, gentle cowboy, was being abused—regularly. Even when he'd used his rope to subdue me it never caused serious damage.

Itsuma didn't answer me.

"Who?" I asked.

He breathed as if trying to calm his own waves of anger. "I think it's best if he stays here."

It was the best answer he could give without infringing on Scott's privacy. I gripped Itsuma, trying to hold onto the last vestiges of my dignity. Too little, too late. Wetness trickled down my cheeks.

"Let's get you back before curfew."

It took me a few minutes to stand. A full-grown adult and it took a kid to help stabilize me. Keep it together, Mori. What the hell? This wasn't the first time I'd seen bad bruises. But seeing them on Scott affected me.

I led Itsuma out to the garage where I kept my white Porsche Boxster convertible and climbed inside. Itsuma folded himself in the passenger seat with the air of a royal Japanese prince.

"No shocked question of how a substitute high school teacher can afford a car like this?" I pulled out of my garage.

He shrugged. Itsuma acted like money got deposited in his wallet every day. Of course, I wasn't one to talk either, but I got the impression he did not have any idea how much things cost.

Itsuma gave me directions to Malibu Canyon as I drove and we talked.

"Does Scott ride horses a lot?"

Itsuma sighed. "That's his job."

"Riding horses?"

"He's an assistant trainer for some stables in Chatsworth. He does the muck work too."

"Does he fall off horses often?" I snarled. It wasn't meant as a rhetorical question, but I was still reeling from my discovery. A part of me held out hope that maybe all that damage really was from an accident.

Itsuma was quiet for a moment and then answered, ignoring my underlying question. "I've watched him. He's one of the best. Even wild broncos can't throw him." Itsuma rustled in his seat. "Pisses me off."

"That he's good at riding?"

"That he'd blatantly lie."

"About?"

Itsuma tsked. "Ask him." He pointed at a road. "After this curve, turn left on the side street."

I turned. "Do you know why he's barely passing?" Scott was a smart kid.

"Figure it out yourself, genius."

Christ, Itsuma's attitude sucked sometimes. "May I ask what your relationship with him is?"

Itsuma's white-toothed smile glowed against my interior lights. "Are you interested, Sensei? Would you like to date us?"

I feigned nonchalance. "Just curious."

Itsuma sat back. "We used to go out, but I fucked up."

"Hmmm… surprise, surprise."

I expected an explosion and got a whispered plea.

"Just be slow with him. He's delicate." Itsuma crossed his arms.

Scott being called delicate might have seemed like a mismatched description, but after seeing him today I agreed with Itsuma.

"Here it is. Pull over."

There was only one side to pull over on. Across the way was a cliff. I pulled off on the dirt road next to a gate. From here it looked like an empty lot. A few lights in the distance proved there was a house out there somewhere.

"Will you be okay?"

Itsuma's narrow eyes made him look like he was scowling all the time. Only his warm smile tipped me off to his teasing mood. "Are you afraid of the dark, Sensei?"

"I'm not afraid, I'm concerned for you. The road is narrow."

Itsuma leaned over between the buckets seats and shoved his tongue down my throat. Just like he had when we were in my dining room. I tried pushing him off, but the headrest prevented me from evading. A hand slipped in between my thighs and fingers groped my balls. My moan of protest quickly died into compliancy. He could have me right here in my car if he continued. Only something drastic would save me now.

I undid my seat belt and opened my driver's side door. I spilled out the open escape onto the dirt bank. "Don't do that out in public!" Of course, yelling about it like a drama queen was just as bad.

"Why? Because we're both men, or because you're a teacher?"

"Itsuma!" I stood up and brushed the dirt off my jeans.

"There's no one else that lives on this road." He opened his side door and got out. "Don't get huffy, Sensei."

"Don't dismiss me like that." *No wonder you fucked up with Scott.* I almost said it. But that seemed too petty.

Itsuma smiled. "You're cute, Sensei."

"Well, you're not." I was being toyed with. It got me irritated as all hell.

"Goodnight, and Sensei?"

"What?"

"You belong to both of us." Itsuma's voice turned velvet, twisting my gut and quickening the pace of my heart. He got out, walked to the gate and slipped inside the property.

I got back into my car and sat there with a raging hard-on. Prick. Leaving me like this so I'd think about him on the drive home. So childish. It worked. Twenty minutes later that kiss was something that didn't leave my mind even as I pulled into the garage. My stiff cock hadn't abated one bit. I turned off the engine and tried to calm down. Scott was inside but I didn't want to go in there like this.

Great. *Go easy on him*, Itsuma said. How the hell was I supposed to that? Put on tight underwear and hope I could keep myself in check? Wait and let this throbbing member go down naturally?

I got out of my car and spied Scott's Chevy truck still parked on the street. A good sign. He hadn't snuck out and left. I pushed the button to lower the garage door and went inside. He wasn't in the kitchen, the living room or the bathroom. But I found a half-naked Cowboy clinging to my pillow sprawled across my bed. A towel covered his lower half and he'd re-wrapped his middle, but what I could see of that back, those powerful shoulders and his muscled arms wasn't helping my wood. *Calm yourself, Mori. He's hurting both inside and out.*

Asleep and burying his nose in my pillow, there could be nothing more endearing. I wanted to eat him. Right here, right now. Keeping myself in check, I crawled on my bed beside him and passed my fingers lightly over a few stray bangs.

Scott opened his eyes. I thought I saw fear in them for a split second, but he smiled and snuggled into my pillow.

"Sorry." His cheeks flushed. "I can sleep on the couch. Can I borrow some pajamas?"

I laughed at his modesty and how completely different he was from Itsuma.

"No." I pulled the covers down. It took herculean effort to keep from fondling his body. He needed rest. "You can sleep here or in the guest bed. I don't think I have clothes in size hunk, so you'll just have to stay in the buff or wear too-short sweats and too-tight t-shirts."

Scott sat up, still holding my pillow. The real feat was that he managed that maneuver without the towel dropping from around his waist. "Is… is that okay? If I sleep with you?"

Shit. I'd expected him to take the guest room. Of course, my heart and my cock agreed about where I wanted him sleeping. The two against my logical brain tried winning over the whole *this is a bad idea* argument.

"Scott…"

"I mean just sleep," Scott rushed in his explanation.

"Like gentlemen."

He nodded.

"This really isn't appropriate."

"I don't want to sleep alone."

He might as well admit he had night terrors and I was his life vest. "Then I'm going to ask questions, and I'll expect honest answers." If that didn't scare him into the other room and he was hell-bent on being next to me, well then, I'd keep to myself. This was my compromise between my heart, body and mind. If he was going to hide, he could hide everything and stay in the other room. "I'll give you a moment to think about it."

I got up, went to the bathroom, and brushed my teeth. I found Scott's jeans, shirt and underwear in the washer and shoved them in the dryer. After my rounds, checking all the doors were locked and lights were out in the house, I went back to my bedroom.

Scott was already under the covers. Well, I'd get answers.

"Do you want anything? Water?"

"No," he whispered.

A flash of modesty washed over me. Scott's shyness was contagious. *Pitiful, Mori, he's already seen most your body.*

I turned off the light and stripped. Normally, I'd wear sweat pants and a shirt to bed, but the lure of touching skin to skin left me wearing only pants. God, I wanted to rub myself all over him. Good thing I turned off the lights or my eyes would have been molesting him before I got in the bed. Then I remembered his bruises. The kid was so banged up I'd be afraid of hurting him.

When I climbed under the covers I ignored the hard hunk of meat between my legs and turned on my side. As I was lounging with my head in my hand it was Scott who started the questions.

"So when you said you were versatile, what did you mean?"

"It means that I can top or bottom." I let him process for a bit.

"Do you like women?"

I chuckled. "I have nothing against women, I just don't get hard for them."

Scott's relieved sigh said much. I knew how it was liking a straight man and then the angst of him finding out and the weirdness that comes with trying to act normal. That whole road was a mess.

"Itsuma liked women. I think he still does." Scott lay there looking at the ceiling.

"Itsuma goes both ways, so don't think you've messed him up for life." That painful road was hell for both sides.

"I wasn't sure about him being bi until tonight."

"Tonight?" I asked. "What about Monday?"

"He was just playing a gag. Revenge for some petty pissing contest."

"Wow. Harsh hazing."

Scott sat straight up. "No, no! I went because I didn't want either of you hurt."

"Scott…"

"Please understand, I didn't expect him to go that far. I was there to keep him… I'm sorry. I reacted too slow."

I grabbed his arm, threw my leg over his hips and planted myself gently in his lap. "Scott, it's okay. Stop blaming yourself."

"But that's not how I wanted to start with you."

"It's okay." I wrapped my arms around his shoulders and pulled him into my warmth.

"I'm sorry."

Shit. What could I say to calm him down? I tightened my grip and held him as he clung to me like a lost child.

"Make it up to me by letting me keep you safe," I whispered into his blond hair.

Scott let out a shuddered breath.

Before he could take hold of the conversation I asked, "So, what's your preference?" *Great, Mori. Such a pervert.* But it was the only thing that came to mind.

Scott looked up at me. "Like, what's my type?"

It was pretty obvious what his type was, but that wasn't what I was asking. "You like them short, tough and with a little bit of an attitude."

He shrugged. Scott wasn't denying my assessment.

"Are you a top or a bottom?"

"Ahhh, well, ummm…" Scott loosened his hold on me. "About that."

He was a virgin? "So you and Itsuma never went that far?"

"No, that's not it. I'm just not sure."

How could he not be sure? Unless… *I fucked it up. Oh, Itsuma.* Sounded like Scott and I shared a similar past. If what I assumed was true, and Scott was a bottom, then maybe his first time was not so pleasant. I could relate. Boy, could I relate.

"So, you've bottomed?" Scott looked at me from under his lashes.

"Yes. I have."

"Does it always hurt?"

I shook my head. "With enough lube and a slow start it's actually pretty addicting. Have you ever wanted to top?"

Scott squirmed under me. "Um. No."

"So you want to be the receiver."

"I'm not sure I can do that either."

His demeanor seemed familiar. Indecisive. Just like me five years ago. Things were becoming clear. "Ah. Okay. Let me guess. You and Itsuma got together, he pushed for sex and wound up hurting you." A past too similar to mine.

Scott nodded. "I was the one who pushed for sex, but it was bad."

Yep. I was right. "You, sir, have bottom trauma." It was a common story. "You're hard up because you want it, but you can't do it because it's terrifying."

The scared, how-did-you-know look in Scott's eyes told me I was right.

My decision was already made. "We'll take it slow. After you graduate."

"I can't wait that long." Scott's breath stuttered. His passionate words smashed a part of my resolve. Strong arms pulled me in and his lips pressed against my chest.

Crap. I can't think clearly when it involves physical pleasure. It got me in predicaments. Even so, this time was different. My heart beat faster. My mind muddled. Scott's light kisses and the way his voice quavered the *couldn't wait* comment made my strength waver. Such a bastard—that was me. I didn't want to wait either, but I must.

Scott nuzzled his way down to my nipples. A sharp bite of teeth had me arching my back, pushing into the pleasure.

"Wait…" We couldn't do this. I had to keep asking questions.

Hands rubbed warmth into my back muscles. His tongue played with my erect chest buttons.

"Scott…" My cock started thumping against my abdomen. "We should really wait."

But there was zero conviction behind my statement. I would stop if he told me too. My plea was the last fight for responsibility. Inside my heart I knew I might regret this weakness.

"I… I need to…" Scott whispered. His voice infused a now-or-never urgency into the air.

Well, shit. "You're my student."

"I'm eighteen and I'm not your student when I'm not in class." He set me on my back and laced kisses down my stomach. Tentative lips traveled further, bridging his kisses between my pants and skin, his breath lulling me into the warmth I craved. The soft sensation washed over me to let my guard down. All the tension in my shoulders relaxed all through my spine. If he were like Itsuma I could fight. But Scott had seen enough abuse. I couldn't bring myself to push at his bruised body.

"Please," I moaned. "Just wait for a little…"

Without any more warning, he'd slipped my pants down and consumed my cock. My tip hit tonsils so hard I jerked up.

"Scott! Whoa. Stop. What are you doing?"

My Cowboy rose up into a sitting position. "Did I hurt you?"

"No, but slow down." This was supposed to be a nice and easy cuddle session. Not all out war.

Scott climbed on top of me. "Would this be better?" He grabbed my hard rod and started guiding me into his back end.

"Stop!" I pushed on his hips. "Damn it. I don't mind you on top, but we need to go slower."

"Did I do something wrong?"

"No!" I panted. "But if you just cram it in I'll hurt you."

"I don't mind." His look of concern was for me. It broke my heart. "If it's you, I don't care if it hurts."

"What? Well, I do!" I reached up, took his face into my palms and looked into his eyes. "Did you think about how I would feel if I hurt you?"

He looked ashamed. "I'm sorry, Mr. Reis."

"Don't be sorry." I calmed down a little and rested my hands on his shoulders. "You can't just dive in. A bottom needs to prepare."

We both stayed as we were. Me leaning my hands against his chest while he tensed those beautiful muscles underneath me. I relaxed when he wasn't trying to force me inside him. It was difficult to let a top climb over me, and it had to be the same for Scott. My Cowboy hadn't been with me, so he didn't know what to expect. Yet he was so desperate he dived in without knowing the consequences. It seemed I found my modesty when it came to Scott.

"Please understand that I don't do this sort of thing just for fun." Not anymore. This kid did "it" for me. I wanted him the right way. Or at least as right as possible.

"Mr. Reis, I'm not playing with you. I'm serious. I meant what I said. If it's you, I can endure whatever."

I closed my eyes. Could he not see how much that hurt me? *Enduring* is not an option."

"I have to. Can't you understand?"

My hands skimmed his wrapped chest. He probably didn't know any other way than pain. I'd teach him the opposite of enduring.

He grabbed my hand and kissed my fingers. "Please…"

His plea battered my heart. "I know it feels like you can't wait, but…"

"This is my only chance with you."

"That's not true." What, did he think I'd walk away from him after he graduated?

"There might not be a tomorrow for me."

What? "That's not fair."

"Life hardly is." He started to press my cock up against his entrance.

"Alright!" He'd suffered enough. "You win. If you're hell-bent on disregarding me, then at least give me the chance to make it feel good."

Scott sat back, his head lowered in shame. "I'm sorry. I thought… maybe Itsuma's right. Maybe I am projecting."

I climbed out from under him and got off the bed. "Sit here." I patted the edge of the bed. "Let me get in between your legs."

Scott moved where I told him and set his feet on the floor. I got in between his knees and admired his amorous cock.

"If I hurt you, promise to tell me," I said, well aware I'd probably have to say it again and again. No matter. I'd use all my senses to gauge his threshold. It was up to me to make sure he never felt anything uncomfortable. My hands glided up and down his thighs. "Making love has nothing to do with pain. Understand?"

He sucked in a breath, and even in the dim light, I could see his eyes widen.

"Do you understand?"

Scott nodded.

"Tell me if it hurts." My hands moved closer to his balls. "And tell me what you like."

He stared down at me like I was making a fantasy come to life. That expression left a heady impression. I stuck out my tongue and licked the underside of his cock. Pressing my thin beard against his velvet underside, I dragged my chin as I stroked him with my tongue.

Scott's reaction was better than I expected. He threw his head back and let out grunts of pleasure. My tongue lavished him in waves, all to hear his ego-boosting cries. I flicked his tip with my tongue and teased his cock head with my mouth, each time checking his response. My eyes were riveted to his face, ready to back off at any moment.

I lipped his shaft, taking his tip in my mouth, and traced the ridges of his cock with my tongue.

Not one iota of discomfort crossed his face.

Scott repeated, "Yes… yes…" at nearly every stroke, flick and teasing of my tongue and mouth. That's when I took the plunge and took his cock slowly down my throat. I didn't force it. Instead, I suckled him, letting the dry parts get lubricated from each pass. Scott leaned back and spread his legs wider. His short staccato outbursts, combined with his glazed-over expression, made me crave more. My heart soared. His sounds, his taste, his skin was an addiction. One hit and I was hooked.

He threw his legs out wider and leaned back onto the bed. With better access, I could now tease his back end. My hand glided over his thighs, down to the business part of his ass, making sure he knew where I was going. His cock flexed when my fingers hinted at the notion of rimming his hole.

"Good," he cried out.

Thank god. He was communicating.

His passionate abandon placed him in the right mental place. Perfect. I kept going while reaching out and opening my nightstand drawer. I felt around until the lube bottle rolled into my hand.

Freeing his cock from my mouth, I stroked him and said, "I'm going to start with fingers. You tell me if it hurts."

Scott nodded, but I wasn't positive cohesive thought was getting past his pleasure haze. I kept pumping his cock while I grabbed a special lubricator with a packet of Astroglide with an attached thin, long tube that helped insert the gel.

"This might feel cool, but it won't hurt. It's just lubricant." There was no sexy way to say it, but I wanted him to know what to expect.

Scott nodded and smiled, but his cock lost some of its hardness. He was frightened. Yet he still made like it was nothing. A chip of my heart broke off and drifted into the *for Scott* part of my soul.

I ripped off the tip of the applicator, slipped the flexible, thin tube up Scott's back channel and squeezed the bladder. He sucked in a breath but otherwise didn't move.

"I'm only touching, okay?" I watched Scott's face for the slightest hint of discomfort.

"Okay," his voice cracked.

"Did it hurt?"

"No."

"Are you okay?"

"Yes." He smiled and those white teeth blazed in the dark room.

"Good." I flipped the lid off the bottle and coated my right hand until my fingers were dripping. I closed the lube, tossed it, took the base of his cock with my dry hand and lavished my oral technique with lips, tongue and suction for his pleasure.

Scott expressed his gratitude by letting loose with seductive panting. "Yes… Mr. Reis… yes." His hands explored the tangles of my long hair and gently pulled my strands back into his loose fist. A few stray locks escaped his grasp, and each time he would gently lift the escapee back up.

I couldn't get enough. My tongue stroked up and down his silky skin. I wanted to excite him until his cock couldn't get any harder. I sucked and teased, watching his expressions. So far only enjoyment crossed his relaxed face.

As he got harder I pushed that cock of his down my throat until I swallowed him to his base at every stroke. His whimpers became my favorite soundtrack. Slow and steady, I kept my pace. He was shaking. The kid was holding back.

"Move your hips. Lose yourself."

He was being too restrained. Too polite. Scott trembled in the fervent shaking from need. "Mr. Reis! Mori!"

Good boy. I smiled while plunging down on his cock. Now was the perfect time to introduce fingers. I stroked a thumb under his balls, pressing against the section of skin above his anus. His cock flexed in my mouth. He was ready.

The twinge of hesitation in his eyes had me reassuring him. "Just fingers."

Our eyes locked as I rubbed the lubricant between my fingers. I willed away the uncertainty I saw in his face. Only a good experience would cast his fear out. I'd make sure to take it easy and blow his mind in the best possible way.

I went back to using my oral skills to calm him. I'd make him forget his troubles. At first I rubbed around his back end, slicking his body and getting him used to the idea. All the while I never stopped letting him feel the pleasure of oral sex.

My forefinger rubbed up and down, desensitizing the trauma area. Scott responded surprisingly well. He let his head fall back and relaxed his legs even further. Once the lubricant spread, the apprehension changed to lust.

"Good?"

"Yes," he panted.

"Just relax. I won't go further than you want. Talk to me." It was the best way to get him over this. He'd have to beg before I'd plunge my fingers in.

"There," he said. "I like it when you stroke me… over my… entrance."

Giving him control worked. He relaxed completely, sliding down onto his back. Letting me work him through his anxiety. Of course I was prepared for him *not* to give the word to go further. Just getting him this far was a triumph in my mind.

Scott moaned and panted but didn't give me any more instruction. My free hand took his cock, and again I took him in my mouth. I stayed in control, bobbing my head up and down his shaft while my fingers grazed his back end in languid teasing.

Scott let out more of that sexy voice. He had an amazing amount of flexibility. His feet spread wide, his thighs spread, he lay there in submission and trust. So sexy.

His hips started meeting my oral thrusts. His hands clutched my bedspread. Good. Seemed like he was letting himself go.

"Mr. Reis, please enter me."

I near choked. *Jeez. Don't say it like that or I'll get the wrong idea.* "Just fingers."

"Whatever, get inside me."

His words short-circuited my brain. *Fingers. Only fingers.* My cock waggled, trying to convince me otherwise. *No. No.* I pushed my index finger inside his back channel. He clenched and I halted.

Scott thrust his hips and moaned, "More."

Brave kid. I pushed in and waited. "Scott? Are you okay?"

He popped his head up. Glazed-over eyes told me enough. He was feeling it. Thank god.

"Your mouth…" he said. "So good."

I smiled and wiggled my finger. "Relax."

He dropped his head back down and squirmed as I rooted for his pleasure spot.

"Breathe, relax."

Scott let out a breath and unclenched his ass.

"Good boy." I took his cock in my mouth once more and gently pushed in with my finger. He gasped and closed his knees, boxing my head in between his thighs.

His high-pitched cries filled my room. "More!"

I thought he'd come, but he lowered his knees back down and gripped the bedspread tighter.

"More!" He sounded desperate.

The lubricant did its job. My fingers could now slide back and forth easier. Fuck, this kid was good. I could get lost in him. He brought out my protective streak. If I wasn't careful I'd fall into a more dominant position and take his ass with my cock. He wasn't ready for that. Even if his insides were warm and soft, even if he could take another finger, we had to go slow. I was going for that special button to send him over. I wanted to know where he liked it, and how far I could go. To find the place that would free him of his bad experience. Just another moment and I'd find it.

Scott's hips tried keeping up with both my fingers sliding in and out, and also my mouth pumping his cock.

"Deeper!" He grabbed my hand holding his cock.

"With my mouth or fingers?"

"Yes!" Scott had a vise grip on my wrist.

Well, if he wanted deeper, I could do that. I added my middle finger and increased my pace a little.

"Good?"

He loosened his grip on my hand. "Yes."

I reined in my control and stayed in a solid, easy rhythm so he could predict my movement. My mouth went back to tantalizing his cock.

Scott pushed at my forehead. "Wait! I'll come."

Exactly the point. "It's okay, let go." I pinned his hand down and continued. If he came while I was playing with both front and back, his bottom trauma would subside a little. Bit by bit he'd be comfortable with more and more. I'd been through the same process.

"No," Scott used his free hand and pushed at my forehead again. "I want you inside me."

I stopped pumping. "That's too much tonight."

"Please," Scott's breathless appeal struck a massive blow to my resolve. His power of seduction might have been the source of his bad experience, but no way in hell would I ever blame Scott. The temptation to taste him was strong. If I hadn't had my own experience with bottom trauma, I might have fallen to my desire.

I pulled my fingers out and climbed on top of him, making sure to keep my cock in check and not press on his bruises. I looked in his eyes and with my firm teacher's voice said, "No."

Scott's face distorted in guilt, "But I have to…" He squeezed his eyes shut and covered his face with an arm.

"Why?" I lowered my lips to his chest, placing delicate kisses over his body. He needed to know I wasn't going to be pushed into hurting him.

He kept his face hidden, but answered. "I know it's childish and stupid, but I want to continue."

"Does this have anything to do with Itsuma?" Immediately I regretted bringing up another man's name in the bedroom.

Scott sighed.

Yes. This had everything to do with the man not physically here. I wasn't into being a replacement. I stopped everything and crawled up next to Scott on the bed. "I don't want to get in the way of your relationship with him," I said.

"You're not." Scott lay there. "If anything it's the other way around."

"What do you mean?"

"I mean, maybe if I were as smart as he is, or if I were interested in giving rather than receiving, then maybe I could compete with him. But I can't even do that."

Oh, I did have it backwards. "So, you're basically wanting to go all the way because of Itsuma, right?"

"Didn't I say it was childish and stupid?"

My turn to sigh. "Scott, you are smart. In fact, you're probably the most intelligent of us all. I bet if you put your mind to it, you'd run circles around him." If Scott could read and think his way around such an archaic history book, he could do the same with anything. "And you're sexy as hell." I ran my palm up his stomach. "With that shy smile and shaggy hair, I bet all your lovers have to yank ladies and dudes off all the time."

In fact, I made a mental note never to bring him to a bar. Ever. He'd be surrounded faster than I could fight them off.

A semblance of Scott's bright smile crossed his face.

"So whatever relationship I have with Itsuma," I said. "I don't want you to compare it to ours. And don't try to keep up. Everyone is different. Everyone relates differently."

"I just really like you."

"And I like you. So don't do things that make you feel uncomfortable." God, did that get through to him? I liked him, not the things he could do or the things he thought he had to do for me.

"I'm not. I really do want you." Scott leaned over to me and planted a lingering kiss on my lips.

I let him take the lead and responded in kind when he deepened the kiss. He laid me back and climbed on top of me. Only this time he gave me room to escape, and he didn't seem so desperate. Thank god. I rather enjoyed this slow seduction. Most of my partners were hot, heavy and casual. Making love was a novelty. Being slow was different and arousing.

As he doled out kisses like chocolate candies, his cock hung low and traipsed around my lower abdomen.

"Here, lower your waist." I grabbed his ass and pushed his hips downward. Our cocks mingled together. Oh, that felt good. Both rods sliding between us, the feel of our hardness against each other. It wasn't long before my hips moved on their own.

"Oh, fuck, we're going to need a towel," I said.

Scott bent his knees and hovered over me. He seemed cautious after our conversation. It gave me the chance to slip my arm between us, grab both our cocks in one hand and start pumping. Scott watched for a while as I stroked. Then he took over the hand job.

I let sensation take me away. "You are so much better at this than me," I said. I didn't hold back; I let him hear the pleasure he gave me. Just as he'd turned me on with his cries, I let myself go. I rolled my hips in a sexual dance, trying to relieve the pressure building from my talented lover. My hands roamed his body. I caressed the dips of his chest, his strong thighs, and the part of his ten-pack abs that wasn't wrapped in gauze. All that rippling muscle under my fingers got me up to my peak.

"Mr. Reis, I want to try."

Reason and logic were beyond my capacity. "Scott…" My weak protest turned into a squeak.

"Don't worry. You won't hurt me." He grabbed my thick rod and started guiding me in.

"Wait!" I rolled up and held him in my lap. If he was set on doing this and breaking down my defenses, I'd at least do the responsible thing. I grabbed a condom from the drawer and strapped it on so fast it could be in the Guinness World Records. I dumped lube over my gloved cock in a wave. Most of the lubricant actually made it onto my intended appendage. But some went everywhere else, like the sheets, on Scott, down between us, on the floor. I didn't care.

"Okay, ready." I lay back down.

Scott chuckled softly. I pretended not to hear. My Cowboy rose on his knees and I helped guide my cock against his hole. I was so hard I throbbed. This was my absolute limit. My rod couldn't get any bigger. Scott was unbelievably sexy. From his long sandy blond locks to the crooked path of curls under his navel, I wanted him.

While he adjusted, trying to find the right place for entry, I casually stroked his cock.

"You're distracting me," he said.

"That's the point." I didn't stop pumping. "May I help?"

Scott nodded.

I grabbed the base of my rod and guided myself until I found the right spot to enter. I set a hand on his hip and helped him lower. His ass spread over my tip. *Oh, so good.* I loved that moment when my head invaded a new man. The first time going inside Scott and going slow made this so much more delicious. His rim was slick and pulsing.

Scott sucked in a breath.

"Relax." I stopped pushing him down. "Breathe."

His lips parted and he sunk further. I let out a whimper as my head plundered my sexy Cowboy. He stopped and held me at half-mast. Watching this amazing display was enough to keep me at my hardest while he adjusted to me. God, I could feel him. My cock was inside, but I desperately wanted more. I kept a tight lid on the urge to move my hips or force him down. I remained occupied by stroking his cock and rolling his nipples.

Watching the twitches of discomfort on his face helped abate the need to sink all the way inside him. This was his demon to conquer. All I wanted was to let him feel how good it could be.

"You're pushing yourself," I said.

"No." He grimaced. "Give me a moment."

Scott lifted a little but then dropped down, taking more of me on his descent.

Much more of this teasing and I'd come. All thought ceased as Scott pumped his way down. My ministrations of pleasuring him stopped. It was all I could do to prevent losing my load. Now I was the one churning out squeaks of pleasure and making stupid faces. Scott's insides heated my cock. He was slick, warm and soft. Pliable yet firm. I was losing my mind.

"Oh please, oh please, oh please…" I heard myself plead. Fuck. When could I start driving in? I grabbed Scott's hips but resisted the urge to push down. I waited, maintaining a low level of conscience as he sunk my cock into his body. Scott's perfectly shaped ball sack nestled in my pubic hair.

"Oh… god…" My guttural cry was a victory. For both of us. I pressed him down with my hands and lifted my hips up. He was all the way down. I was all the way in, and at the edge of my control. Shit. I'd ruin his trust if I couldn't prevent the natural urge to pound him like a rabbit.

"Scott!" I yelled out. "Don't move."

"It's okay." Scott's calm voice anchored me.

"No, I'm not going to hurt you."

"Like I said, Mr. Reis, if it's you I can bear it." His breathy voice didn't have any hint of discomfort.

I ran out of words. My brain could only handle so much. There was only one way to regain any composure. I'd have to come. Fortunately, I was close to my release. I had to keep from going wild on Scott.

"Can you move a little?" Even a wiggle would do.

Scott lifted straight up and slid down, seating himself as before. His ass tugged at all the right spots, building the pressure needed for my orgasm.

"One more," I said.

When he dropped down again my wail held no evidence of masculinity. I'd be done with one more.

Scott rotated his hips. "Anything for you, Mori." Then he rose up and slammed back down.

My release spilled over. My legs spasmed. My core tightened. I pushed up as far as I could inside of Scott.

Scott let out a bellow. Wet splotches hit my face and chest. He was rubbing out the last of his orgasm. *Oh god. We came at the same time.* A certain amount of relief washed over me. The kid had done it. He'd made us feel good and gotten over the first hurdle of bottom trauma.

He collapsed on top of me. Scott weighed a ton. My arms wrapped around his back and I kissed his neck.

"How was that?" I asked.

No response.

"Scott?" I nudged him.

Damn. He felt like dead weight. I turned us over. His eyes were closed and he breathed slow and heavy.

"Scott?"

No way. He was asleep. Out cold. Good night, sweet darling. *Oh wow. After his orgasm he fell unconscious.* I was speechless. If that wasn't some ego boost. Hell, we were still connected. My heart warmed. I rubbed my face in his chest and giggled.

"Thank you, lover," I whispered. "We both really needed that, huh?"

So much for the rest of my questions. I kissed him lightly on the lips and pulled myself out. Disposing of my condom, I used a damp towel to clean myself up. I did what I could to clean up Scott, but he didn't wake up. I managed to roll him under the covers and joined my Cowboy in sleep.

♂♂♂

I woke to slow, deliberate, probing kisses. Scott's breath tasted minty, like he'd just brushed his teeth. The room was dark. I was disoriented, but this was one hell of a great way to clear my mind. Or rather lose my inhibitions. I wasn't used to having a guest in my house or being woken before sunrise.

"What time is it?" Had I overslept? The clock read four a.m.

"I have to go to work," Scott said.

Oh, but my cock was saying, *stay*. "Why?" I clung onto my lover like a child trying to prevent his overnight friend from leaving.

He held me close and his low chuckle ruffled my hair. "Horses need to be fed, stalls need to be mucked."

"I'll give you some muck."

Again his amusement tickled my ear. His face was so warm. "Next time I'll last longer."

"You were amazing," Tingles still ran up my spine at the thought of his powerful muscles gripping my cock.

"Get some rest." Scott set me down.

It was easy to sink back into the fluffy pillow, but not so easy to ignore the growing hardness between my legs. I listened to him walk out of my bedroom, then out the door. I snuggled deeper into my mattress and fell asleep before my lower half kept me awake.

Chapter 7

Walking from my car to my classroom proved I hadn't had sex in six months. I was out of practice. All the muscles in my lower back, my ass, my balls and my cock reminded me of Itsuma and Scott's extracurricular activities last night.

The real mystery of it all was, why was my stomach so sore? I trained every day. Yet one or both of those boys made me work muscles I didn't know needed training.

But I was happy. Smiling like a fool happy. Walking on air happy. I guess certain frustrations had piled up. Which was why I let two students have their way with me. Of course, I was the responsible party. This circumstance was a disaster. Still, I couldn't bring an ounce of *give-a-fuck* to the situation. Those two meant more than anything to me. Which was why I had to protect them.

It wasn't going to be easy, and it meant a whole career down the toilet, but I had to do something about the abuse Scott endured. Tonight, we'd discuss the topic specifically. I'd get Scott out of his predicament. We'd get Itsuma to take what he wanted to do in life seriously. I'd resist them until graduation. Until then I'd keep it in my pants. But I would have to tell Principal Ellis.

I'd be blacklisted. I'd lose my CIT gig. And I might have to move to Belgium, but if Scott and Itsuma were with me it'd be worth it.

Shocking how my thoughts went long-term—with both Scott and Itsuma. I didn't want to give either one up. Not for the other. Package deal. The way Itsuma presented this whole debacle *they* wanted me. Well then, it was *their* fault I was possessive over the two of *them*.

I hadn't thought about long-term since high school five years ago. The proposition was welcome. The dam of logic holding back consequences and reality started showing cracks. No, I shouldn't think this way. Itsuma was just playing with me. Scott…

Just a little more time. A little more of this lighthearted feeling. Tomorrow, the world would come crashing down. But the taste of long-term had an enticing flavor. I'd stopped being the wild child, the versatile short-term partner passed around like a party favor, but I hadn't stepped into having a permanent lover mindset either. Both Itsuma and Scott held equal footing in my heart. I shouldn't touch either one.

Even knowing Itsuma would leave after graduation, I resolved to firmly set rules for our relationship. Setting a no-sex-until-graduation rule was top on the list. Getting them through the year and off to college, or wherever, was top priority.

♂♂♂

When the time for homeroom came, Itsuma casually walked in like he always did, except he was talking on the phone. He stopped beside my desk, listening to whoever was on the other end. My Prince didn't look happy. Not the usual *you embarrassed me* unhappy but more like a grim acceptance.

"So, you're not coming in at all?" Itsuma said to the person on the line.

A pause.

"What about after?" Itsuma glowered at the ground. "Don't be a douchebag."

More listening.

"Then I'll meet you at your place."

I heard a distinct voice on the other end yell out, "No!"

Itsuma pulled the phone away from his ear, giving the device an expression of disbelief.

The voice on the other end of the line was Scott.

"Okay, man, okay," Itsuma said into the phone. "But you better meet me there or I'm coming to get you." Itsuma tapped a thumb to his phone, cutting off the call in the middle of Scott's protestation.

"Scott's not coming to class," Itsuma said.

A spike slammed into my heart. Painful waves of nausea spread over my body. Was Scott embarrassed? Had I hurt him? Or maybe he felt it was a mistake to sleep with me. I felt my face drain of blood. It was like my life force was being sucked dry.

"Why?"

Itsuma shrugged. "Guess he's working."

Working? He was a student. His full-time job was education.

Heat warmed my cheeks. *Get ahold of yourself, Mori.* After two breaths and a mental chokehold on my emotions, I reverted to my usual teacher mode.

Don't think, just do.

My Prince went to his seat and the buzzer rang. Routine would save me. With a hand bracing my forehead, I started roll call. When I got to Scott's name, I'd gone numb. I remembered to skip over his name, but when it came time… I called out, "Itsuma Karter."

I sighed. Disgusted at myself I just checked the box for present. *I'm an idiot.*

"Ohayō," Itsuma said.

My heart skipped. My mind froze. I blinked several times and continued roll, the rest of the time internally freaking out like a girl. Did he know I was ready to cry? Was disappointment written all over my face? Was he trying to calm my nerves? Did he know about last night? Did Scott tell him? Internalizing my bitter displeasure, Itsuma's leeway relieved my stress the tiniest bit. It was enough. I could kiss him. *Thank you. Thank you. Thank you.*

After I confirmed attendance I dared a glance at Itsuma. A melting glower that both seduced and frightened me twisted my gut. His eyes hinted at a darkness sexual in nature. My body responded. *Yes, yes, yes. Make me submit. No. No. No. Forbidden fruit. No sex. Bad sensei.* My insides were jittering so much I thought my guts would crawl out my ass.

I tore my eyes away. No doubt Itsuma would claim victory and laugh. Visions of being tied from ankle to elbow sitting before Itsuma and "forced" to suck his cock ran wild in my thoughts. Shit. I'd have myself whipped up and ready for the taking by the time he got to my place tonight.

Itsuma's phone call replayed in my mind.

What about after? Don't be a douchebag. Now the comment made sense. Scott wasn't planning on coming this evening. My heart lurched into a free fall. I'd hurt him. He didn't want to come back. I'd taken it too far. His trauma was probably worse. How could I have been so stupid? I wasn't strong enough to resist. My weakness for pleasure hurt Scott. I couldn't forgive myself.

"Mr. Reis?"

I lifted my head from my hands. Susan, a student, stood on the other side of my desk. The class was emptied out, save a few stragglers. The bell had rung without my notice.

"Yes?"

The frail, tawny girl with sad eyes and a mothering way about her probably couldn't help herself when she saw someone so desperately miserable.

"I just wanted to make sure you were okay. You went pale all of a sudden."

"Thank you, Susan." I set my hands down. "I'm fine."

"Okay then. See you later."

I gave her my best smile and nodded. Itsuma caught my eye as he walked out of the classroom. He acted as if he couldn't care less about me. Good. He was playing it cool. As much as it hurt, we needed to keep a certain distance. But I wanted to know about Scott.

Go to hell, Mori, you weak bastard. You can't even keep your hands off a student. You're the worst.

Ultimately, the high I rode in on didn't even last half a day.

Chapter 8

My swollen, raw fists hit the punching bag over and over. For the last ninety minutes I'd been hitting the leather bag in the training room of my house. The knuckles of both hands stung at every blow. I'd wrapped my hands, refused gloves and beat the hell out of myself to feel pain.

I'd kept my composure through the day, but I'd gone straight home after last period. I wanted this self-loathing out. It wasn't containable anymore. I'd failed Scott. Failed myself. And failed Itsuma. I hadn't gone to the principal because I was weak, and because I wanted to take a pound of flesh out of myself. Maybe I should get a chastity belt, or get a Prince Albert so sex would hurt for a while. I shuddered.

Sweat burned the open sores on my hands, but the pain wasn't enough. Nothing had quenched the thirst for revenge on myself. White-hot, molten inward hate cooled to a simmering lifelong contempt after my hour-and-a-half workout. The clock said five. Itsuma would be here in another hour and a half. Sweat dripped off my brow. I should get cleaned up and make dinner.

♂♂♂

The doorbell rang as I took the lasagna out from the oven. My stomach churned. I set the pan on a cooling rack and took off my mitts. As I walked to the door I pushed my hair behind my ears. Was it Scott or just Itsuma? My heart fluttered. Nerves screamed there was danger on the other side of the door. For all I knew it was a SWAT team ready to take out a teacher that has sex with his students. *Fine by me. Time to face the music.*

I swung the entrance open and Itsuma's rage-filled eyes stared back at me. Of course. Scott had told him what I'd done. I deserved to be punched in the face. Itsuma stepped forward. I stepped back. Then Scott slunk inside without even looking at me. I closed the door and murmured, "Hello."

Itsuma grabbed Scott by the arm and turned him to face me. "So this is why this noppo didn't come to school today."

Noppo? Was Itsuma trying to make a joke? "Isn't *noppo* a bit of outdated slang for a kid?" I narrowed my eyes at Itsuma. Then I looked at Scott. A prominent, very dark shiner enveloped Scott's left eye. My heart twisted tighter than a strand of yarn wrapped around underwear in a dryer. I held onto the urge to yell. A boil of heat enflamed my cheeks. The machine gun of questions jammed up my muzzle. Scott's good eye watched me. Assessed me. Fear.

Had I put that despair on his face? My hands started shaking, but I had a handle on the nuclear explosion that went off in my gut. All of it got shoved in a bottle called *later*.

"What happened?"

Scott smiled. It was a wide fake crease across his beaten face. He was trying to convince me everything was alright. No, things were not alright.

"This?" He pointed at his eye.

"Yes." I wanted to belt him one.

Itsuma crossed his arms and glowered at his friend.

"Oh, well, this…" Scott shuffled and put his thumbs in the pockets of his jeans. "I got caught up with some guys…"

"Stop." I held up a hand. "You don't know this about me, but I don't do outright lies." There was a time and place for little lies like *No, honey, I didn't get you anything for your birthday* or *that shirt looks slimming*. I wasn't talking about omissions to protect friends and family. When I asked a direct question, I expected my partner to pony up and admit everything.

"I wasn't lying, I did go to work after…" Scott cut off his own sentence and shuffled from foot to foot.

"If you can't tell me the truth…" I bowed my head, railing against my own principles. I wanted to give Scott a chance, but if he couldn't be honest he'd shatter me. "Then get out," I whispered.

Scott's eyes widened. "No, wait…"

I turned, planning on showing him my back if he continued this charade. I made it to the dining room and gripped the back of a chair for support. I wasn't breathing. The room started spinning.

"After what?" The wood under my fists groaned. "Start over."

"After I got up this morning, I went to work." Scott's voice shook.

I hated the fear in his tone. Here was the truth of his story, and I turned around and faced him as a man should when listening to his lover.

"I fed the horses and cleaned stalls." Scott shuffled his feet. "I was asked if I could work the full day because we have a show this weekend. Sometimes I take off school so they have help. This time I said no and went home to change for school."

Scott paused, and I wasn't sure if he was going to continue. He started shaking and staring off. A marker of abuse. There was no way I could ignore this. I'd have to report it to Principal Ellis. But if Scott was eighteen, could he do anything for him?

Itsuma stepped closer, caressed Scott's arm and gently took hold of his hand. Touch seemed to ground my Cowboy, and he continued. "When I got home to shower... *he* was there. Waiting for me."

"He?"

Itsuma answered, "His father."

"He asked me where I'd been." Scott looked at me with one good beseeching eye. "But I was stupid. I told him."

Itsuma grabbed Scott by the shoulders. "You idiot! You told him! He's going to come after Sensei now!"

"No! No!" Scott shook his head. "I only said I was with my lover."

"Fantastic." Itsuma threw up his hands. "This again. Well, if he comes after me I'll kick his ass just like before."

"No." Scott violently shook his head. "He won't come after you."

"Motherfucker, how do you know?"

"So, your father did this to you?"

Scott squeezed his one good eye and hung his head. "I'm sorry. I'm proud to be your lover. I... should have said something else."

He looked up at me. Every pore of his body pleaded for forgiveness. Scott also seemed nervous. He wanted me to acknowledge us. My heart went to mush.

"It's okay," I said. "I want to shout from the rooftops about my two gorgeous lovers too."

Itsuma paced, mowing his short black hair back with his hands. "You're an idiot," he said to Scott. "We're supposed to protect Sensei, not yell each blow-by-blow of our sexual experience."

Scott winced.

"What comes will come," I said.

"No," Scott shook his head. "I'll be more careful. I gave him the excuse."

More careful? An excuse? I reached out my arms—a little too fast. Scott flinched. His reaction blasted a hole in my chest.

"Come here," I held out my arms. "I won't hurt you."

It took him a moment, but then Scott flew to me and wrapped his arms tight around my body. In return, I was gentle, knowing he probably had new injuries. Even pressing on a bruise would maim my heart.

"Nothing you said is excuse enough to beat you."

Scott held me tighter and buried his head, hiding silent sobs in my shoulder. I let him cling to me as I stayed strong for his sake. Itsuma stood back with his arms crossed, shifting uncomfortably. Scott needed the support of all his friends right now. I held a hand out to Itsuma. Encouragement was all that was needed. My Prince dropped his bad boy attitude and hugged the both of us from the side.

I wanted to protect them. Both of them. I wanted to know the story about Itsuma and Scott's dad. The hint at an altercation between them had me curious. I got the feeling I'd want to pat Itsuma on the back and buy him a beer after hearing the story.

Scott's guttural attempt at trying to stop crying squeezed at my heart. My Cowboy was still trying to be strong through all the bullshit he'd been put through. Questions swam in my head, making laps around the murk of my imagination. I wanted to wait to ask until Scott regained his composure, but I wanted answers. I flicked my eyes over to Itsuma.

"How long has this been going on?"

"Since fourth grade," Itsuma said.

It was obvious this had been going on for a while, but I was shocked to know for how long. "And no one noticed?" My anger started to rise again.

"Oh, trust me, we've tried," Itsuma said. "There have been several teachers that reported it. The officials come and they're always sent packing. Plus Scott's legal now. They won't do anything for him."

Unbelievable. "Sent packing?"

"Let's just say his dad has influence."

Scott tried to pull away. I didn't let him. *No way. Cry more.* All this toxic crap inside him needed an outlet. My shoulder was safe.

"Don't go back," I said. "Stay here."

Scott managed to pull away from both me and Itsuma this time. "No, I can't." He wiped his eyes, keeping his head down.

"Yes, you can." I bent my knees and searched for his eyes—or rather, his one good eye. "If you're worried about me, don't. You're welcome here."

"No." Scott backed up away from me. "I have to go."

I grabbed his wrist. "I'm not comfortable with that. I won't touch you if you're worried."

"No." Scott shook his head. "That's not it at all. I have a sister and a brother and my mom. I have to go back."

Itsuma straightened. "He's not… is he going after Tommy?"

Scott still wouldn't look at either of us. "I have to go back."

Shit. He was being a shield for his family.

"I'll get them," I said. "You can stay here."

Even to myself I sounded desperate. Get them? How the hell was I going to do that? *Hi, Mrs. Cooper, I'm Scott's teacher. Come live with us…* still, I turned towards my kitchen to go to the garage.

Scott grabbed my arm. He still wouldn't look at me. Dead eyes stared firmly at the ground. "Mom already tried moving us once. He found us all the same."

"I'm not going to let this stand as it is."

Scott snapped his head up. "No. Leave it. It's fine."

"So what are you going to do?" Itsuma threw a hand in the air. "Get beat to shit? Do you even fight back?"

Scott threw a dirty look at his friend. "If he's hurt, he can't go to work."

The aura in the room turned from dark to worse. This conversation had the feel of past scars seeping into the argument.

"I'm not sorry for defending myself." Itsuma spit out the words. "Spending my freshman summer in court was wild fun."

Scott sighed and raked a hand through his hair. "I have to get back. I can't stay."

All the blood left my face. He was going back? Into that hell? Why didn't he want me to do anything?

"So when do I get to see you?" I didn't want him going back there. All this training and I couldn't even use it to vanquish his demons? I was useless.

"At school, I guess."

The blow I suffered was Scott's look of resignation. But I didn't pay attention to fate, stars or whatever rules were written in the book of life. A miasma of a plan was already forming. I calculated risks, factors, steps to take, action plans and possible counter-maneuvers for both Scott's resistance and his father's fury.

First step... assess the problem. What type of issue do we have? What's the best method to solve it?

"Okay then," I said distractedly. "I'll see you tomorrow."

"Sensei?" Itsuma eyed me. "You're just going to accept this?"

My eyes flicked over to him. I gave him a dark sneer. Accept? Never.

Itsuma stepped back and blinked.

Scott, forlorn in his troubles, turned to go. I touched the back of his hand and he grabbed for the support. *Cowboy, if you think you'll be doing this alone you are so very, very wrong.* I lifted his hand, palm up and kissed callouses.

Scott caressed my face. "I promise I'll be back once this whole thing cools down."

With that he turned to go.

"I'm staying." Itsuma turned to me. "But I'll be right back."

The nanosecond they left I made a beeline to my cell phone. In my calculations, I thought about what the school principal would say. Itsuma indicated there were other reports about my Cowboy's abuse, but Scott's legal age was now a hindrance to the legal process.

Still, there was one man I knew that could help me. Whether or not he would was in question. Kai was one heartless son-of-a-bitch. After graduation I'd never wanted anything to do with him ever again, but Scott was in danger. I gripped the cell phone and squeezed my eyes shut. *This is for Scott.*

I dialed the number.

It picked up on the second ring, but I didn't hear anyone on the other end.

"Kai?" I said.

A pause. "Moriel?" The smooth, cold voice sent a chill down my spine.

"Ah, yeah. I don't have much time, but I need to ask a favor."

Another long pause. Damn. After all this time, I thought he wouldn't affect me like this.

"Kai?"

"If it is a favor then it should be face to face."

I grit my teeth. "Fine."

"You are still at the same place?"

"Don't come here." I preferred to meet him someplace public. With bright lights. Or better yet, during the day. With a crowd of people. Preferably police around too. "What about the grill?" Where we always used to meet.

"Now?" His voice was cool, saying tonight would not be a good time. But that was Kai.

"No…" Actually, never was a good time. "At ten-thirty."

A pause. He was so freaking annoying.

"This is a favor," I huffed. "Not a booty call."

"I see."

Fuck you. Well, that wasn't fair. I was calling him out of the blue after years of silence. But I figured he owed me.

"Don't push yourself." I wanted to hang up and go to Plan B. Only, Kai was the fastest way for Scott to be extracted from his father.

"Ten-thirty at the grill," he said in his monotone.

"Thank you." I pushed the end button and hugged myself. *It's going to be okay. There will be people around. I won't put myself in a compromising situation with him again.*

Itsuma came back in as I tried getting a handle on my nerves. I immediately went to the kitchen, fishing out two plates. China rattled together in my hands until I set the dinnerware on the counter.

Itsuma folded his arms and leaned against the kitchen column divider. "So what's the plan?"

"I just called a friend. I'm going to meet him and see what, if anything, he can do." I pulled out a knife and spatula.

"What does he do?"

I started cutting lasagna in large chunks. Calling them squares would be a stretch. The knife jittered so much in my hand I couldn't make straight lines. "He works in child care protective services."

"Sensei?" Itsuma stepped forward. "Why are you shaking?"

Like I'd done for Scott, Itsuma wrapped me in his arms. His warmth and strength held me up. His confidence became my shelter. Safe in his arms, I hadn't noticed how much I'd come apart just from the incident with Scott and talking to Kai. My body melted in his embrace. *Breathe, Reis. Breathe.* As I leaned heavily on Itsuma, he became my rock. It was his carefree attitude. Even though he was as sick about Scott's situation as I was, he was so calm. I expected him to pull his perverted tricks with me, either take advantage or lighten the mood. But he let me be. Gave me relief from the perfect storm raging in my gut. Itsuma didn't ask me any questions. Didn't try to get information from me. His hands didn't wander and he didn't try to take advantage of the situation. He was there, with me, in the moment and taking care of me.

"I told him you weren't going to let this slide." Itsuma whispered in my ear. "I said you were different from all those others that turned a blind eye."

"What did he say?"

"I think he's half hopeful and half dreading. He asked me to convince you not to do anything."

"Is that what you're doing now?" I pulled away and picked up the spatula. He let me climb out of his embrace, soft, no grabbing. No demands.

"I told him not only would I help you, but that he could go fuck himself if he thought we'd just sit there and do nothing."

I chuckled. It would be just like Itsuma. "You did not."

"Yeah, I did."

Of course he did. That was Itsuma. It was a relief to know exactly what he was thinking. He wasn't truthful to be mean. The opposite, actually. It was the lies that killed. This kid naturally knew that.

"I might lose him again." Itsuma's tone held sadness. "But it's better if he's safe."

"Again?"

"Ah, yeah. Our first encounter didn't go well."

I spooned the "squares" of food onto plates.

"I've done research since. But I'm afraid I hurt him. We sort of drifted apart after that. I've been trying to win him over since."

Once the food was served, we moved to the dining area. "You think his dad might come after you?"

"I hope he does." Itsuma pushed the math books aside and set his plate down on the table. "This time I'll let him hit me if it helps Scott get free of the bastard."

"This time?" So this kind of altercation happened before?

Itsuma sighed. "Yeah."

He stabbed his food, filling his mouth before he could say more.

"There's a story there."

My Prince swallowed and answered. "He found out Scott was gay, beat him within an inch of his life, then came after me." Itsuma said it like it was all in a day's work. "I kicked his ass. He couldn't work for a week. Then the guy tried to sue me and my parents."

"Class A citizen."

"Yeah." He eyed my plate. "Are you going to eat that?"

"Yes." I stabbed my food.

"Are you going to stop shaking like a little girl now?"

"Screw you, dude."

"Later." He wiggled his eyebrows.

His bad-boy attitude helped calm my nerves. Yet, even though we joked, I felt sick to my stomach that Scott lived under such severe conditions.

"We can't just let him go back," I said. "He's not safe." A part of me felt that I'd failed just by letting him walk out the door.

Itsuma's mood soured. "What are you suggesting? Kidnapping his family? Bringing them here? He's an adult. We can't force him to leave his home."

"Should we have just let him go? Is his father going to beat him again?"

He shook his head. "That's not his pattern. Scott's dad is probably drinking his woes away. They'll be safe for a couple days."

"Days?" How did I not notice Scott was getting a weekly beating?

"Sensei, do what you have to do to get him out. But he's probably safe tonight."

The advice was in total contrast to what Itsuma would do. "How can you sit there knowing this and do nothing?"

Itsuma stopped eating and stared at me. "Really? You think I've done nothing?" His face hardened. "You weren't there through the harassment, the police, the court trials, not to mention my mother crying on my chest asking what she'd done to turn me gay? Yeah, the conversation with my father? Just peachy."

"I'm sorry."

"Scott's problems with his dad didn't start as all out brawls. Slaps turned into punches, punches turned into beatings, it escalated slowly."

"You're not making me want to stay in my chair."

"Well, then tell me the plan." Itsuma resumed eating.

♂♂♂

The time went by like a Friday-night date. I explained what I'd do to extricate Scott from his father. Not that I wouldn't try the official way first, but I was afraid the school system would look to child services and child services would raise their hands in defeat saying Scott wasn't a minor. Same thing if I went to the police. Domestic disputes were dealt with only when the victim reported the abuser. Most the time, a child would not out their parents. Scott's attitude proved he had someone to protect. He wouldn't implicate his father. So, while there was Plan A and Plan B, I had suspicions Plan C would be implemented. And that's where Kai fit in.

He might be able to pull in a favor and do something. What that something was, I didn't know. This didn't mean I wouldn't report my suspicions and myself to the principal, and retire. Just that I wasn't necessarily all that hopeful. Still, Scott was a student at Cerilia High School.

"So you won't be Sensei anymore?" Itsuma's face went ashen.

I shook my head. "No."

"Why?" He grew angry.

"I don't deserve to be teaching anywhere." I had given up that right the moment I grew too weak to resist Scott or Itsuma.

"That's not what we planned."

"Whatever plans you made, you didn't include me, so…"

"This is bullshit. You didn't do anything wrong."

"Adults pay for the mistakes they make." I hung my head.

"You're still thinking of me as a kid. I'm an adult!" Itsuma slammed his fist down on the dining table. "You're saying I shouldn't be the one who pays? I was the one who was supposed to get in trouble."

"Why did it have to be you in trouble?" There was a name for a certain type of troublemaker who wanted to be punished for his crimes. Neglected. Itsuma's attitude screamed he wanted attention. Yet he also wanted to be the *good student*. He wanted praise by his teachers. He also wanted to push the boundaries.

"Do you not understand how this goes?" I said. Our fiery gazes met over the table. "It doesn't matter who approached who first. The fact that I…" was a scumbag and let temptation rule meant I was the one who should be punished. "You should stop coming here for a while."

"You're pushing me out?"

"No!" He'd said it like I wanted him to leave. Staying away from me was for his safety. His anonymity. "When I

S.N.McKibben
♂♂♂
98

report myself for—having sex with you, I'm probably going to jail."

"They can't do that. I'm legal. So is Scott. We can make our own decisions."

I looked hard into Itsuma's eyes. "Are you jealous of what we did last night?"

He laughed. "Only that I wasn't there to watch. You're both mine, Sensei."

Really. "Does Scott know that?"

"We had a little talk during your conversation with your friend." Itsuma smirked. "If he had any confusion before, it's cleared up now."

"What?" I frowned. "What did you do?"

"You want me to show you?" he purred. His hands reached for me.

I slipped away. "Itsuma!"

"How long do I have to stay away?" He gritted his teeth and stared at me. "I'm being shipped off in two months. This is my only chance."

"Only chance to what?"

He lunged for me. His lips met mine and his tongue swirled in my mouth like an angry eel.

"Itsuma!" I pushed him off. "This isn't helping."

He collapsed into my chest, hugging me tight.

"Sensei," Itsuma whispered into my chest. His voice soft. Tender. Concerned. "I'm sorry. This isn't what I wanted. I like you, Sensei. This summer is all I have. When it ends I have to leave you. I have to leave Scott. I have to make things right before I go."

A sincere Itsuma was too much. Like a gentle Prince. If he acted like this, with words so painfully conscientious, how could I resist? Madness. That was my only excuse.

"Baby, I know you've tried hard." My voice cracked. "I know you've been a model student. The most painful thing to see is that you're just throwing yourself away. And for what?"

He turned his head up and looked into my eyes. "What do you mean?"

"You're not even sure what university you're going to. And why are you interested in an old man anyway? You should be chasing after Scott. Anyone's more respectable than me."

"I told you. I like you." Itsuma lifted his chest, his face determined. "I like you both. You're both mine. It's my consolation for being a good boy and following what my parents want for me. That was the deal. I do what they want me to do. If I don't get to choose my life, then I don't have to choose between either of you. I get you both."

He'd broken my heart admitting he had no control. Decisions were made for him. He'd been going along with what his family wanted. Deep inside, Itsuma was a good boy being played as a pawn with his parents at both ends of the board. "But will that make you happy?"

"You know what would make me happy." The cocky Itsuma was back in full force with his mischievous smile and taunting words. He attacked with his mouth again. Everywhere there was exposed skin, his lips desperately covered every inch of my body. Teeth might have nibbled a bit. Itsuma brought my hard-on to full culmination.

"We shouldn't…"

"Not this again. If you're blowing the whistle on yourself, then this is my last chance." He unbuttoned my jeans and pulled down my zipper. His hand slid up and under my t-shirt. Our eyes met and held. The fire in his gaze melted my insides. His desire fueled me with uncertainty. His admission of his helplessness on the course of his life gave me pause. I'd been fighting Itsuma since day one. Now that I looked back it was attraction.

He'd known it from the start. It'd taken me a while to realize. The switch from seeing him as a student to a lover was a valid reason. It was the same as when you met a new person and put them in the friend, fuckable or datable category. Once placed in the friend slot, it was hard to climb out of that mire and into the fuckable or datable place-mark. I resisted with everything I had, but Itsuma was digging his way through to my heart.

"Close your eyes, Sensei."

"Why?"

"Because this is a dream. You're not responsible for dreams." He trailed kisses along my neck and whispered into my ear. "Yes, having you would make me happy. I could do anything if I had you."

I shivered in anticipation. Why I liked Itsuma was a mystery to me. He was pushy, cocky, arrogant. Yet those were all the reasons why I really liked him. Self-confidence was sexy. A man who knew what he wanted couldn't be denied.

Think, Mori, for just a moment. "We shouldn't…"

"I'm clean," Itsuma said. "I was tested two months ago, five months before that."

My eyes flicked to his face. "That's an awful lot of testing." What was he, a porn star?

"When my parents found out I was *sexually active* they took me to a doctor." His fingers tickled my thin beard. "Fact remains, I'm clean."

"Chriiii… oooommony…" I covered for my swearing. "They test you every three months?" They treated him like he was having sex with the whole school. If you knew the kid, you'd know he was good with that mouth of his but was a total virgin when it came to penetration.

"Like I said. The conversation with my pops was wicked fun."

A man who spoke his mind, didn't hide his anger and showed every emotion on his face was a man I could trust. If he said he was tested, I believed him.

Itsuma crawled down, trailing soft, burning kisses until his nose skimmed my cock. On the way up, his tongue licked my shaft from base to tip.

I inhaled sharply and let out a relieved breath. "Oh god, that's good."

He seared me with those lips along my chest. Itsuma put a hand over my eyes and kissed me. "This is just a dream."

Itsuma didn't let me speak. Didn't let me push him away. He held me tight, his talented tongue tossing my common sense away. He held my cock and stared like a lost child. Our eyes met and he swallowed.

"Sensei, what do I do? How do I make you feel good?"

He might have "researched," but theory and practice were not necessarily the same things. He was a contrast of contradictions. Pushy then meek. Cocky then unsure. I didn't think his confidence was a front. He was honest. He charged up to the point of his understanding and then looked for guidance when he was uncertain.

"Stand up," I said.

He lifted from his knees while I sat. Our eyes remained locked on each other. I smiled up at him and locked my arms around the back of the chair. A Cheshire grin spread across his face. It was his way of acknowledging his understanding.

Itsuma revealed a very pristine, thick, glorious cock. I nearly swallowed my own tongue in anticipation. The lure of how he'd taste spiked my lust all the way down to my balls.

I took his cock and plunged my mouth all the way down his tip. Itsuma's head slid past my tonsils. As I lathered my new tongue depressor, I spread my legs apart and let one hand wander over his abs and chest. The other hand helped me pump Itsuma breathless. Fuck. I shouldn't be doing this. I hated myself for feeling so good. Desperation bargained with morality, pleading its case with ethics about base needs and opportunity. While I sucked and got off on Itsuma's encouraging fingers tangled in my hair, demons laughed at my weakness. My eyes wandered to the outside windows, double checking the curtains were closed.

"Sensei…" The gentle Prince caressed my face. "We'll find another way. I won't be able to stay away from you."

With a soft pop, I let go of his cock. "You may not have a choice."

"Say we overpowered you."

"I wouldn't say that!" I burst out with my first thought.

"What? Can't stand even the thought of losing a fight to me?" He wrapped his lips over mine. He was trying to comfort me. Give me an easy out. But there was no way I'd let either one take the fall for my inability to deny them.

"We face the consequences together." Itsuma's eyes softened and the gleam of high intelligence shone with affection. Another side to Itsuma I hadn't seen before. He was a diamond showing me the different facets of color inside. This diamond could get me to do anything. It was as if our souls touched. Mine asked, *Are you falling for me as hard as I am for you?*

"We'll protect you, Sensei."

The promise washed my anxiety way. Hope bloomed in my heart. *No, I'll be the one to protect you.* It was too soon to ask if this was more than curiosity or a fleeting infatuation. Before I could go down that line of thought, Itsuma teased my cock, stroking his thumb over the tip.

Pre-cum spilled over and he rolled the natural lubricant paste around the rim of my prick. Then his mouth was sucking on me and blowing my mind.

His oral skill made my body shudder in delight. Oh, this was bad. The quickness of my response wasn't just from lack of a partner. This kid was exceptional. Between my moans, Itsuma stripped me naked and pulled my ass forward. Both butt cheeks teetered on the chair's edge. His technique made me so distracted I didn't notice he'd climbed on top of me until his tongue was down my throat and his cock pressed against the crack of my ass.

"Itsuma!" I scrambled to get out from under him. An old twinge of fear had me in a panic. "Get off me!" I hooked my arm around his neck and flipped him. We were both on the ground with me straddled above him. "Haven't you ever heard the term *bottom ready*?" I panted.

Itsuma looked up at me dumbfounded. The kid seemed in shock that I could overturn him so fast.

"I'm sorry." I leaned my head against his. "Don't just climb on top of me."

Itsuma raised his hands in defeat. "I got it, Sensei. You're in control."

My dismay faded. There was a saying I'd heard—a bottom is never ready. For me that only applied when a situation was out of my control. I'd been hurt before. But I didn't want the past to screw up future opportunities, so I made sure all parties involved were safe. Only when I knew a top understood me would I let him have me on my back. It was that way with everyone. Even my Prince.

"First, just let me prepare." I rolled us over to the back of the couch and lifted the top of one of the hidden compartments. Lubricant, condoms, and those special gel applicators with the long nozzles were stashed in my couch's emergency can't-wait-till-the-bedroom alcove.

"Just so you know, I'm clean."

He smiled. "You would have told me if you weren't."

"How do you know?"

"You're the scrupulous type." Itsuma picked up the lubricant and eyed the bottle while I grabbed the applicator, cut the top off and straightened.

"What is that?" Itsuma gave me a perplexed look.

"Hmmm… that's telling." I smirked. "I thought you said you had experience."

"I do, just not with toys," he said. Good to see Itsuma's bravado manned up.

I inserted the long nozzle inside me, and with a squeeze, gel spread into the cavity Itsuma wanted to put that bad-boy of his. Tossing the applicator aside, I grabbed the condom, ripped the foil and strapped the rubber down his shaft.

"This is for your protection."

"But I want Sensei bareback." Itsuma smiled and wiggled his hips.

"Deal with it." I took the bottle from his hand, flipped the top and tipped the opening upside down.

"Sensei, you are a sly fox." His hands glided up my sides, making my cock jump. Gel spilled over his gloved manhood, balls and abs. A little too much gel.

"Stop distracting me."

He chuckled and ran his fingers up and down my skin. God that felt good. It had been so long I'd all but forgotten how it felt to have a knowledgeable lover touch me, last night excluded. But where Scott's touches were exploratory, Itsuma's were skillful. He knew where to touch, where to skim, where to squeeze.

I lifted up and positioned his staff to my entrance.

"Sensei?" Itsuma asked with breathless disbelief. "Are you sure?"

That gave me pause.

His eyes widened. "No, I mean, I want to, but I… I don't want to hurt you."

Was he afraid? "Don't worry, I'll be gentle."

Itsuma rolled his eyes. "I'm fine. It's you that's been fighting this since day one. You're the one I'm worried about."

Ah. I'd never thought Itsuma might have been scarred over the first-time incident with Scott.

"He told you, right?"

I nodded my head. "Yes."

"I don't want to hurt anybody again." He held my hips tight, as if I'd pull away.

"You won't hurt me, I promise."

"Then teach me how to make it feel good." Itsuma pulled me down.

I felt the burn of his tip separate the ring of my ass. This part of me hadn't been spread like this in so long. I was careful and lowered myself in increments. Slamming down on him was out of the question. The shock alone might be too much for a newbie, let alone my own ass. Hell, I might break him if my body didn't give enough.

In small waves I endured inch-long triumphs as I sunk his flagpole. Itsuma arched his back and gave out little sighs while I pushed him inside me. As I went down my cock got hard all the way down to my balls. His arms shook. His head listed to the side, but his eyes never left my face. Those thighs of his seemed locked, straining to remain still. Finally, my pelvis met his hips and I gave him a satisfied smile.

"All in," I said.

Itsuma gave me this arrogant gaze, as if he were thinking *look what I can do with a good partner*. Smug little troublemaker.

I rose and came down, repeatedly, slicking his pole until the initial ache subsided. But it was nice and easy, letting our bodies figure out their compatibility. Itsuma stared at our connection, never moving and letting me take control. Thankfully, he got it. I didn't want him "helping" me. Once I felt looser I went all the way down and swirled my hips, stirring him inside me. I grabbed his shoulders and met his eyes.

"Ready?"

His eyebrows rose. "There's more?"

"Oh, yeah." I balanced my feet on the ground. "Talk to me, Itsuma. How are you feeling?"

"Fucking fantastic." He smirked and settled his hands on my hips.

"Good." I started bouncing. Straight up. Straight down. "Still good?" I couldn't tell if the faces he made were from pain or pleasure.

He grunted and nodded. "Yeah. Fuck. Yeah."

Shit. He *was* a total virgin. With his confidence and talent, I'd thought he'd have some experience. He'd fooled me. Guess he'd only tried once with Scott. But Itsuma gave me a green light, so I continued to pound as hard as I could.

"Still okay?" I panted.

Itsuma leaned his head back, eyes closed, lips parted. I found my Prince's expression unbelievably erotic. My heart soared. This time I'd get him off. Then we'd see how my smug Prince looked when I gave him an orgasm.

I pumped up and down, my hard cock slapping heavily on his six-pack. Fuck, this was good.

A soft bush of hair grazed my balls, sending every nerve on hyper drive. My body hadn't forgotten these dance moves. My cock was thrilled. Hands caressing my chest and abs sent waves of pleasure crashing into my mind. The only thing that might be better was if I had a nice, hot, hard rod in my mouth.

Itsuma shifted and grabbed my hips. He now thrust into me as I slammed down.

"There!" I cried out. "There! Oh fuck. That's it." I threw my head back. Itsuma found my spot. The place where, when stroked at just the right angle, I went mindless. His hands kept me on course to strike my weak spot over and over.

"Sensei, you like it there." He smiled with that superior air.

I couldn't help my reaction. My cries kept on, showing a more lusty side of me than he'd ever witness in the classroom.

"Sensei," Itsuma breathed. He sounded as if he were reaching his limit.

In an instant I was flipped on my back, my legs thrown up, the back of my knees hooked around the crook of his elbows. He'd never pulled out of me during the maneuver, and kept going. Pumping me into oblivion. Making me scream. Turning my mind into scrambled eggs.

Itsuma placed his hands behind me, giving him leverage to sink into my ass as deep as his cock could reach.

"Sensei, you make it hard to control myself with that erotic face."

His eyes stared down with such intensity that I knew he was claiming me as his property.

"Fuck, your cock is so good." So good I wanted to cry.

He pounded into me so hard I thought I'd become one with the floor. Every time his hips thrust he destroyed the pleasure button inside me, driving me insane. His position changed slightly as he lifted up and held my ankles. My legs spread wide, splitting me open, making me feel vulnerable, making me his sex slave. With each cry I acclaimed him the victor. Controller of my body. Those eyes dared me, captivated me, devoured every wail I made in honor of his glorious cock sending me into oblivion. His oblivion.

I gripped Itsuma's shoulders. All thought flew out. I moaned at Itsuma stripping away my rational mind.

"Yes," I moaned. "Good. Good."

Itsuma crashed into my ass harder.

"Sensei…"

I looked to my Prince. His sultry gaze commanded attention.

"Your face warms my body." He wanted my eyes on him.

Attention whore.

But damned if I could say more than one-word sentences. Soon only our cries filled the room. My cock bobbed and jumped in time to Itsuma's strokes. His face got closer as he leaned over me, leaving his dignity behind and letting pleasure show on his face. Endearing. He was pounding me a little harder, a little recklessly.

I squeezed his shoulders. "I'll come soon. Hold out for me."

This would be worth it. He might not understand the significance, but I was going to come just from having his cock. No hands needed. No friction. The effect of an orgasm achieved without having to stroke my own penis was always profound. I'd done it enough to be known for it in certain circles. It made me popular with men. But it only happened for those I really liked.

Shit. I'd spurt at any moment. Itsuma wasn't pulling any punches. Exposing himself like this. Did he know he was stirring me up inside?

"Sensei, Sensei…" Itsuma pleaded. He was warning me.

My breath caught. "Wait!"

This was happening too fast. *Please, more. Hold out for more.* But the desperation of release won. My cock bobbed. My ass spasmed. I felt Itsuma's cock convulse. A burst of come shot out my rod. The bittersweet release both hurt and pleasured. Spurt after spurt, cum shot onto my chest, my face, my hair. Fuck. I thought I might faint.

Even before I could get my huffing under control the flow of ecstasy drained me. My body settled into deep relaxation. My mind buzzed with pleasure. My heart soared. My arms wrapped around my lover and remained locked. I was simply unable to move.

Itsuma lay over my chest. His cock remained inside me, proving this wasn't a dream. A glow of warmth shined in my heart that he didn't just toss me aside for cleanup. I didn't want another convenient lover while I waited for "the one." It made me fall for Itsuma just a little more.

♂♂♂

"Slave driver." Itsuma sat at the table working out math problems while I cleaned up the kitchen. After we'd shown ourselves a good time, I insisted he hit the books.

"As much as I love getting crushed on the floor, we still have an agreement. You study. I tutor."

His head popped up, a grin on his face. I'd cast him a browbeating before he made his comment.

When I looked at the clock next it was ten after ten. Shit. I'd be late for my appointment with Kai, but maybe I could make up some time with my Boxster.

"I've got to stop you here." I rounded the kitchen and leaned against the pillar between the dining room and living room. "I've got to go."

"That's fine." Itsuma grinned that wicked, sexy smile at me. "I'll stay here."

"No. You have a curfew."

"Damn." He looked at his phone. "Yeah, it's time I go anyway." He stood up and eyed my Calculus Four tome. "Can I borrow this?" He held up the book.

I gave my own smirk of triumph. "Of course."

He shoved the book in his bag and then grabbed the back of my neck and pulled me in. His kiss was a surprise attack and left no room to breathe. His tongue skillfully dropped my IQ to zero, but my cock was turning into a genius.

Itsuma pulled back. "Sure you don't want a quick one?"

My eyes could barely focus. My words slurred. "I gotta thing…"

"Yes, can we use your *thing*?"

"Noooo…" But my head nodded yes. Then I came back to a state of semi-consciousness. "No. Can't." But I was forgetting why.

"Okay, go meet your friend."

That sobered me up. Kai. I was meeting with that sadist bastard. Itsuma gave me a subtle once-over but said nothing. He shoved the rest of his things in his backpack and gave me a flip of his chin for a goodbye. "See ya, I might come by tomorrow."

Seeing as tomorrow was Saturday, he must think I'd be waiting for his arrival. "You think I'll be here?"

"You're a teacher," he said, as if that was explanation enough.

"Screw you. And if you think that nod in my direction qualifies as a goodbye…" I wrapped my arms around him—pack and all, "… think again." It was all an excuse to touch him, to shove my nose in his neck and breathe in his scent.

He chuckled and hugged me back.

So much for rules. But Itsuma and my weakness for physical touch wasn't conducive to rules. This was so dangerous. I wanted him again. Instead of pulling him in for another kiss, I pulled back before he could feel my chubby turning into a full-blown hard-on and walked him to the door.

I stood there in my entryway watching him until he got into his pearl-white Lexus and drove away. As I turned back inside, the crunch of footsteps on gravel spun me around. Out from the darkness, fading in like a stealth ninja, came my demon from the past. He walked towards me just as he pleased. My heart jumped out my chest and ran for dear life while my feet grew roots. Shock drained the blood from my face.

"Kai!" As if my voice broke the spell, I was able to move and I stepped back. My heel tripped over the doorway. I was falling backwards. Kai rushed forward and caught my wrist. My other hand grabbed for the doorjamb and I was saved from falling. I would have rather landed on my ass then been touched by this man.

Being this close to Kai brought out all the bad memories, the pain, the trip to the hospital, the heartache, rejection, and betrayal. Really, could I call him a friend? I hadn't in a long time.

"Are you alright?" There was no concern in his eyes, only his stubborn poker face.

I regained my balance and tried to push him away as forcefully as I could. He might as well be bolted to the ground. He didn't even move under my hand. It was me who stumbled away. This time he didn't motion to grab me. Thankfully I didn't trip this time.

My body went numb. My mind went blank. My only urge was to run, flee, escape. The body shakes returned in force. There was no Itsuma to hold me this time.

"If this is how you act around me, what is the point?"

"You were supposed to meet me at the grill." I tried holding myself to put back the pieces of my failing courage.

Kai stepped into my house and shut the front door. "I would rather speak in private. I have something personal to say."

Fucking Kai—doing whatever he pleased. He hadn't changed.

We stared at each other. Kai looked the same as he had five years ago. His black hair still shined. His short locks waved and shifted like a damn shampoo commercial. Those golden eyes pierced with a laser focus that seemed to be able to physically push people away. Narrow chin, slight nose and a perfect complexion made him devilishly handsome. Operative word being devilish. But that face wouldn't fool me anymore.

"So, I have a favor."

"What? No how is life? How have you been? What is new?" Kai folded his arms as if he had a right to be pissed.

"Fuck you, you goddamn asshole! You're five fucking years too late. Go to hell!" I screamed my head off. Wetness trickled down my face. Shit. I couldn't look at him. Not like this.

"Communication runs both ways."

My head snapped up. "Communication? Well, then you're the worst listener ever."

Kai breathed a sigh of relief.

My trembling became a source of energy. Energy enough to continue. "No, you don't get to come here and find resolution, fucktard. You used me like a goddamn toilet…" My knees wobbled. I caught myself and leaned against the back of my couch. *Oh god, why did I call him?*

Flashes of memory came rolling in. Five years of trying to forget him and what he did came rolling back like it was yesterday. Kai staring at me like he'd never seen blood in his whole life. The hospital. The nightmares. Watching him sling an arm around a girl, ignoring me as they passed. The pain of rejection when I needed answers and he wouldn't return my calls.

His voiced snapped me back into the present.

"Granted, I probably deserve your ire—"

"Probably?" I screamed like a woman who'd been cheated on. "Ire? No, you son-of-a-bitch, there's no probably about it. What you did doesn't just cause ire, fuckface."

"You always did have flare for theatrics."

His words gave me the will to push off the back of my couch. I'd been using it as a crutch. My goal became grinding his face against pavement. I crouched low and went after him.

Much like in high school, he knew my moves before I could think. He grabbed my wrist in a lock, spun me around and shoved me into the dining area.

"Good," he said. "Let us have a go for old times' sake."

My blood ran cold. He was the national wrestling champion. I was blinded by rage. This wouldn't go well for me. "No. Get out." I pointed at the door.

"After all this you are giving up? If you are so troubled over seeing me, and it took courage to call me, then it must be important, right?"

Yes. Scott was important. I had to do this. I could ask and be done with Kai. He owed me this much. The torrent of anger still pursued me, but I restrained myself enough to explain what I wanted. "I have a father that needs to be pulled from his kids."

Kai walked over to my dining room table and pulled out a chair. "Sit."

"This is my house, jackass."

"Sit, please."

"No, thank you." I folded my arms.

"Moriel Liel Reiss, sit down." Kai bared his teeth and his eyes flamed up in anger.

Holy Mary, "The Wall" Kai is actually showing emotion. He had changed. I wanted to piss my pants. He used my full name like an angry mother. The petulant child part of me wanted to flip him the bird. But if we were going to make a deal, then it would require civility. "I feel more comfortable standing."

Kai nodded and conceded the point. *Yay team Mori. One point.*

He walked past me to the kitchen, opened the refrigerator and grabbed two microbrews. He searched around in my drawer and finally found my pop top. The hiss of the beer caps made me want something stiffer.

Kai came back and set a beer next to me, then took a long draw from his own lager.

"Help yourself," I snorted in disgust.

"I will." He took another draw.

"Douchebag." I walked past him, using all my self-control to remain calm. What I really wanted to do was plaster my ass against the wall and slide out of existence. But I strolled into my kitchen, pulled out the stepstool and opened the liquor cabinet above the refrigerator.

Kai was right about the alcohol, but it would take more than three percent to calm me down.

"Want any help?" He stared at me with dispassionate eyes. Underneath he was probably laughing at me.

"Ha-ha." Well, I was short. Go ahead, laugh. Even Itsuma, of Japanese descent, was taller than me by an inch.

I grabbed a shot glass and the bottle and put them on the counter, then put away the stepstool. I poured and downed the shot, refilled and slugged a second. Then a third, and finally a fourth for good measure.

"Mori." Kai sounded annoyed. "That is enough."

"I'm not in twelfth grade anymore."

"Then do not bitch at me when you pass out on the floor and I have to touch you to get you over to the couch."

"Just leave me on the floor, then." I didn't want to admit he could be right. I was a lightweight. I left the hard stuff on the counter and went back to the dining room. Now I could sit in his presence.

"Let us begin again." Kai walked to the opposite end of the table and sat.

"Whatever."

The sarcastic Kai I'd known throughout high school came out. "Hi Kai," he said. "Long time no see. It *has* been a while. Do you still work as a protective custody social worker?"

I grumbled. "As if you'd be anything else."

All the years I'd known Kai he had two facial expressions. Bored and sarcastic. It hadn't bothered me in high school, but I thought I knew him then. People would look at Kai and describe him as serious, dependable and stern. But they hadn't seen the monster inside of him. His straightforward ways hid his darker side.

"Yes. I am still with CPS. Are you a professor yet?"

"Halfway there." But all that was going to be over once I turned myself in to the principal.

"So this kid that needs his father taken away, was it the cutie that left?"

"No." I narrowed my eyes at him. He wasn't going to get any information about Itsuma.

"Tutoring awfully late, are we not?"

"That's my business."

"So, he is a student."

Kai held my glare and we had a showdown of will. His golden eyes never wavered. Staring his opponents down was the way he won half his wrestling matches. Old and conflicting feelings came back that made me lose the staring contest.

"You haven't changed much," I said.

Kai crossed his arms and remained silent. It was the only discomfort he'd show. Good. I wanted him to feel uncomfortable. Since he barely showed emotion on his face, I relied on the tiniest of body language he gave away. Still, trying to assess Kai was like trying to play against a professional poker player.

"Say something," I prompted.

"That seems to upset you, so I am listening."

Ha. Right. He was never one for idle chit-chat. We were polar opposites. In high school we complimented each other. I'd spoken on his behalf when people mistook his shy nature for rudeness. We were like brothers. At least that was how I felt before...

That blind spot of mine was an endless void. After the incident—after graduation I no longer had a clue as to what he thought or felt. I'd convinced myself I'd interpreted his feelings and desires wrong. But him being here was not about how he felt about me.

"As I was saying, I have a student who shows signs of abuse. He's admitted it's his father," I said.

"Then report it through proper channels."

"I will, but I have reason to believe it won't be enough."

"What do you want me to do about it?"

"Aren't you an investigator?"

"Yes."

"Then can't you say you received an anonymous tip?"

"You do not want involvement?"

"He'll hate me if he knows it was me." Scott would probably suspect me anyway. But if I took Itsuma's words correctly, I'd need to get this done from the inside.

"If he is an enabler it will not go the way you plan," he said. "How old is the child?"

"Eighteen."

A pause. "That is not a child."

"He's still under his parents' roof."

"The problem is no longer under CPS jurisdiction, and if the adult does not press charges then there is nothing the police can do either."

Frantic, I realized Kai was right. "There's two other children involved. Both of them are underage."

If I could get his other family members safe, then Scott wouldn't have to shield them.

"That I can do something about," Kai said. "Have there been other complaints?"

"I believe so. How long would it take?"

"If the situation is apparent, immediate action can be taken," he said in that lifeless monotone. "If the situation requires observation, then it can take weeks or more."

How could he be so cold? "Are you really a child care investigator?"

"Yes." Kai answered without irritation. I wanted to see something from him, but he was just as calm about everything.

"Will you help or not?" I put my head in my hands, ready to give up on him.

"Do you understand what you are asking for?"

I raised my head. "I'm asking for your help."

"Yes, but the way you want me to do this bypasses all regulation. It means I have to go through the registry, in which you *believe* there are records of previous reports. If so, the job is easier. If not, then what will be required could call the attention of my superiors. I like my job, Mori."

"So no, you can't do anything."

"That is not what I said." Kai set his elbows on the table and leaned forward. "What I am saying is, if I do this the way you want, which is immediately, then it is up to you."

"What do you mean it's up to me?" I didn't like this. It felt like I was watching his endgame unfold. "What do you want?"

"I want you to forget that night," he said.

I stared at him. My body went cold. "Oh, you mean the night you pinned me down and used me like a glory hole? The night I screamed over and over for you to stop? The night I almost bled out and died? Or are you talking about the night that I ripped my stitches out from a nightmare and had to go back into surgery? Or maybe you could specify what night you want me to forget?"

Kai took my scathing lecture in as if he'd heard it all before. Unmoved.

"I panicked," he said.

"What?" Not possible. "I'm not convinced. You want to tell me the great Kai Akiyama, who competes in a wrestling class above his own weight, panicked?"

"I saw the blood and it terrified me. I had no idea what to do."

My mouth hung open for a moment. Then I regained myself. "Even after you left, why didn't you call an ambulance?"

"Because when it comes to you I am *useless*."

Was I going mad? This was a joke. "Right. You, voted most capable, that makes sense." Still, I was sure his pride had taken a blow when he called himself useless.

"I am saying I love you."

Words escaped me. But my thoughts ran a mile a minute. "So you love me, but you'll let me bleed to death." Sand clung to the roof of my mouth. "Why?" I croaked out.

"I just do."

"No." I cleared my throat. "Why didn't you come see me in the hospital? Why didn't you come anytime afterward? Why did you ignore me?"

"When I found out, I was ashamed. When I finally did try to talk to you I was told you did not want to see me. I thought I was complying with your wishes. I realize now I was being a coward."

"So you didn't even think an apology was necessary?"

Kai took in a deep breath and let it out with a sigh. "Moriel, I have spent the last five years regretting my inability to act in a suitable manner. I have been gutted and plagued ever since that night. Not seeing you was as if the sun never rose after the last time I saw you." Kai stood up from his chair, walked within three feet of me and dropped to his knees. "I beg your forgiveness."

Seeing the proud boy I loved before me on his knees brought out an old pain in my heart. I'd have bet money against ever witnessing Kai conceding to anyone. I reached out and stroked his soft hair. Hair I had wished I could touch so many aching times after the incident.

"Kai… forgiveness? That's… I don't know. It's a tall order."

"Then I accept your punishment."

I pulled my hand away and raked my own locks. "I can't do that either." The feelings I'd held for him tangled with fear and hate. But any possibility of reconciliation with Kai died a long time ago. I could forgive him, but things would never be the same.

Itsuma. Scott. They were my golden blooms. My hope. My future.

The alcohol was starting to kick in, and I was getting tired.

"Why did you not press charges against me?" Kai remained with his head down.

"I can't do this right now."

"Why?" His fierce tone woke me up, showing me something special. Something rare. Anger. It was terrifying. His intense glare held me speechless. Then his expression went back to its bland nothingness. "How could you just let me get away with it?"

Shit. Not pursuing the person who'd done me wrong… wasn't I the same as Scott, then?

"Are you looking for redemption?"

"What if I am?" Only Kai could be crouched below my chest and yet loom over me. "If I cannot erase the memory, then let me replace it. Let me replace that night with another one."

I pulled back. Horrified. "You want a do-over?"

"I am much better at it now." He reached out and gripped my hand. "I have practiced."

Practiced? I pulled away from his grip. Whatever he proposed, I wanted nothing to do with it. "So you're telling me you fucked a whole bunch of people in the hopes you'd get back together with me and make it right?" As if you could make something like that better.

"When you say it like that, it sounds cheap."

"This isn't even funny."

"This is not a joke."

"Kai…" I stood up and out of my soberness. "Go home."

"Fine. You can give me an answer later." He stood and backed up. "Do you recycle these?" He picked up the beer bottle.

My head spun. "Just leave it."

He set the container down and ran his fingers through his black hair. "Think about it."

As I tried to keep from falling down, Kai let himself out.

Chapter 9

This had to be the worst predicament a teacher could face. After the last period, instead of catching up on my paperwork, I closed up my classroom and headed to the principal's office.

It was my duty as a teacher to report any suspicious activity. Scott admitted his trouble to me, but in confidence. He wasn't going to appreciate me talking to Principal Ellis about this. Scott probably saw his predicament as all his fault. But I was required by law to report it.

As I trudged down the corridor I heard Mr. Goyas's deep voice. "Hey kid, whose funeral are you going to?"

"Well, since I'm going to be dead meat after my conversation with Principal Ellis, mine, probably." I stopped in front of his burly chest, my head hanging low.

"Hey, Mori." Mr. Goyas said more seriously. "What's wrong?" He set his big hands on my shoulders. "Kid, are you crying?"

"I'm not crying," I said, a bit too fast and earnestly. "And stop calling me a kid. I'm twenty-three."

He chuckled. One of Mr. Goyas's meaty hands lifted my chin and made me look into his eyes. His ever-present soft smile greeted me, but real concern shone through his eyes. "So what's got the happiest guy I know down in the dumps?"

I wanted to lean into him, set my forehead against his strong front, but I left that temptation aside. People believed talking about their problems made them better. This was not one of those times. "I have to report an abuse case to Ellis."

"Damn. It's the Cooper boy, isn't it?"

I stepped back, a little angry. "How did you know?"

"That kid," Mr. Goyas shook his head. "Do what you have to, but don't expect a lot of sympathy from the principal."

"What? Why?"

Mr. Goyas scratched his thick beard. "Let's just say you won't be the first one to report things like this on that family."

"Then why hasn't anything been done?" I was almost yelling.

Mr. Goyas winced. "Child services has gone over several times."

"And?" I rubbed my forehead.

"And nothing changes. Rumor has it every teacher that reports it has been transferred out."

"Well, I'm only temporary anyway."

"Mori, are you sure?"

"Yes!"

Mr. Goyas held up his hands. "Okay. There's something that doesn't add up with that boy."

"Like?" Now it was a matter of pride. That was my lover he was talking about.

"He's too quiet. He's smart but doesn't use it."

I couldn't disagree, but the way Mr. Goyas was talking about Scott didn't sit well with me. "So he's a quiet loner. What's the problem?"

"I know, but there's something about him I can't put my finger on." Mr. Goyas was reflecting on his own musings.

The first thing I thought was, *finger on what? That he's homosexual? Unbelievable.* I wanted to shout the words at him. The urge to get away from my old shop teacher moved my feet forward.

"Mori…"

I kept going. "I've got to go."

"Mori…"

I didn't stop.

If he knew about me, would he treat me differently? The whole conversation angered me enough to leave Mr. Goyas standing there and stomp into Paul Ellis's office.

"Shut the door." The back of a red leather chair faced me. The commanding presence of the high school principal emanated from behind the desk. The man was frightening. Maybe because he was the principal or maybe because Principal Paul Ellis could pin me down with his stare.

I sighed and closed the door. "Principal Ellis?"

The red leather seat turned. "Mr. Reis." His silky voice could gain my attention, but today I needed him to listen.

The greying older man leaned back in his chair and assessed me with blue-grey eyes. He was intimidating. The type that grew strong with age. I didn't know about other people, but I always felt like a rabbit in the talons of an eagle in his presence. Not a man to piss off.

"I need to report a suspected abuse case."

"Who?"

I straightened. "Scott Cooper."

Principal Ellis steepled his fingers. "On what grounds?"

Oh shit. I hadn't realized I'd have to justify it. This could get dicey. "I saw him limping. I asked him about it and in the process saw bruises on his body."

"Scott has a dangerous part-time job with horses. It might have been that."

The blood drained away from my face. This shouldn't be in question. "I considered that, but if you recall, I'm familiar with these types of bruising."

Ellis stared at me with his steel grey eyes. The clock on his wall ticked away. A bead of sweat ran down my back.

"There's not much I can do since he's of legal age."

"But he's a student of this school."

"Yes, he is," Ellis said, as if he could see right through me.

Damn. Mr. Goyas had been right. No sympathy. I stood, waiting. Ellis didn't move. He didn't take his eyes off my face. Could I turn and run now? But even fleeing wouldn't be possible. I was within his grey gazing grasp.

"Thank you for your concern." Ellis broke the spell of silence. He looked down at his desk and opened a file.

I blinked. Had the principal of Cerilia High just brushed me off? Stunned wasn't the right word. Shock was different than this. This was worse than being yelled at. I was being ignored. Cast aside. "Sir?"

Principal Ellis flicked his eyes up with a *you're-still-here* look. "I'll take care of it."

Confusion swirled around in my head. He'd just lied to me. What the hell was going on? How the hell did my student deserve this kind of treatment? It was like he was a lamb to slaughter so that the machine could run its smooth course. I was in a nightmare where I had no voice, watching behind a glass wall as the love of my life got shit kicked.

"I also need to report mysel—"

Ellis pounded his hands against his desk and stood. "Mr. Reis, I promised your father to help keep you out of trouble, since you seem to find it so easily. Since I owe him so much I'm happy to comply."

"But—"

"I've also maintained this school and its reputation for the past six years. I will not have a temporary drag my school through the mud for something so mundane."

"Mundane?"

"You've done nothing wrong." Principal Ellis stunned me silent. "Adults can do as they please. But do keep your personal business outside of school."

"You knew?"

Principal Ellis pointed at the door. "Out."

"You're endangering students."

"As far as I'm concerned, Mr. Reis, you provoke them, and you reap what you sow."

"This isn't right."

"How do I say this so you understand?" He was vibrating in rage. "It takes a special type of person to piss off a normally mild-mannered genius who is the pride of the school. Get. Out."

I stood there in shock for a moment. I'd heard of the teacher being blamed for a student, but this? It made me second guess everything. Everything except helping Scott.

"Scott Cooper needs to be removed from his home."

"Not by this school."

"Why are you so hell-bent on seeing him suffer?"

"I'm trying to protect both him and you." Principal Ellis picked up his phone. "Or should I call your father to let him know before another of your scandals is out?

Should I alert the media and have Scott's life ruined because you're too hard up to keep your hands off him? Wouldn't it be fantastic for you to leech from your father, having no career because of your righteousness? And what about Itsuma? You think he'd appreciate being dragged down into your mire of rectitude?"

Speechless, I could only stare.

He dropped the phone in its cradle. "Keep your mouth shut and get out."

I tried working my voice. No words came out. Principal Ellis would be of no assistance. I walked out, defeated. I'd thought I'd be taken out of here in handcuffs. Dazed, I went back to my classroom.

Mr. Goyas leaned up against my door, waiting for me. "Did you talk to him?"

"Yeah."

"What did he say?"

I didn't reply. I just kept walking down the hall.

Mr. Goyas caught up, spun me around, trapped my shoulders in his massive hands and looked into my eyes. "What did he say?"

"Nothing." I didn't have the will to tell him. Not after mustering every ounce of courage to talk to Ellis. Not after being so thoroughly rebuffed, blamed and dismissed.

Mr. Goyas sighed. "Well, kid, it's as you said. You'll only be here for a while." The warmth of his hands seeped through my shirt. "Promise me you won't pursue it more than this."

I pulled back, away from his grip. "I don't get you."

"Mori, you're going to be a professor, right? You won't have this worry there."

"I want to be alone." I held my hands up and backed away.

Mr. Goyas nodded. He turned away as if someone kicked his puppy.

I'd never felt so utterly crushed. Not for someone else. I loved them both, Scott and Itsuma, and I would fight for them. It looked like I was the only one that would.

Chapter 10

Both Scott and Itsuma arrived at my doorstep at six-thirty. It took every effort to act normal, as if I hadn't ratted Scott's father or myself out to the principal. A load of good that had done. I might have been trying to act nonchalant, but my Prince saw right through me. He looked like he wanted to ask what happened many times, but he finally slipped the question into the middle of a rhombus formula.

"Sensei, are you alright?" Itsuma eyed me suspiciously.

"Yes, I'm fine." But I was too curt. I tried to go on. "So if you take a kite…"

"How did your meeting with your friend go?" Itsuma laid over the book and notes, blocking my attempt to bowl over his first question.

"What friend?" Scott glared at me over his book. His interest was an earmark of overprotective jealousy. Normally I'd find it annoying. But Scott was different. He made me feel wanted.

"I don't feel the need to answer." It was a knee-jerk reaction. I had a habit of running away from guys with a possessive attitude.

"Oh, Sensei," Itsuma tsked. "Now you've done it."

"Who is he?" Scott closed the history book and tossed it on the table. The gentle Cowboy I knew disappeared.

"How do you know it's a he?" I had to stop this. I was being too defensive. Scott didn't deserve this. But I'd been mulling over Kai's request and it rattled me every time I thought about it. His offer seemed closer to an option.

"What's his name?" Scott leaned forward, giving me a death glare.

"Why is it your concern?" *Stop, Mori. Don't yank his chain like this.*

"Christ, Scott," Itsuma said. "It's just a friend."

"That he met over the weekend?" Scott turned his laser focus on Itsuma. "What time did you leave Friday?"

"How did you jump to the conclusion it was Friday?" I said.

"Why would Itsuma know about something that happened over the weekend? Wouldn't it make more sense you told Itsuma he had to leave early for your date on Friday?"

Whoa. Scott was sharp *and* suspicious. "And here I was thinking Itsuma might have a jealous streak."

"I've got nothing on Cooper." Itsuma folded his arms.

Scott stood up and hit his fist on my dining room table. "Answer the question!"

Dumbfounded, I stared at Scott. "Where is this coming from?"

"Don't I mean anything to you?" Scott's face turned red.

"Yes!" No hesitation. I didn't think I'd hidden my feelings towards Scott and Itsuma, but I couldn't understand why my calm, reserved Cowboy was so upset. "You mean a lot to me."

"Then why are you seeing other men? Are you done with me already?"

Why was he spiraling into this pit of despair? What did he need me to do? I looked at Itsuma.

"I'm confused," I said. "You watched me and Itsuma, hell you tied me up and let him—I "

"Zuma is different," Scott said.

"Oh-kaaay…" I looked from one to the other. Itsuma gave me an *I-don't-know* shrug.

"Are you worried because I'm a teacher? Do you think I'm going to go around sleeping with other students? I'm not abandoning you." I was doing everything in my power to protect him. But maybe he needed the words. I held out my arms for him. "I love you."

The vulnerable Cowboy made an appearance, but then Scott shook his head. "Don't distract me with pretty words."

"Come here and I'll answer your questions." My arms remained outstretched.

After a moment's hesitation, Scott shuffled over and I wrapped my arms around him. I looked at Itsuma, who hemmed and hawed, pretending not to watch. I held out a hand to him and said, "Hey, jackass, I love you too."

Itsuma took my cue. He stood and held the both of us.

Scott laid his head on my shoulder. "See, you're still avoiding my question."

"His name is Kai Akiyama. He's a high school friend. He was on the wrestling team with me. I hadn't seen him since graduation and was catching up with him."

"I don't like it." Scott held me tighter.

"Ummm…" What could I say? Itsuma was right. Scott's jealousy added up to extreme insecurity.

"High school *friend*?" Itsuma could say so much with so little. He drew out my guilt.

"We have things to deal with," I said. That didn't sound suspicious, bad or dubious. Not at all.

"What things?" Scott wanted specifics.

Sighing, I said, "I'm not going to lie to you, but it's not your business."

"The hell it isn't," Itsuma weighed in.

I cleared my throat and put on my stern voice. "Both of you, I've let you have your way with me too much. Granted, I've given in to my desires, but there needs to be some rules laid out."

"Spoken like an adult to a child." Itsuma pulled back.

"What's that supposed to mean?"

"If you want a discussion, I'll gladly hear you out. But don't treat me like a child."

Good point. "Okay, look, you're my students. I should not be having sex with my students. So none of that until you graduate."

"That's not gonna fly," Itsuma said.

"Excuse me?" *Don't fuck with your Sensei.*

"You know why. My parents bought a one-way plane ticket to Japan. I leave the day after graduation."

Scott jerked his head up. "You're really going?"

Itsuma cast his eyes away. "As far as I'm concerned, I'm not holding back."

His words hung in the air like a death sentence. So this was all the time I had with Itsuma. I stepped back and leaned on the backrest of my couch. "So we have about two months."

Summer would go by like the wind.

"So you can screw anyone else you want, but I'm going to get my fill of Sensei before I leave."

Scott and Itsuma looked at each other. The gleam in their eyes made me nervous. Then they both stalked me like hungry wolves. *Oh shit. I'm in trouble.*

"Hey…" I threw my hands up. Trapped between a sofa and two desperate teenagers, I had no confidence I could

talk my way out of this. "Wait. You guys, we shouldn't—
"

"Why should we wait?" Scott grabbed hold of my shirt and pulled me to his lips.

I clenched my jaw in protest. It was futile. His tongue played with my mouth and smoothed over my teeth. I pushed away. "I reported myself today."

Scott froze.

"You went to the principal?" Itsuma eyed me.

"Yes."

"And?" Scott pulled back.

"He told me my personal business is my own." I narrowed my eyes at Itsuma. "He also said to do it off school grounds."

Itsuma laughed.

Scott shook me. "Why did you do that?"

I looked him straight in the eye. "Because I'm having sex with my students." It was the decent thing to do. I glanced to Itsuma. "The principal seems to think you walk on water."

My comment only made Itsuma laugh harder.

"The only reason why I haven't gone to the police yet is because I'm afraid of what it would do to you." If the media got a hold of this, nobody would have privacy. I wasn't sure my dad could take another incident of his son being in the news again. Mother would have a heart attack. But if that happened, Scott's predicament would be exposed. He might be able to escape.

"Don't." Scott shook me. "I don't like the look in your eye."

Itsuma's laughter ceased. "Sensei wouldn't do that." He looked at me. "You wouldn't do that, right?"

"If it got the abuse to stop, I would."

"No. It wouldn't. He'd just wait. Then…" The fear in Scott's eyes overtook his concern.

"But we could get you out of that situation."

"I told you, I have my family to take care of. I can't leave my sister. My brother. My mother—he'd kill her."

"Wouldn't that be a reason to go to the police?"

Scott violently shook his head. "No. Promise me you won't do that."

"Scott…"

"Promise me." He shook me.

What was I going to do? "If you move out of there, I won't."

"I can't do that either."

"Then we're at an impasse, aren't we?"

Scott stepped back. "I've got to go."

"Running away?" Itsuma spat.

"Please, don't!" I grabbed Scott's arm and held it close. Just like a girl holding on to her childhood sweetheart. "Don't go back there."

He lowered his head and gritted his teeth. "I have to." Scott tugged at my hold.

"Right now? Can't you stay just a little longer?"

I could see the war within him raging over his face.

"You should stay." Itsuma sighed and stepped to the kitchen table. "At least finish your assignment." He looked at me. "Cooper aced his last history test."

My head spun to Scott. "Really?" We'd only read books on Washington so far.

Scott's smile was coming back from extinction. "Yeah." A blush formed over the bridge of his nose and spread outward.

"Well done." I'd have to get with his history teacher and find out what topics were next.

"Mr. Reiss," Scott said with an air of importance. "I'm very serious about you. I pay attention when you talk."

I pulled back. "When you go to college things might change. I'd expect you to experiment."

"What do I have to do to make you see me?" Scott brushed his hand over my cheek.

"Scott…" I leaned into his hand. I knew what he meant. He was a man. I was treating him like a kid. I didn't doubt his devotion. But I held my reservations once summer school was over. I'd never be long-term. I wanted to try, but once he had a taste of college life things would be different. It would crush me if I started thinking about him as mine. Losing both of them would destroy me.

"Until you graduate, you're still my student." I glanced at the healing bruises over his body.

"Are you embarrassed to be with me?"

"No." I made sure my voice was clear and definitive. "I'd like to crow all about us."

"You should have seen him Friday," Itsuma said.

I groaned. "I was pretty obvious."

Scott eyed us. He hadn't been there that day. That was the day he'd taken off after his father got *a hold* of him.

Itsuma explained. "You didn't see his freshly fucked glow…"

"Itsuma!" I scolded. "Seriously, language. You sound like a short-order cook."

Scott laughed, his arms holding his sides. Even I let a smile crack the stark state of my mind.

He wrapped his arms around my neck and set his head on my shoulder. The intimacy dashed away apprehension of the future. We were here and now, enjoying each other.

"I need to go," Scott said.

No. No, no, no, no, no. Sending him back to that place was my hell. "So soon?"

Scott pulled away. "Yeah."

The hands on my clock read a little after eight. I didn't like this. Ever since he spent the night he'd been going home earlier. "You won't stay?"

My Cowboy turned away, avoiding my eyes, and swallowed. "I can't. I have to go."

His hand slipped from mine. I didn't doubt his feelings for me, but family needs outweighed selfish desires. That I understood. Still, when he picked up his pack I thought my insides were doing a freefall. Like a trapdoor opened below me and plunged me into darkness.

Scott put his shoes on while Itsuma and I watched. Neither of us gave protest.

After he collected what he needed, my Cowboy sauntered over, leaned a hand on the couch and swept me in a kiss. I forgot words. Language. Coherent thought. Our tongues caressed each other in a dance of mindless instinct saying *I will return*. He'd better. Dizzy in my stupor of love, I watched Scott pull back, turn to Itsuma and give him the same as he'd given me.

Watching the beautiful Cowboy and the Japanese Prince left me breathless. Their eyes watching each other, their lips tangled in a gentle battle. The kind of goodbye that left a man gasping and sent blood pressure soaring. If Scott didn't concede to Itsuma soon, we'd find ourselves back at the beginning, with them trying to pounce on me.

Scott finally pulled away. Itsuma smiled up at him, claiming his victory, tempting his classmate for another round. But their ardor for each other rang clear in their eyes. Scott pulled away and gave me a lopsided grin.

He leaned over and whispered in my ear, "Goodnight."

His salutation wrapped around my cock and stroked from base to tip. I couldn't move. Couldn't breathe. His whisper froze me in place. Holy shit. His voice was a bourbon whiskey aphrodisiac. Yes please, may I have another?

My Cowboy walked across the room and half my heart went with him out the door. We sat there for a moment in silence.

"Bastard." Itsuma flashed his impish grin.

I eyed my Prince. "You're not leaving so soon, are you?"

"Baka, he made sure to leave us wanting."

"Don't call me an idiot. No more bad words or I'm putting out a jar."

Itsuma tsked and crouched. His agenda had nothing to do with eating or studying. It didn't seem like he wanted sex. No, his body language suggested something physical, but not carnal.

I narrowed my eyes at him. "What's your angle, Karter?" I wasn't prey and I refused to relinquish control. The jitters I'd get before a match roiled in my stomach. My muscles tensed in preparation.

"You know," Itsuma said, "Scott's goodbye technique is effective. It's what got me thinking about him." He stared at me with unblinking eyes.

"Jealous?" My heart rate sped up. Excitement skittered up and down my spine.

"No." He held still, a panther ready to pounce. "You know better, Sensei. We need to have a discussion."

"About?" I tried to look harmless as a hare. *Yes, come get me. I'll fight you for the top position.*

Itsuma held his unnerving smile, a technique all the best mental fighters possessed. Confidence intimidated opponents. But I had my own techniques. I knew better. And yet I wanted so badly to take that smile off his face, or ravish those lips. Scott may have left us wanting so we wouldn't fight, but his plan wasn't going to work out. I wasn't sure what we were fighting for, though. Was it for Scott? Dominance? Losing face? Or was he still being petty over his precious iPod?

We both lurched at the same time. I had him on his back in an instant, but he rolled with my momentum and somersaulted us over until he was on top. I expected as much from a black belt.

"So who's this Kai Akiyama?"

Crap. He remembered Kai's full name. He was probably going to google stalk him later. There wouldn't be much to find.

"High school friend."

"Yeah. Like me and Cooper are high school friends. I got that. What do you two have to work out?"

"I said it's none of your business." I swept his arm and leg, rolling us over, fighting for dominance. I stretched out on top of him. Itsuma raised his middle. *Damn. I didn't expect him to know wrestling moves.* I kicked his feet out from under him and we slammed down, me still on top. I had him pinned.

"Did you play with him like this?" Itsuma said.

Before I realized what was happening, I was on my back. He had the concept down, trying to flatten my legs so I couldn't gain ground, but I'd been trained for this and he was still an amateur at wrestling.

"It wasn't like that." I hooked my arm over his neck and crawled over his back, wrapping my arms under his and locking my hands over the back of his neck.

He struggled. Itsuma tried to flip over. Crazy ass kid. It was difficult matching his speed. But I was able to keep him unsteady and unbalanced.

Itsuma coughed out. "Is he gay?"

Not really. "He's like you."

"The hell he is!" Itsuma twisted his body like a contortionist. He gained more speed and energy. Because of that we rolled and I was on my back with him on top. "Sensei, you need to learn to take me seriously."

Yeah, as if. "Well, you do like to horse around."

"Tell me what you and your *friend* have to work out." Itsuma wrapped around me with his arms and legs, holding himself so even a strand of hair couldn't get between us. He'd reversed our positions, only he didn't put me in a chokehold. He held onto me like a monkey, using his hundred and sixty pounds of muscle to keep me turtled. He was incredible. It made me hot for him.

"It's personal." I struggled, using grappling methods to get out from his hold.

"Then I'll find a way to get in your business." Itsuma turned me over and ground my head into the floor.

"Why are you so angry?" Ouch! He'd dug a knee into my back.

"Oh, I'm not angry, Sensei," Itsuma said, but his tone specified he was more than pissed off.

"Alright! I'll tell you. Let me go." Although his punishment was intoxicating, the thought of my Prince angry with me didn't sit well.

He let go.

I immediately felt the loss of his body heat. "Kai is in child care services." I flipped over and sat up, using the side of the couch as a back rest.

Itsuma stared at me with a mask of noble indifference. He didn't get it yet.

"He can charge Scott's father with child abuse."

"You mean he can put him in jail?" Itsuma's eyes sparkled with malicious intent.

Don't like the idea too much. "Basically. Or get his children taken away." The second situation could go awry.

"But wouldn't that mean Scott would be separated from the rest of his family?" Itsuma said.

"I won't let that happen."

"So the two of you are conspiring against Mr. Cooper." Itsuma crossed his arms.

"Essentially."

"Scott won't like it." Itsuma crawled closer. "He might not forgive you."

I sat there waiting for him to pounce again. "I could lose him, yes. But I'd rather him hate me than the alternative." Voicing my thoughts on the worst-case scenario would only make me worried.

"Better than him going to the hospital." Itsuma slid a hand up my leg.

"Or being carried in a pine box by six," I whispered. The worst-case scenario always inserted itself no matter how hard I tried.

Itsuma's hand gripped my calf. "And Kai will do this for you?"

For a price. "Yes."

"Why?"

Great. Uncomfortable questions. "He owes me."

Itsuma scowled. He grabbed my ankle and stood up, taking my leg with him.

"Karter!" I was upside down. Only my shoulders and head were on the ground. "Put me down!" I tried kicking free.

He grabbed my other leg and spread me open. "Sensei, I'm going to make sure you understand who you belong to."

Oh shit. This was not what I had in mind for the night. I had no control. My students were doing whatever they wanted to me. All my rules were being thrown out the window.

"Itsuma, let me go!" I tried wiggling free. No use.

"Not until you stop saying his name like he's the one that got away."

"What?" I looked up at him in horror.

"It's obvious you loved him." Itsuma lifted me up and threw me on the couch.

I bounced with my furniture. "Past tense, Itsuma. Past tense!"

Itsuma grabbed my wrists and sat on top of me. "Why do you think Cooper went kamikaze on your ass?"

Really? Ridiculous. Kai betrayed me in the worst sense. "He was… my first. You don't forget your first, okay?"

Itsuma slid down, grabbed my ankles and spread my legs open. "Then I'll have to do my best to drive him out."

He turned me on my side and rummaged around in the hidden compartment of my couch. When he came back with the lube and started unzipping my pants I lifted my leg and hooked an ankle over his shoulder. My other leg hooked around between his thighs.

"Wait. Itsuma. Condom. It's not safe."

He cut the top off an applicator and lubed my ass. "I told you, I'm safe."

"I wasn't saying you're not safe."

"Ah, the truth comes out."

Cool gel spread inside me. "I haven't been with anyone else except Scott."

"Since when?"

"Six months."

"You were tested?"

"Of course. I'm clean, but—"

"Good." Itsuma undid his fly and, without preamble, proceeded to push his thick cock inside me.

I whimpered. His slow penetration took over my senses. Being fucked sideways changed how my hole accommodated his wide rod. Being stretched like this made me feel like a virgin again, only without the pain.

He nestled in deep and shifted so we were perfectly cradled together between each other's legs. Itsuma moved his hips, showing me no mercy. That's when I realized he'd been holding back before. Oh my god. Talk about hip power. This was the real Itsuma pounding into me. His hand gripped my middle, using me for balance. Showing his strength.

My body wasn't sure how to register this intense fucking. Pain. Pleasure. I'd have it all from Itsuma. Watching him let go, trusting my body to him, I accepted the sexual monster inside Itsuma showing his true colors. His beast intoxicated me. Having this as a first time would be frightening, but after so many partners Itsuma's deviation from the normal was refreshing.

"Sensei?" Itsuma watched me. He seemed concerned.

"Good," I wheezed. "More."

He smiled in relief. Even though I'd asked, I hadn't expected Itsuma to be able to give *more*. And yet his pounding became harder, faster, deeper.

I cried out a salacious "Oh fuck!" and tried grabbing the cushions. My arms flailed, finding nothing to hold onto. My entire body belonged to Itsuma. I was truly helpless. Knowing my vulnerability heightened my senses, Itsuma continued to crash down, impaling me, filling my mind with all of him.

"I… I… yours… yours…" I whispered.

His eyes widened. My limit was getting close. With nowhere to go, my only outlet was my voice.

"Yes, Sensei, let me hear you."

His permission released the floodgates of restrained wails. Holding it all in, I'd thought I would burst.

"Such sweet sounds, Sensei," Itsuma rasped. "You drive me to my limit."

"Yes, yes!" *Please cum inside me. Stretch me more. Shove your cock down further. Fuck me. Use me. Hurt me.*

My heart pounded as my true desires emerged. These hard-to-face emotions only opened me up to Itsuma more. If he could see my insides, would he curl his lip in disgust or accept me in a way that even I hadn't? He sure was giving me everything he had to offer.

Sweat rolled down his back, making it hard to keep hold with my leg around his shoulder. Still he continued to fill me with every stroke. I couldn't explain how this change of angle cracked my heart open. His cock felt bigger, almost unbearable. But it made me feel closer to him. Our connection slammed straight up to my brain. I understood his ferocity. He poured his frustration into me. If I could help him pump away his demons, then I was more than happy to let him go wild.

"Do you get it now, Sensei?" The devotion in his eyes clamped onto my heart. "You belong to me," he said. "You belong to Scott. You're both mine."

"Yes," I croaked.

Shit. Owned. Possessed. Mastered. By a kid. I'd been looking for this since Kai abandoned me. Fuck. My sight grew watery. I'd let my control go and now everything was rising to the surface, including goddamn tears.

Itsuma froze, his eyes wide in fear. He started shaking. "Sensei did I hurt you?"

His concern overwhelmed me. Inside my heart, a door of utter gratefulness opened. More water leaked from my eyes. "No. I'm fine. Keep going."

Relief and his soft smile of understanding consumed my vision. He threw his arms around me and buried his head in my neck. "Thank god. Thank god."

My shoulder felt soggy. I wrapped him in an embrace, hoping to convey my understanding.

"It's okay, baby. It feels good. Let go. Don't hold back."

He hid his face, but his voice sounded hoarse, as if he were crying. "You sure? I don't… I can't… hurt you."

When it came down to it, Itsuma was humble. The desperation. The bravado. It all made sense. He didn't want to hurt anyone. Never meant to. The enigma of *the good child* wanting a life of his own. Itsuma tried to be both the straight A student *and* the bad boy. A case of trying to please everyone—except himself. Mistakes happened when you tried to be all things to all people. I'd bet Itsuma attempted to assure Scott by acting knowledgeable during their first time, only to have it blow up in his face.

"I'm okay," I said. "You're doing fine."

"Then should I teach you what I've learned, Sensei?" Itsuma stroked my cheek with his thumb and started pumping again, ramping up his downward stroke, pounding his *lesson* in further. He pumped so fast there was no cadence to my moans. A long, low whimper leaked from my throat. One long wail matched up to a dozen of his strokes. Maybe more. I wasn't counting. Then my balls started tightening.

"Fuck," I gritted out. My cock hadn't been accustomed to this much attention since college. Sore and aching did not give justice to describe my sensitive manhood. The start of my end rose. "Wait, Itsuma!"

Fearing my orgasm, I braced for impact. This was going to hurt. Still, I couldn't look away from Itsuma's

Cheshire grin. My one-eyed cannon aimed straight for my face.

"Come for me." Itsuma kept going, gleeful in his pace.

"Great, I have a front row seat to the money shot," I hissed.

Itsuma laughed without breaking stride.

A speeding train was eating the tracks of my urethra. The initial burst was liberating. The first splat landed on my nose. I turned my head and was rewarded with cum over my cheek, beard and ear. God, I was going to convulse from pleasure.

"So beautiful, Sensei." Itsuma bunny humped me into oblivion.

My whole body felt like a limp noodle.

Itsuma clutched my leg, sporting the most unapologetic *O* face I'd ever seen. His exposed rapture and vulnerability was a comfort. Oddly enough, I felt it was an honor as well. Itsuma poured his soul into me. Blown away by his fearless act of sensuality, I didn't feel so embarrassed by the stickiness on my face.

"You okay, Sensei?"

"Yes."

My heart, now firmly belonging to Itsuma and Scott, felt secure. I wouldn't have to worry about being torn apart in choosing. They were both there for me. Granted, I had to shove the notion of Itsuma not being here for long and Scott's future, but I could enjoy this moment.

Itsuma groaned and kissed my leg. After scraping his teeth along my calf he released me. My thighs screamed *never again*. My back went one more step and said *I will fucking kill you for this*. In fact, now that the fun was over, every joint in my body registered complaints.

Itsuma lay on the couch on his side next to me holding his head up with a hand. He grabbed a nearby towel and wiped my face.

"Sensei, you're not telling me everything."

I closed my eyes and remained silent.

Two minutes went by before the brush of fingers chased away wild strands in my eyes.

"Sensei…"

I grabbed his hand in both of mine. "I love you. You have me. There's nothing that will change that. But I have to save Scott."

His cat eyes narrowed. "I don't like this."

"Well, I don't like that Scott cowers every time he says he's going home." The meek attitude was another sign that my Cowboy wanted help. Well, I was going to give it to him.

Itsuma closed his eyes and breathed in and out. "You're just going to do what you're going to do."

"I will do anything to save Scott. I would do anything to save you."

"Including getting tossed in jail?"

I threw my arm over my face, letting the crook of my elbow cover my eyes. I didn't reply.

"That's stupid. You can't help him when you're locked up."

He had a point.

"What if I turn myself in after all this?" At least my conscience would be clear.

Itsuma shook his head with an expression of pain. "Sensei, I'm taking a shower." He got up and walked his pert naked ass out of my living room.

This was serious. Scott's safety was in my hands—not the school's, not the officials'. But maybe, with Itsuma's and Kai's help, I could save Scott. I gathered all my strength just to get on my hands and knees to crawl to my cell phone.

I dialed Kai.

He picked up on the first ring.

"Mori?" Kai's bland voice infused nervous energy in me.

"I'll do it. You. Whatever," I blurted.

"Tomorrow," he said. "I will pick you up at four."

Desperate much? "Fine." I wanted to throw up. My jitters around Kai were as bad as ever, and he wasn't even in the room.

He hung up. Typical Kai. No salutation. Just the cold, hard facts.

What the hell had I ever seen in him?

Chapter 11

Nausea prevented me from eating. A deep cleansing prepared my body, but my mind was a complete mess. I trembled from the inside out. My gut twisted every time I looked at the clock. Breathing techniques didn't help. As I sat in the dining room, I reassured myself that Kai wasn't going to rip my ass open again. That I'd learned how to *receive* without pain. Fuck, was I crazy or stupid?

The doorbell rang. I jumped. *Here goes.* Forcing my feet, I moved to the door and opened it to Kai's beautiful form. Damn my jitters but he did have a fine body. His grey slacks flowed with the breeze. A matching jacket with a black shirt formed an elegant ensemble. Shit. He'd said he'd pick me up, and I assumed we were going out, but I'd only worn jeans and a button shirt.

"I should change," I said.

Kai grabbed my arm. "Do you have your wallet and keys?"

They were in my back pocket. "Why?"

"That is all you will need." His cold glare was a shield. One he'd never learned to put down.

"Okay." My heart raced and my body felt warm.

He pulled me out of my house and shut my door for me. He turned and appraised me for a long look.

"This pisses me off." But his expression didn't show anger. He wore his usual poker face.

"What?"

"You are terrified."

"No, I'm okay." I did my best to stop my inner quaking. My hands vibrated with anxiety.

Kai stared at me for a while, then said, "We are switching to Plan B."

"Huh?" I didn't like this. "What was Plan A?"

"You cannot eat, right? I bet you would throw up if you drank alcohol. Am I right?"

"I said I'm fine." I put anger behind my words.

Kai grabbed my hand and hauled me with him to his silver Beamer. In high school, he'd always had the newest model. Nothing had changed. "No, you are not okay. You look ready to bolt."

I ripped out of his grip. "Well, what do you expect?"

We stared at each other, and then I saw something miraculous. Kai swallowed. A visual indication of his nervousness. It was enough to calm my nerves.

"I would expect you to hate me," he said. "I expected you never to call me again."

The emotionless voice I'd known through high school remained the same, but it didn't mean Kai didn't feel. I knew better. All the more, what he said broke my heart.

"Now that you have called, seeing you like this—all for a kid." He shook his head and avoided my eyes.

"I don't hate you."

"But you are terrified of me."

"I'm fine." I clenched my hands. "This is something I have to do anyway."

He lunged so fast I couldn't react. He crushed my wrist and yanked me forward. "Something you have to do?" He turned and pulled me along. "Fine, then."

Shit. Things were not fine. Kai was pissed. There was nothing more frightening than an opponent staring me in the face, staying calm five feet in front of me, but this... He hauled me over to his sleek silver BMW.

"Kai, let go. You're hurting me."

He stopped dead in the middle of the sidewalk, not letting up on his crushing grip. "Well then, since all I do is hurt you, you should be used to it."

Kai turned back and pulled me out to the street in front of the passenger door of his car. He clicked a fob, pulled the handle and shoved me into the bucket seat.

"Stay here. I have to make a phone call." He slammed the door.

My heart beat fast as a racehorse. Fuck. It was difficult to deal with my own issues and his at the same time. I trembled with an old anxiety. This feeling inside was that familiar self-loathing, like a villain one loved to hate. Even his name held power over me. We had to talk this through. He shouldn't have left me that night. But as unforgivable as his betrayal was, I had to get past it.

I breathed in the scent of the boy I'd loved. He was embedded in this car under the new leather smell. I closed my eyes and tried to remember the good times in high school. He was the unshakable wall. I'd confessed I liked men to him just to see him stutter. All he'd said was, *What do you want me to do about it?*

The driver's side door opened and Kai slipped behind the wheel. "Thank you for waiting."

He started the car and drove. I kept my mouth shut.

After a few streets, Kai broke the silence. "I apologize for hurting you."

Which time? No. As much as I wanted to spit the words at him, making matters worse was hurtful and childish. "Apology accepted. Please try not to do it again."

Subtly, but enough for me to notice, he sighed. The man was showing more emotion in the last fifteen minutes than I'd ever seen him display in the three years of loving him.

"You've changed a little." I appraised him anew.

He grunted.

Yep. Just a little.

"Where are we going?" I watched the traffic go by. We were headed toward Santa Monica as far as I could tell.

"Common ground."

"The bar?" I was hopeful.

"A hotel."

His words felt like a sucker punch. Still, I made light of it. "What, no flowers? No dinner? No movie?"

The tiniest upturn of his lips made me feel better. "Demanding for someone whose first words to me were not even a salutation."

"Humph." I crossed my arms. "Like you're any better."

"Such the girl."

It felt like old, good times. "Kai, what I said earlier… about needing to do this—"

"It is fine."

"How about letting me speak."

He shut his mouth.

"What I said earlier, don't take it the wrong way. I think that if I can do this then it means I can move past…"

Fuck, I didn't want to bring up that night. I'd wanted it, and he given himself to me. The very fact should be beautiful, but the outcome hadn't been what I'd thought it would be. We were inexperienced. I tried to take more than

I could. He got carried away. The experience left us both scarred. It took therapy, years of healing, and a patient, older gentlemen lover to show me the joy of taking it up the ass before I got over my bottom trauma.

I watched for his reaction. He said nothing. No emotion. God, how did he do that? I hated it. I also hated myself for opening my mouth again. I'd just pointed out how much he'd hurt me. He might not show it, but even Kai had to feel something.

"Did you go back to girls after me?" I couldn't just shut up. Trying to drown out the hurt with more words was like a drunk trying to drink himself sober.

"I fucked a lot of people after you."

Great. This was turning out to be a mutual hurt fest. "People?"

"Men. Women. Anyone who would let me."

"Do you talk to any of the guys from the team?"

"From high school?" He glanced at me. "No. After they abandoned you I cut ties with them."

"Oh." That was shocking. The guys on our wrestling team hadn't taken it well when I admitted I was gay.

"So, umm, do you still train?" Ants started crawling in my stomach. How far was the hotel? Could I do this without running the moment the car stopped?

"You get diarrhea of the mouth when you are nervous." Kai settled a hand on my knee.

I froze. What was he asking?

"Please just drive." I set his hand on the console between us. Scott and Itsuma's faces never left my mind. Especially now. I was having serious doubts. Jail time looked more reasonable than this deal Kai wanted.

"There were no complaints on Mr. Cooper. However, there was an empty folder."

"An empty folder?"

"Yes. I found it curious."

"And?"

"I had a colleague research him in the database."

"You found a lawsuit, didn't you."

"Yes."

I knew about that. "So, how do we get him away from his children?"

"It is best I leave out the details of such an operation."

"So, you don't really have a clue."

Kai cast a deadpan glance my way. "When have I ever not had a plan?"

There was that. "Heaven forbid you wing it." I smiled. Old-time nostalgia helped calm my jitters.

He set his elbow on the console divide and hung his hand upward, offering me to take it but leaving it a non-threatening gesture. My breath hitched. This man, before he'd hurt me, had accepted me the way I was. Holding onto the past kept me from moving forward in some ways. Time to forgive and shed old memories. I slid my fingers down his cool palm and clasped his hand, accepting the peace offer. I looked out the passenger side window, blinking away the sting in my eyes.

"We are here." Kai pulled into a circle drive, put his car in park and let the valet take his ride.

Kai took my hand and led me through the hotel lobby.

A flood of *rules* came back to memory. Terms and agreements about our relationship, what was possible, what was unacceptable, all things I understood as conditions for going out with him came rushing back. No PDA. No looking at him "weird." No excessive touching. Definitely no *hand-holding*. It was a difference in him that made me nervous.

"Kai, we're in public." Besides that, his fingers were freezing.

"I do not care about that."

What? "But the rules," I whispered.

"Forget them." He wasn't whispering.

Hmm. Okay. Let's test this theory. He'd been so reserved in high school it made me doubt he'd changed so much. I closed my hand around his and kept pace. We went past the check-in desk and straight into the elevator. He hit a button, but the doors remained open.

"You already checked in?" I said.

"Yes."

I see. He wouldn't let go of my hand, so I stepped closer and set my chin on his shoulder. The elevator was wide open for anyone to see.

He gave me a sideways glance. "Watch yourself."

"Ah…" I smirked in childish triumph. "So forget the rules means only you get to break them."

"No, it means I have been waiting five years for another chance with you. Do not entice me too much."

Stunned, I pulled back. There were no words. On one hand I'd thought I was a one and done for him. He'd gotten inside me and called it good. At least that's what I'd thought. But he really did mean for me to forget that night. Did he think we could start over just like that? My jitters returned.

"Those other people I had sex with were practice," he said. "This time, I will make you beg for more."

I huffed. "Good luck with that."

The elevator was empty except for us when the doors finally closed. I got a case of fireflies buzzing in my stomach sending little electric jolts. *Breathe. Shit.* My anxiety bubbled. I thought I'd break out in hives. *Fuck.* This was becoming real. I wasn't so sure I could go through with this. If I refused, would it be like last time? This whole mess was all my fault.

"Kai…" my voice trembled. "I'm sorry. I staved you off so many times. When I finally got the courage to let you have me… I should have realized you were frustrated." Kai, the wall, was not without his limits. Nor was he an unfeeling machine like so many believed. But I feared he'd get me in a private room and go off on me again. *No. No. I was a virgin then. I can take it this time.* But the fireflies became angry bees.

He lifted my hand and kissed my knuckles. "It is not going to be like last time. I will be gentle."

"No." My body started to shake. "Just give me two minutes to prepare and you can plunge in." *Oh god. I can't do this.*

Kai froze and stared at me with his cool gaze. "I do not want that."

"Kai, just…" *Crap. Just get it over with.* "Do what you want, okay?"

He cupped the back of my head and pushed me against the elevator wall. The metal handrail on the side dug into the small of my back. Kai's cruel gaze seared his next words into my brain.

"I told you. I do not want that."

My mind went blank. It didn't stop my mouth from running off. "What do you want?"

The elevator chimed and Kai jerked away, turning to the door and letting me have my space. I panted and put my one thought back in order.

The doors opened as Kai held out a hand and I let his fingers envelop mine. I thought nothing, felt nothing, letting him pull me along. *Just relax and let Kai do what he wants.* But thoughts started becoming clear in my mind. This was for Scott. But would he want me to do this? Was I doing this to get over that one night? No amount of justification was making this scene okay.

He opened the door and waved me inside. For a hotel, the room had space. Not your usual Motel Six. A breeze lifted the gauze-like drapes from an open sliding glass door. Beyond the balcony, a gorgeous view of the ocean cast a serene atmosphere. Light cast a romantic aura around a California king-sized bed. Opposite the mattress hung a flat screen TV. This room was more like a love nest than a place people stashed their baggage for a trip.

"Wow."

"You like it?" Kai leaned against the front door.

"You chose well."

Despite the elegance of the room, I started remembering all the things Kai liked—sexually. I went into panic mode. When we were going out, seven years back, the rules were simple. He didn't mind if I sucked his cock, but I was not to expect him to return the favor. No fingers and absolutely no penises near his ass. He was like Itsuma in that regard.

I remembered the real reason I was here. Scott. I turned to Kai and watched him watching me.

He stood there, arms folded, staring at me with his expression of indifference. Nothing ever fazed The Wall. At least on the outside.

His eyes roamed my body in a slow sweep. He wasn't moving. Even for Kai he seemed oddly stiff. Was he holding back? Geez. What was going on in that mind?

"Are you okay?" I said.

A pause. "I am fighting with myself."

Fighting himself? About what? Feeling more and more like I'd entered the lion's den without a care, I berated myself for being so stupid. I pocketed my hands, hiding the fact they were shaking like I were going out to my first tournament. "Fighting?"

He raised a hand. "It is not what you think."

"Explain it then." I'd never seen him tongue-tied. Kai was honest and blunt to the point of offensive. He never held back his words. Hell, if he had, it really would be like talking to a wall.

"I want to show you, but it is hard."

"Show me what?" My nerves were starting to get the better of me.

Kai stepped forward. I looked into his face. Oh god. I saw fear. No. Not Kai. Anything but fear. It was like watching my god fall from grace.

He swallowed that little bit of emotion and I understood. He was trying to express his feelings. Trying to break free from the shell of his upbringing. *Don't show empathy, don't show weakness, don't let anyone see the chinks in the armor.*

For a fleeting moment, I saw inside Kai Akiyama. Then he shut down. He was his namesake, The Wall, once more. My body buzzed with tension.

"Thank you." I didn't have to explain for what. He'd shown me something amazing. That he was human.

Kai nodded and started taking his jacket off. "Sometimes I see myself from the outside. I walk around like a robot. I watch people express themselves, people like you, and I wonder if I have anything like that in me."

I wanted to die. Yes, Kai had feelings. For so long he'd been told what not to do. It was probably a record going on in his head until it was background noise. Don't tell people who you love. Don't cry. Don't smile carelessly. Don't tell. If ever down, get back up. Don't admit defeat. Show nothing. Be a wall.

He stepped forward. I stepped back, leaning my back against the door. His finger traced my chin-strap beard all the way up to my ear and brushed the tussles of my shoulder-length hair aside. He gazed into my face, taking me in, and smoothed his fingers over my imperial mustache.

"It suits you," he said. "Otherwise, you look like the pubescent high school boy."

I snorted. "If you want to compliment me, tell me I look manly." *Not this half-ass bullshit.*

The Wall stared back at me.

"Kai…" *I can't do this.* No matter what, I loved Scott and Itsuma. Doing this would betray their faith in me. I'd find another way. My hand reached for the door handle.

"They tell me you are especially careful and hygienic." Kai gripped my hand.

"They? Who is they?"

We stared at each other, face to face. "I would approach your ex-lovers and ask them questions. Some would oblige my request and show me what you liked."

"Show you?" My jaw dropped. *Stalker much?* "That's just a little creepy." The man was a stickler for detail, investigating every option. Seeking to understand. Once he set his mind, he was thorough.

"I apologize," he said. "I wanted to know."

"You should've been a detective."

"There is a lot of research that needs to be done in child care. My talents are not wasted."

I gave him a weak smile. Kai, in his own way, had just made a joke. One of those kinds of jokes that I'd have to explain if people didn't know him.

"So, they showed you?" I wondered what kind of demonstration he got. I liked a lot of things. "But you're straight."

"What does that have to do with anything?"

He leaned into me. I couldn't move. *No. Definitely can't do this.*

Kai gave a slight grunt. "Maybe I am bisexual."

Un-fucking-believable. Bi?

His poker face was flawless, but I knew better. He was pushing himself. I grabbed his waist and forced him back. "I can't do this." I turned around and squeezed the mechanism escape. He pushed the door closed and shoved me into the wall. I was face-first against plaster with my ass pressed against Kai's bulging hard-on.

"Please, if you can, stay like this for a minute," he said. "I will do anything you want."

Terrified, I held still, keeping my instincts from kicking in. Or kicking Kai. I didn't want to hurt him. I just wanted to get away. "I can't… Kai, I can't do this. I'm sorry. I have to go."

"I know," he whispered. "I know."

My heart broke. His voice held more emotion than his stony face ever could.

"Do you think we could go back?" Kai said.

"Back?"

"To before that night?"

That's right. He wanted to erase our first time. The nostalgia of going back to high school days, starting over, having our first time. If that night were done right…

"Kai, I'm sorry, but even with my scars, I've moved on."

He gripped me like he'd never let me go. "My first memory as a child was when I cried and my father slapped me. I was so shocked I stopped crying, and my father said *good*."

I knew a little about Kai's stern upbringing. He'd been nicknamed The Wall for his lack of emotion. Even when I screamed two inches from his face he never showed fear or anger.

"I know you've been trained not to show emotion."

"That was not it. I have been trained not to feel at all."

"You're upbringing was cruel."

"That does not matter."

Anger sunk in. Kai couldn't get mad at his father or about his situation because he'd been trained that way. It made me all the more angry *for* him.

"What matters is I had been pushing emotions down for so long that I… was not dealing with things."

"Maybe that's why people depended on you so much."

"Yet look what happened with you and that time—our first time."

Yeah, leaving me during that emergency wasn't the best thing. I could rationalize how he panicked. Someone trained not to feel. That doesn't work. He must have overflowed with emotion and shut down.

"I get it," I said. "Men in general don't deal with *feelings* well in the first place. For you it was probably like being a med school student on their first day told to go do brain surgery on this person and oh, if you don't he'll die."

"You brought them out."

"Brought *them* out?"

"Yes." He loosened his hold on me. "I am dealing with the repercussions of my upbringing. I see a psychologist three times a week."

Oh, he meant his inability to even admit he had feelings.

"If it were not for you, I doubt I would still be here," he said.

I turned around in his arms. "What do you mean?"

He stared into my face. I could swear I saw hairline fractures over his mask.

"In high school you showed me another world." He gripped my waist. "You got through to me. I would be in a psychiatric ward if it were not for you. Or dead. You taught me love. I am grateful and I am in your debt."

I gaped at Kai. His hand slipped into mine as his eyes gazed at me. Kai's fingers were no longer cold. They'd absorbed my body heat through his caress. He laid his head on my shoulder with a content sigh that ruffled my hair.

We stood there together, me hugging him, both of us lost in our memories of the past. Neither of us caring. This conversation was long overdue. I could have been married to this man if things had gone better in the beginning. But I wasn't and it hadn't. Itsuma and Scott were my world.

From today on, I would move forward to be a dedicated partner. This side trip had been an exchange. A learning experience. I could no longer be the popular party favor. Scott and Itsuma only. I'd never get another chance with them, so this was the only time to get close to them. I wanted to get back to them. Itsuma had a tournament and Scott had a show today, but I wanted nothing more than to get home and be a good boyfriend. Committed. I started liking that word.

"Kai…" What could I say? "You know, this is… I mean… I have someone I like." Even if they were just playing with me for now, I still wanted to be with Scott and Itsuma.

"That kid, I know."

"Yeah. Uh… him and… one other."

"Ah. I see."

Thankfully his tone wasn't condescending.

"Room for one more?" His whisper tickled my ear.

"Uh… it's a unique dynamic."

"Mori…" He pulled back. "It was a joke."

No way. Kai *had* changed. A joke? That was a joke. A good one, too.

"Besides, I would not be able to share you with anyone."

"Oh." I should have realized. He was straight, at first, and possessive.

"So I will wait," he said. "Until you are ready."

"You are so troublesome." I sighed. "Don't wait for me. You're wasting your time."

He kissed my shoulder. "Loving you is not a waste of time."

My heart ached.

"Kai," I whispered, sad and apologetic.

"Shh…" He held me. "I understand. But even you cannot change my heart."

"What have I done to you?"

He put a finger over my lips. "Do not say such things."

♂♂♂

Kai pulled up to my house and parked on the street.

"Need help getting in?"

"No." I sighed, spying a familiar white Lexus sitting across from my house.

Kai trapped my hand between the drive shift and his palm. "I will still help you."

"Thank you." I mumbled.

"You love them?"

I nodded. "Yes."

"Then, at least, I am partially redeemed."

It was safe to say I was gun shy when it came to love. That night in high school I'd trusted Kai and received nothing but pain. Physically. Emotionally. Psychologically. He'd left me as scorched earth. Looking back, I understood why and forgave him.

"Kai, it's the past. Don't beat yourself up about it anymore. You don't owe me anything."

"I can owe you this."

I hung my head and thought about it. "Okay."

Kai squeezed my hand and let me go. After a demur goodbye, I got out of the car and faced Itsuma.

My Prince leaned his sexy ass on the passenger side door, his muscular back to me as I walked across the street. Smoke twirled up and over his head.

"Are you smoking?" I rounded on him.

His hand trembled as he took the cigarette from his lips and blew smoke up into the air. "So I see what kind of favor he owes you, Sensei." Itsuma took another hit and crossed his arms. "No wonder you insist on a condom. Here I thought you were more innocent."

"Stop." I grabbed the cigarette from his lips, tossed it on the concrete sidewalk and stomped on the thing till it went out. "No more of this bullshit."

Itsuma pushed off his car, anger rolling in his wake. "I thought I made things clear to you. You're ours."

"I didn't do anything."

"Oh, right. How is the Marquis Hotel? Did you have a room overlooking the ocean? I bet it had silk drapes."

"You followed me?"

"I thought you'd go to the police, so I was going to stop you. Now I don't know whether to fuck you till you bleed or shove you in a vat of Clorox. But I think it best if I leave."

"Fine. Run away. But I'm not going to apologize for giving everything I have to save Scott."

Itsuma turned around. "You think Scott would want this?"

"You think I'd do *nothing* when Scott is an inch away from being beaten to death every night?"

"Why did you have to do that?" He threw a hand to where Kai's BMW had been. "Why do you throw your body away?"

"Says the man who tries to fuck me in class."

Itsuma stared at me. He was angry.

"What?" I said. "You want to hit me? Hit me."

He lifted his index finger. "One. You're allowed this one. Next time I will break his penis and then you'll shit out of your ears when I'm done with you."

"I didn't do anything!" I raged. "I couldn't, because I love you."

"Good," Itsuma said. But he was still pissed, and I didn't think he was listening. "You should run inside now. Clean yourself. You stink." He turned and walked.

"What, no make-up kiss?"

Itsuma flipped me off as he reached his car. He opened his door and glared at me. "Sensei, I'm not letting you off lightly. Prepare yourself." Malice lingered in his dark gaze.

I fumed, watching him leave. He too had considerable restraint seeing as how furious he was with me. But Scott's safety was worth more than my shattered heart. More than my used-up body, my pride, or my career for that matter. We'd be getting him out. Tomorrow.

Chapter 12

So many students asked if I was okay that I finally wrote on the chalk board *I am fine. Please don't ask*. Yet the clowns and wise guys still asked anyway.

"I fell and landed on my tailbone," I replied. That seemed funny to them. Truth was, Itsuma's pounding of me the night he wanted to know more about Kai was the real reason I was sore. That was two "tutoring sessions" ago and I was still tender.

Itsuma glowered at me all through homeroom. Scott looked mortified and glared at Itsuma. When my phone rang after lunch break, the only reason I answered was because it was Kai.

"It is done." Of course he didn't give a greeting.

My students jeered at me. "Hey! How come we have to turn ours off?"

"Teacher privileges."

"Must be nice."

I rolled my eyes at all of them, covered my phone and said, "Hush! I have an emergency."

"Thank you," I said into the phone.

"He will be released in twenty-four hours. Maybe sooner. It is the best I could do."

"Okay. Thank you." I expected the usual dispassionate disconnect.

"Mori?"

"Yeah?"

"If you ever need anything, I am here."

"I'll keep it in mind." Hopefully I conveyed compassion without giving him hope for more.

The line went dead and I addressed my class. "Thank you all for your understanding." I pushed the off button on my phone and showed them all the shutdown screen. "I'm now turning off my phone."

♂♂♂

The last bell couldn't come fast enough. Eager to get the hell out, I had my students lock the classroom. They were all too happy at my distracted pace. I got on my cell phone and called Itsuma. Bad student that he was, he had his phone on. Thank god.

"Ohio." Itsuma's greeting calmed my nerves.

"I'm on the move, are you alone?"

"Hai…"

Great. He was distracted. He started rambling in his native tongue. I understood enough. Apparently, Scott's mom called Itsuma to talk to Scott. After their conversation, Scott left a blazing trail as he exited the classroom saying he had a family emergency.

"Can you come with me, or is that not a good idea?"

"I better come with you; otherwise, you're not likely to get in the door." Last night's anger was still under the surface, but Itsuma repressed it over the phone.

"It's okay?" I said, trying to get a feel for how pissed he was at me.

"Waunita likes me." His grin could be heard through the line.

"Who?"

"His mom. Jeez, did you plan this through?"

Uh. Now I felt like a fool. "Some. Meet me at my house."

"Hai. Hai."

A flood of doubt now ate away at my good intentions. But like they say about the road paved with good intentions—I'd find out if we were in hell soon enough.

This was just like me. Jumping in. Not holding back. Justification didn't mean I was in the right. It just showed what kind of lines I'd cross for Scott's sake.

God, what would I say to Waunita? *Hi, I put your husband in jail for your getaway.*

What if she was like Scott and didn't want to go? She was probably just like him. What if this was all in vain? What would I do next? I'd been too much in my head to really think. This could be a complete disaster. But I was too far along in my plan to stop. I'd already tried getting Scott away from his dad. None of my attempts had worked so far. In fact Scott was in more danger now than ever. So what was I hoping to do? Separate a man from his family? No, I couldn't think that way. This was about shielding victims from an abuser.

When I pulled up my driveway Itsuma was waiting outside his car. Just like last night he leaned his beautiful ass up against the passenger side door. He pushed off, walked over and got in the seat next to me with a judgmental thud.

I leaned forward and put my forehead on the steering wheel, praying to higher powers above for guidance.

"Sensei? Are you okay?" Itsuma's words were uncharacteristically gentle.

"You're right. I don't know what I'm doing." I stayed bent over, shamed to look at him. "I think I'm going crazy."

He ruffled his hair. "With interfering with people's lives, or running around behind your boyfriends' backs?"

Harsh. That was Itsuma.

I lifted my head up. "Is that how it looks?"

"It seems no matter what I do you never take me seriously."

"Itsuma, we never talked about our relationship."

"I thought you got it…" His sarcasm oozed Itsuma style. "But I guess I wasn't direct enough."

"Pinning me against a couch and ripping an orgasm out of me isn't sitting down and having a conversation. You shoved your demands on me. You didn't ask me what I wanted. You didn't say you loved me. You haven't confessed anything aside from moments of passion— which, by the way, does not count as a proclamation of love. It only means you're enjoying the sex. Giving me pleasure isn't a license to my heart. You steamroll me at every turn. You're damn right I don't take you seriously. You're not out of school and you're fucking leaving the day after."

Itsuma pulled back with hurt eyes but said nothing.

"Let's talk about this later, after we get Scott out of that house." I put my car in reverse and rolled onto the street.

"Sensei, I've tried this type of thing before and it backfired. If you do this, Scott will find out."

"It's already too late." I put my car in gear and started driving. "I've accepted I've already lost him. But I have to do this." I prayed I hadn't already lost Itsuma too. "I've tried to pursue other means," I said. "I've tried turning myself in. I've tried sheltering him."

"Yeah, I know, which is why I'm only going to punch you in the gut once when this is over." He smirked. Itsuma's joking was just as intense as the man.

"What for?" I gave him a sideways glance.

"For trying to do it alone."

"Don't expect me to just take a beating."

Itsuma harumphed at me.

"Which way to Scott's house?"

♂♂♂

The quaint, one-story, everyday suburban home was not really what I expected. Not that I equate abusers with trailer parks, but the way Scott portrayed his family life, not having a cell phone, bringing lunches from home and his old, worn-out clothes created a different impression of his family life. The grass was green, the neighborhood was descent and the place was clean. Your regular middle-class lifestyle.

"Not what you expected?" Itsuma smirked at me and started climbing out of my parked car.

"Shut it." I closed my own gaping mouth.

Everything I'd planned on saying flew out of my head. "Itsuma?"

He turned to me.

"Am I doing the right thing?"

He looked at me and shut the car door. "This is the way I see it. The way you did things, I don't completely agree with."

"Oh I see, Mr. Breaks-the-rules gets high and mighty when it's my turn." I stepped out of my car and pressed the fob's lock button.

Itsuma kept talking like I hadn't said anything. "But I understand that you're trying to help him when he can't help himself. He sees no way out. It could cost him his life if he stays."

"Knowing that, how can you not want to take him away from all of it?"

"Because it's his choice." Itsuma raked fingers through his hair.

"His choice to die?" I pulled back and pinned Itsuma with a glare.

"I don't want him to get hurt, but what you're doing could also put him in a bad place."

"Thanks," I said with enough sarcasm to compete with the Prince himself. "That makes me feel better."

"But I think it's admirable that you want to help him."

"Yet you believe it would be better if he asked for help instead of forcing it."

"Yes."

"But you said he'd never ask."

"Because he won't. He's got too much macho pride."

I snorted. *Yeah. I guess mixed in with that submissive trust, Scott also has a stubborn streak.*

"So really the choice is let him have his pride and watch him be a punching bag, or go in, try to save him, but lose him forever."

"Yep." Itsuma sighed.

"How was losing him before?"

"Hell."

"And how is watching him get beat to death?"

"Unbearable."

That settled that. "Yeah, I'd rather lose him but have him safe than watch him suffer."

"Either way this goes, we'll all suffer."

I supposed he was right, but I resolved to do something rather than nothing. An army of rats climbed the walls of my stomach. I was terrified. Hopeful. I stepped up to

Itsuma and we walked up the path to a solid wood door. As I pressed the ringer, a jolt of static electricity went through me and I jerked my hand away.

Itsuma snickered. "That shock wasn't coincidence. That's Aubrey's idea of a joke."

"Who?" I shook my hand, trying to get rid of the pain. "Scott's sister."

The door opened a crack and a girl, maybe fifteen years old, leaned against the doorjamb in cut-off shorts and a spaghetti string top.

"Speak of the devil!" Itsuma grinned at the girl.

"Zuma!" The girl threw open the door and launched herself into Itsuma's arms. "You finally came to ask me to marry you," she said with a laugh.

"In your dreams, sprite." Itsuma held her in his arms and twirled her around. "Besides, didn't you want to hook up with a rich guy?"

"You *are* rich." She laughed.

A knowing grin and a spark of mischievousness in her eyes made me bet her teachers had a handful with her in class. But despite the playfulness my hackles rose up. *Get off my boyfriend, you hussy.* Geez. Jealousy. Hadn't felt that in a while.

They stopped spinning and she gave me a questioning look. "Hello," she said. She let go of Itsuma, stuck out her chest and her hand. "I'm Aubrey."

Sorry, sister, shoving your tits at me does no good. I wasn't rude, though, and I shook her hand. "I'm Mori."

She squinted her eyes like she knew me. "Have we met?"

"Not unless you go to the same high school as this guy." I pointed a thumb at Itsuma.

"Next year," she said. That would put her at about fourteen.

"Aubrey?" A timid voice called from behind the door.

"Mrs. Cooper." Itsuma straightened and bowed at the waist.

Holy crap. He could be a proper Japanese prince. Now I wanted to see the person who could make the sarcastic bad boy pull out his congeniality. I stepped next to him and saw a tan, thin woman with strong Indonesian features standing behind Aubrey.

"Hello." The woman gave me a cautious smile. She was stunning. Even a man-lover like me could say this woman was attractive. But beyond her striking features were the dark circles under her eyes. Her slim build was near anorexic. Her full-length dress covered her from wrists to neck to ankles. That had to be a bit warm for Southern California.

"Hello." I smiled. "My name is Mori Reis."

"Ah, the tutor." Her smile curved more in a friendly warmth.

Er? I was at a loss. I hadn't expected Scott to talk about me.

"I'm Waunita Cooper," she said. "Scott's mom. Come in." She stepped outside past Aubrey and looked both ways out the door.

Itsuma ushered me inside to a sparse but clean living room. On the right an old couch separated the entryway from the living room, making the hall look longer than it really was. A small TV and entertainment center sat positioned opposite the couch. A recliner and a beanbag chair were the only other furniture.

Family pictures lined the wall to my left. Each framed photo showed the procession of three children growing up. I recognized Scott right away. But as he grew older, his eyes changed from the beaming wonder of a child's to those of a man who'd seen repeated hardship. Even

Aubrey's young exuberance in the first pictures faded into a mask blocking life's burdens. But what broke my heart was the third and youngest child, the one I hadn't met. Even in youth, the littlest one's expression was of wary concern, as if there were something around the corner ready to snatch him away.

Waunita, in the first pictures, had a shy expression, but one of hope. By the last picture she looked reserved and withdrawn. The man I guessed was Scott's father was broader than his eldest son. With each passing photo the man gave off a meaner look. The line of pictures told a story of a family disappointed in the world and each other.

"Please sit," Waunita offered me the couch.

I took a seat next to Itsuma. From behind the couch, Aubrey draped her arms around Itsuma's neck. Itsuma, the epitome of relaxed, sat back and skimmed his fingers along Aubrey's arm.

Motherfucker. I could hear him now, saying *payback's a bitch*. Yeah, his taunt to rile me up worked. *Get off each other. Do you enjoy molesting little girls?* I wanted to fling comments, but I just couldn't bring myself to say it.

Despite it, Aubrey and Itsuma seemed close. He gave me a sideways glance and smirked. *Fuck off.*

Aubrey sighed. "It's bugging me. I know you. You said your name was Mori Reis?"

"Yeah." Butterflies fluttered to my chest. I wasn't well known, but why would a fourteen-year-old know me?

"It'll come to me," she said. "I don't forget a face."

Waunita had disappeared and now returned with a tray of bottled waters. She set the tray down on the modest wood coffee table. "I wanted to thank you. You've done a lot for my son."

Oh crap. I was never good with mothers. All the blood rushed to my face. *I've done a lot to your son.*

"Ah, I don't know about that."

Aubrey's indiscriminate staring wasn't helping my nerves.

"Since he's been with you his grades have improved." She smiled sweetly. Was she inwardly laughing? Did she know how embarrassing this was?

"Been… been with me?" Shit. I was totally choking.

"Tutoring him," Waunita said.

"Uh…." My mind went blank. Mom jitters.

Itsuma burst out laughing. "Sensei… she knows."

Knows what? That made me feel worse. I raked a hand through my hair. *I'm a bad man. I lead little boys to the road of sin.*

"Itsuma." Waunita pinned him with a calm, serious expression.

He stopped laughing and dipped his head. Still, a grin shined on his face.

"Mr. Reis," Waunita turned to me. *Oh god, here it comes.* "I'm well aware of who my son is. I know he wouldn't do anything he didn't want to."

"That's what I'm afraid of, but I can't help but feel he bears a weight that might break him."

Waunita stiffened. She was on the defensive.

"Please hear me out," I said. Now or never. "I want to protect Scott, but he wants to protect his family, so if I can shield you that means… that means a better life for him." *Oh god, did I say it right? Was I too direct?*

Waunita fiddled with her hands. She remained stiff but she looked into my eyes. I held my ground and didn't cast my gaze away. Or flinch. Or breathe. Her eyes searched within me for some kind of signal, or perhaps how much I could be trusted. Her expression remained soulful, determined. Waunita was a strong woman. She was not a victim; she was a hostage. The one who took the brunt for the rest of the family.

"That night," she said in a low tone. "When he didn't come home till morning, I was so worried. But then when he came back he was so happy. My happy little boy came back to me after so many years." She wrapped her arms around her waist. The air laid a heavy weight on my shoulders. Aubrey pulled away from Itsuma and stood there like a helpless child not knowing what to do.

"My poor little man can't seem to catch a break," Waunita whispered.

Itsuma tsked. "Don't you mean heal from them all?"

Scott's mother flashed him a nasty scowl.

"I've come to understand his father has a nasty temper," I said.

The blood drained from Waunita's face, and her expression turned to stone. She was going to tell us to get out.

"Please let me help you, any way I can. You can stay with me. Leave right now. You never have to see your son in bruises again."

"He has a bit of a difficult job, you see… with horses." It was a blatant lie, and one told as if she were a recording. I ignored it.

"I know that he suffers." I scooted up on the edge of the couch. "Please allow me to help."

Waunita shook her head and lifted a hand to her face. "I've tried."

"I can do better."

The woman wasn't crying yet, but my heart wept for her.

"I don't want to break up my family," she said.

Unable to sit there, I leaned forward onto one knee. I wanted to hug her, but I stopped short, not knowing how she'd react to a stranger touching her.

"I don't want to break up your family either. But isn't it better to keep your children safe first?" I tried to take all judgment out of my voice. "I can get your husband help."

She shook her head. "He won't do it."

Frustrated and desperate, I nudged myself closer. "There's another way than this."

Again, another shake of her head. Anything I was going to say she'd block out. I wasn't getting through to her. This was hopeless. Scott and his family would forever be ensnared in a vicious cycle. I wanted to pound the walls and scream. I wanted to grab her and all her children and bring them home. Why did she have to be so stubborn? What was she going to do? Have her and Scott be the wall protecting the two youngest forever? And if the two siblings did escape, would Scott and his mother be left as shells, exhausted from a life of torment? No. I couldn't allow that. I couldn't see the shine of Scott's eyes die.

I stood up, took one step forward in front of her, dropped to my knees and bowed my head. In a raised voice, I said, "Mrs. Cooper, I am desperately in love with your son. His happiness is my main concern. But his happiness lies with his family. Therefore, I want to take responsibility for his family. I will do everything in my power to keep you all safe. Please come with me now to a better life!"

I panted in the silence. Unable to wait for an answer I looked up. Waunita stared at me with watery eyes. Her hand covered her mouth.

"Wow, Sensei," Itsuma broke the unease in the room. "A true samurai couldn't have done better." He was serious. I did not hear any hint of amusement. Finally, Waunita spoke in broken patches.

"It's just… there's no way… we can't… I…"

Footsteps thundered behind me and Aubrey sidled up next to me. With hands on her hips in a triumphant gloat, she said, "Moriel Reis! Twenty-three years old, currently contracted to be a professor at California Institute of Technology in the fall term next year. Son of real estate mogul Christopher Reis." She pointed a finger at me. "Five years ago you were treated surgically for an anal fissure."

My body turned to stone. "Did you have to include that last part?"

"See! I knew you from somewhere!"

"How?" I was mortified.

She beamed. "I'm studying to be in Public Relations. I've got to know everybody, so I keep up with the news." She pulled forth a printed newspaper column that reported my horrible night with Kai.

"That was so long ago." My face burned.

"The point is," Aubrey challenged her mother, "he can take care of us."

"Huh?" Itsuma said. "Go back a bit. Why does Sensei going to the hospital mean he can take care of you?"

Aubrey swung around. "Did you miss the 'son of Christopher Reis' part? Do you know who Christopher Reis is?"

Itsuma shrugged. "Everyone knows who he is." Itsuma pointed at me. "But this guy isn't related. He's a high school teacher." Itsuma looked at me. "Right?"

Oh god. Might as well own it. "You got a problem?" I sat up and folded my arms.

His face fell. "So…" Itsuma stared at me like I was a whole other person.

Aubrey turned and started walking off.

"Brie?" Waunita warned her daughter.

"What?" The teenager whirled around in dramatic fashion.

"Where are you going?"

"To pack my bags. I'm going with the billionaire's son."

"Our problems shouldn't be dumped on a stranger." Waunita's soft voice and statement had merit.

"I don't have to be a stranger." I turned to her. I pushed myself towards her seat. "I'll marry Scott. I'm prepared to propose."

Aubrey stomped off in a huff. "Oh my god! Why does Scott always get the rich guys?"

I'd stunned Waunita. Itsuma looked like he was still trying to mentally link me to my father—Christopher Reis. We stared at each other until Aubrey came back with a backpack and headed for the door.

"Young lady, where are you going?" Waunita said.

"With the man who has the balls to try and right this family."

"Leaving would be a mistake." Waunita folded her hands, becoming a statue worthy of Mother Theresa.

"Why?" Aubrey turned to her mother.

"Your father would track us down. You know how he is."

"So living in fear under his roof is better?"

"Life isn't that simple." Waunita raised her voice.

"You just want us to hurt as much as you!"

Scott's mother was on the verge of tears. "That's not true."

Itsuma sat up at the edge of the couch. "Mrs. Cooper, doing it alone might not have worked, but—"

"Get out." Waunita flashed an angry look at both of us. "Get out before I report you to the school."

That sent me reeling. Fuck. That's just what I needed. Another controversy. Dad would kill me. He'd been understanding about Kai, my sexual orientation, but this? His son back in the tabloids would make him furious. Not to mention his money dumped down the drain into the career I'd worked hard in attaining. But if it got Scott and his family out, I didn't mind. All I cared about was what would happen to Scott. If I couldn't get him out from under his father, what would happen to him?

Defeated, I stood and glanced at Itsuma. He was watching me to see what I would do. I sighed and turned for the door. I'd find another way.

"Aubrey!" Waunita shouted.

"I'm going with or without you. And Tommy is coming with me." Aubrey stomped over to the door.

Right then I saw a younger version of Scott clinging to the hallway corner. I recognized him as the youngest in the photos. Only in person he wore a shiner and his left arm was in a cast. I couldn't help but stare at his broken arm. How old was he? Eleven? Beat up and broken already.

"Neither one of you is leaving this house," Waunita said to her daughter.

"Don't tell me what I can do!" Aubrey shouted back. "If I want, I can get emancipated."

Kai clearly had talked to Aubrey. She was now spewing legal jargon at her mother.

The little boy blushed and turned his head. Adorable. And probably realizing he was interested in men. He gave off that feeling that he was like me. I was the same age when I started realizing I didn't want a conventional relationship.

The young man turned his face enough for me to see his bright red ears, neck and profile. One eye peered at me in coy curiosity. He didn't want to be seen, but he wanted to look. The arm that was in the cast moved, bringing my attention back to the state of affairs.

"I hurt myself playing baseball." His voice was small and uncertain.

Inside, a piece of me died for this child. Half of it was that he didn't even wait to be asked. Another was his defense of what happened to him. "So young, and yet you lie so well it chills my heart."

His eyes grew the size of pie plates.

"Tommy," Waunita said. "Go back to your room."

"No, Tommy." Aubrey stomped over to him and held out her hand. "We're leaving."

Without question the little boy put his good hand in hers.

"Aubrey!" Waunita swooped in and grabbed Tommy's shoulders.

"Let go or you'll hurt him." Aubrey let him loose, clearly not wanting to pull her brother in a physical tug of war.

"Aubrey," Itsuma said. "This isn't the right time."

"Then when is a good time? When Scott isn't around and it's me he goes after?"

Itsuma straightened and balled his hands into fists. "He's gone after you?"

Aubrey set her hands on her cocked hips. "Yeah, when he *accidentally* mistook me for Mom."

"That's enough," Waunita said.

Itsuma shook. His eyes locked on Waunita as if he would attack. His lips compressed. I didn't think he cared about leaving no matter what I did or said.

Tommy, very calmly, stepped out of his mother's grasp, walked to me and put his good hand in mine. "Did you mean what you said?" He stared up into my face. "About going to a better life?"

I went down on one knee and looked up at him. My legs would've collapsed if I hadn't. "Yes. I meant every word."

"Tommy." Waunita's warning tone went ignored.

The little boy searched my eyes. I wasn't sure what he was looking for, but I willed him to see my sincerity. I was prepared for a do or die scenario if they went with me. Maybe Scott would forgive me someday if I sheltered his siblings.

Tommy found what he was looking for and turned to his mother. "I want to go."

Aubrey stepped beside her brother and crossed her arms. With Tommy's words, I regained the strength to stand.

"You can't just leave," Waunita said. Beads of sweat started rolling down her forehead.

"I don't think it's so bad," Tommy said. "Besides, why would dad come for us? He doesn't love us."

Waunita slumped down on her knees just as I had. "What are you talking about? Of course he loves you."

"No, I don't think so." Tommy shook his head. "He thinks I'm a freak, just like my brother."

"That's not true." Waunita pressed a hand to her chest.

"Even if it isn't, his place can't be as bad as here." Tommy looked up at me.

I squeezed his hand. *Well said, kid.*

"Mom?" Aubrey dropped her hands.

Waunita breathed in heavy gulps, placing a shaking hand against the back of the couch.

"Mom!" Aubrey crouched down to her mother's level.

Waunita's eyes rolled to the back of her head. Shit! She was passing out. I let go of Tommy's hand and lunged forward. *Thank you, fighting reflexes!* I was able to catch her.

"Mom!" Aubrey cried.

I put two fingers on her wrists and felt for a pulse. "She's okay."

Aubrey let out a sigh. "She's been having these spells lately. I think its stress. It's like she can't handle life anymore."

I lifted Waunita up and jostled her small frame till her weight was even in my arms.

"Where are you taking her?" She might be at odds with her mother, but she cared for her more than she let on.

"I'm taking her to the hospital."

"Wait," Aubrey said. "I have a better idea."

Both my eyebrows shot up. I looked to Itsuma. He seemed to have calmed down and shrugged at me.

"A better idea than taking a sick woman to the hospital?"

Aubrey squared off, blocking my way to the door. "Yeah, if you weren't blowing smoke up her ass about leaving right now."

I shook my head. "She didn't agree to that."

"If you take her to the hospital, then me and Tommy are hitting the road. We aren't staying here. Do you really want to be the one telling her she's never going to see her children again?"

"You'd leave your mother like this?" Did she trust a stranger to do the right thing by her mother? After all, I was a stranger.

Aubrey rolled her eyes. "She fainted. She's not dying. Put her on the couch. She'll wake up in half an hour."

"How do you know I'll take care of her?"

She laughed. "Zuma would kick your ass if you did anything to Mom."

Itsuma tsked. "I don't know about that right now."

Aubrey grimaced.

A tug on my belt loop got my attention and I looked down. Tommy latched a finger around one of my belt keepers with the broken arm and held a small case in the other.

"What's with the bag, little man?" Itsuma said.

Tommy turned to him without letting me go. "Aubrey said we were leaving."

Itsuma snorted. "You do everything your sister tells you?"

"No." Tommy's belligerent answer put a smile on my face.

"So are you taking us or not?" Aubrey said.

I shifted Waunita in my arms and looked to Itsuma for guidance. He smirked and raked a hand through his jet black hair.

"I only have a two-seater," I said. "Well, the third seat's big enough for a dog." God, how unprepared was I?

"Let me fix that," Itsuma pulled out his cell phone, dialed and started rapid-firing commands in Japanese. After a thirty-second conversation he hung up. "Transport is around the corner."

I narrowed my gaze at him. "You had backup?"

He cracked his knuckles. "I was hoping Mr. Cooper was here."

"So you were going to gangbang him? That's sporting of you."

Itsuma only gave me a lazy shrug in response.

I shifted Waunita once more and turned my gaze to Aubrey. "I meant what I said. Go get a few changes of clothes."

Aubrey patted her backpack. "I have everything I need."

"You really did plan on leaving, didn't you?" I headed for the door.

"Yeah."

I wondered if that had anything to do with Kai.

"Hey, open the door," I said. "She might not weigh much, but dead weight gets heavy."

Aubrey did as I asked and I side-stepped through. Tommy held onto my belt loop. As my partner in crime walked through the door I mumbled, "Could this be called a kidnapping?"

"You're asking moral advice from the guy who went along with helping his friend rope up a teacher?"

"That was Scott's idea?" I recalled the first time Itsuma had a taste of me.

"Well, I was pissed at you. He came because he didn't want me hurting you."

An SUV pulled over to the curb behind my Porsche. The view from Scott's house got exceptionally better as three guys from Itsuma's Judo team stepped from the vehicle. I gave an inner sigh. Thank goodness Itsuma had a backup plan.

"Let me take Mrs. Cooper." Itsuma held out his arms. "She'll be more comfortable in a bigger car."

I let Itsuma cradle Waunita, and as soon as she was in his arms, Tommy put his hand in mine.

"I want to ride in a Porsche!" Aubrey pointed at my car.

Tommy squeezed my hand, giving me the impression he wanted to ride with me. I looked down and gave him a smile. He blushed and played coy, hiding his eyes. If his mother woke up in the car, I wasn't sure she'd appreciate the fact her youngest was with an older man she didn't know. Of course, she probably wouldn't be okay with her daughter coming with me either.

Itsuma saved me. "Tommy, why don't you come with me and your mom."

The little guy nodded and bravely followed Itsuma, giving a backward glance to his sister.

While Waunita was being packed into the SUV, Aubrey stepped up to my car like it was a wild animal. Her fingers trailed the passenger door's edge and pulled the handle. She was careful of the door hitting the curb as she lowered herself in the seat. Walking to the driver's side, I got in and waited for Itsuma and his buddies before pulling out and leading the way.

"So where are we going?" Aubrey asked.

"Logically, we should go to the hospital."

"Logically," Aubrey copied my professor's tone, "we should go anywhere but the hospital. First, we don't know when my dad will be home, and a hospital will call our house. Second, we can't afford that."

"Don't you have insurance?"

Aubrey stared at my profile. "Do you know how much the co-pay is? Oh, wait. Sorry," she snorted. "I forgot who I was talking to. Of course you wouldn't think about money."

"I would pay for her care."

"She wouldn't want you to. She'd probably refuse medical treatment. Plus, dad would find her and take her home whether she needed to stay in the hospital or not. Trust me, that would be bad."

"Okay, so Plan B. I have a place."

"Your house?" Aubrey sounded way too hopeful.

"I live in a more modest place than you think."

"So not like Zuma's?"

"I've never seen his house." Technically that was true. I'd dropped him off in the dark. "What do his parents do?"

"Wow, random question," Aubrey said. "They do investment, I think."

Damn. I had access to a kid who knew all about Scott and I couldn't think of what to ask.

"Has Scott been okay?" I hated that my voice trembled.

"He's been, ummm… distracted, yet focused. I don't know. It's hard to explain."

"Uhhh, okay."

"Well, things make sense now." Aubrey fiddled with the center console gadgets. Granted my car had loads of buttons everywhere and wasn't a safe place for curious minds while driving, but she was acting a bit ADHD.

I slapped her hand. "How so?"

"Like he's got a boyfriend." She leaned over and ogled the steering wheel. "Getting up early. Staying out until the last minute before dad gets home. Things like that."

Her input made me both elated and guilty.

"He's still going to his part-time job?"

"Oh, I don't think he'd give up horses." Aubrey said. "At least not for good."

"Does… does he have a favorite food?"

She burst out laughing.

"What?" I said, a little defensive.

"You're adorable." Aubrey snickered. "Have my mom teach you how to make broccoli cheese casserole and he won't ever leave your side."

"Broccoli cheese casserole, huh?" I'd have to confirm that.

Aubrey looked around. "I must look like a high school kid being driven around by a college student in a car daddy bought him."

"Anyone who thought that would be wrong," I said. "You're not in high school, and this car was my mom's gift after I graduated from the university of her choice."

"Wow." Aubrey looked over at me. "I should be so lucky, but her choice?"

I nodded. "I owed her."

After the crap with Kai went down, me scaring the shit out of her and the scandal while I was in the hospital, I owed her that much.

"Because she'll never have grandchildren?"

If I could have gotten away with gagging her, I'd have pulled out the duct tape. "Can you not wield that verbal sword around?"

She sat back in her seat, her face pale and her hands clasped together. "Sorry," she whispered. "I didn't mean it like that. I'd be the last person to throw stones."

Her sincerity had me thinking she was just a person that spoke whatever came to her mind. I pulled off the freeway and turned right at a green light. A sign saying *Welcome to Woodland Hills* greeted us as we passed. The 27-highway had light traffic, and it was better than trying to muscle my way through the 405 traffic to the top west corner of San Fernando Valley. I pulled up to an iron gate with a guardhouse dividing the driveway.

Security stepped out and recorded my plate number, then walked up to me. He wore a blue uniform and was built like a linebacker.

"Hello, Mr. Reis," the man in blue said. "Who is your companion?"

"This is Aubrey Cooper." I gestured to her and looked in my rearview mirror. Itsuma and his friends pulled up. "The guys behind me are with me too."

"Very good," the guard said. "Everything in the house should be set."

"Thank you."

The guard walked back and I pulled out my phone and dialed Itsuma.

"Don't give him any flak," I said. "He's instructed to take down anyone who refuses to co-operate, you understand?"

"Yeah, I got it," Itsuma didn't sound happy. "She's still not awake."

"We'll deal with that at the house." I glanced at Aubrey. "A few good points were given to me as to why going to a hospital wasn't a good idea. I told him you're with me," I said into the phone. "But you'll have to show ID if you want to visit without me."

"One of those places." Itsuma's sarcasm dripped over the phone. "Do you think it will keep Mr. Cooper out?"

"Hopefully he'll never find the place."

Itsuma grunted.

The guard wrote down the SUV's plates and stepped up to the vehicle behind me. I heard them talking as I listened over the phone. After a round of names, the security guy opened the gate and I ended the call. I led the other car to one of my empty rental houses.

"You said you lived in a modest house."

"I do." I pulled into the driveway of a three-car garage, two-story house. I should have said this wasn't my house, but her assumptions made me want to tease her.

"This is what you call modest?" she sputtered.

The place was an awesome pad, but the five bedroom, three bath house was too big and too secluded for my taste. My three bedroom, bonus room and one bath flat was perfect.

I got out of the car and pulled out a set of keys. Itsuma carried Waunita. Tommy followed, and Itsuma's three friends milled around the car.

"Wow, Sensei, whose house?" Itsuma stepped up next to me with the still unconscious mother in his arms.

"Mine," I said, and waved to the three members of the Judo team. "Hey guys, thanks for helping out."

"No problem, Mr. Reis," the tallest of the three said. Todd was in my fourth period class.

"They won't say anything, will they?"

"Nah. They don't have much love for Mr. Cooper."

I unlocked the door, turned off the alarm and ushered everyone inside. Just as I instructed, the rental company I worked with put in sparse furniture. A few beds, a couch, a dining table and chairs, and an entertainment center. Most of the bedrooms were up the stairs on the left, before the den. The master bed and bath was on the first floor, but the other rooms were upstairs. I wanted to check to make sure they had everything.

"Want the nickel tour?" I said.

Aubrey stared up at the vaulted ceiling. "I'd pay a dollar."

"Dining room is straight past the living room." Though that was obvious. "The stairs lead to four bedrooms and two baths." I pointed. "There's a bedroom on the first floor," I said, leading Aubrey and Tommy around. "The kitchen is behind the den. You have a fridge, a washer, dryer, and dishwasher, and as you can see, room to put stuff if you need." Which reminded me they needed bed sheets.

Aubrey went through the empty cabinets.

"Don't worry," I said. "I'll get you some food. You won't starve."

"I thought you lived here," she said.

"I told you." I took a towel and poured water on it in the sink. "I live in a *modest* house. Not all of us with trust funds are stupid flashy with the money we have." I took the wet cloth, wrung it out and walked over to Itsuma and Waunita in the living room.

Scott's mother looked troubled even in her unconscious state. As I lowered to the white carpet near Waunita, Tommy clomped around upstairs, going excitedly from room to room.

"Whoooooa! This room is even bigger!" His cute staccato voice echoed against the bare walls.

I set the towel on Waunita's forehead. Aubrey came in and sat next to me.

"How long has she been out?" I regretted not taking her directly to the hospital.

Aubrey sighed and lightly slapped her mom's cheeks. "Mom, time to wake up."

Waunita slowly opened her eyes. Thank god. She blinked at her daughter.

"I'll tell the guys they can leave." Itsuma got up and went to the door. Good thinking. If there weren't enough cars to take them back, maybe they'd stay.

"Where am I?" Waunita gingerly sat up.

"It's where we're staying," Aubrey said.

Waunita glanced around. Tommy rushed down the stairs. "Mom! Mom! This place is amazing!"

The mother of three startled as her son jumped into her lap. He didn't seem to care about his cast arm or that she'd just woken up from fainting. "I want to stay here, can we?"

Her eyes flashed a glare to me as she answered her son. "We'll talk about it."

"Great!" Tommy burst out of her lap. "I'm going to check out the backyard!" He ran towards the kitchen's sliding glass door and, like an escaped cat, ran out onto the green grass of the two-acre backyard.

"Why don't you stay here for a while? You can leave anytime. I don't want to separate you, but maybe some time will help you as a family." Okay, I was spouting things I didn't really know about, but anything to get her and the children away from their father. "At least stay until Tommy heals that broken bone."

"No way." Aubrey stood up. "I'm staying here. Mom, you can go back. I'll take care of Tommy."

"A nine-year-old shouldn't be without his family, and neither should you, for that matter."

"Then it's settled." Aubrey crossed her arms. "We'll stay here."

I massaged my temples and said, "You two stop and actually talk to each other for a moment." Women are frightening. It's these moments that make me grateful for loving men.

"No kidding," Itsuma said. "Girls can be vicious."

My thoughts exactly.

Waunita turned to me in exasperation. "I know you mean well, but why?"

"My motivation is only Scott. There is nothing more than that. I want the best for him. You've got to know your family is in trouble and the problem is escalating."

Waunita didn't look at me. A shaky hand covered her forehead.

"Everything that's important to Scott is important to me," I said.

Waunita looked up, her expression tense. Her words challenged mine. "Even his father?"

"Especially his father," I said. "I'll do everything I can to stop the violence. We'll get him counseling. Even if Scott wants nothing to do with me, you'll still be welcome here, and I will always give you my support." I ran my hand through my hair. "But right now, to fix this, your husband needs a wake-up call. And being away from him will keep you safe."

Waunita was silent for a long time. Her narrow eyebrows twitched and her beautiful eyes searched my face.

"Please just let me take care of you."

Finally, her lips parted to speak. Before she could I turned and ticked off my to-do list to Itsuma. "The beds need sheets and the kitchen needs food. Stay with them until I get back. And don't tell Scott or his father where you are. Not yet."

"I'm coming with you." Aubrey made a beeline to my side. "Unless you want to guess at what we eat."

"Good point." I beat feet and got out the door before Waunita could oppose the plan. Aubrey was smart enough to follow. Once outside I pulled out my phone and typed in a message for Itsuma. *Don't let her leave.*

"So you approve?" I opened my car door and dropped down into the leather seat.

Aubrey plopped down next to me. "As long as you treat my brother right, I'm happy."

"I meant about the house?" I rolled my eyes. But having the girl's approval felt good.

"Oh, that… I thought that was clear."

I pulled out of the drive and started for the gate. "Aubrey, it would be best if you didn't go back to your school. Tommy as well." As a teacher it pained me to say such things.

"Yeah, I shouldn't go to my usual haunts, blah, blah, blah. I know. Mom couldn't leave everything behind. That's how dad found us before."

"You're a smart kid."

"Oh, you just noticed?" She elbowed my arm.

"Ow." I flinched. Bony girl.

"OMG. You're such a wimp."

"I'm delicate," I said with a lisp and bent my wrist over.

She laughed.

Aubrey wasn't hard to figure out. She'd become the strong one. The fighter. The voice of reason.

Her laughter died down and she clasped her hands together. "Ummm… but there is one thing I have to get from the house."

"Oh?"

"Tommy's medicine."

"Then we should get it now." I didn't want the chance to meet Mr. Cooper yet, but I also needed to talk to Scott. God, how was that going to work out?

"Okay." Aubrey's courage seemed to evaporate.

I wanted to ask so many questions, but I was equally afraid of the answers. Had she ever suffered broken bones? Was she attacked regularly? Or was it just Scott? The comment about her father mistaking her for her mother churned my stomach. Empty silence continued until I asked for directions.

"If you see a truck parked in the front of the house, don't bother, just drive on by," Aubrey said.

But when we pulled up to the house, there weren't any cars in sight.

"I'll be right back." Aubrey jumped out of the car before I put the engine in park.

"Hey! You're not going in alone. What if he's home?" I parked and jumped out of the car.

Aubrey put her hand in her shorts pocket and the jingle of keys rattled.

"So lame," she said. "I left for good, but I still have the keys."

We were walking across the lawn to her front door when a familiar old pick-up pulled to the curb and parked across the street.

"Oh shit." Aubrey rushed to the door, rattling keys as she unlocked the deadbolt. My heart pounded in my ears. *Okay. Minor development.*

The driver's side door swung open and Scott's brown boot stepped onto the asphalt. He shoved his black outlaw's hat on, looking haggard, all the while glancing at my car with a concerned expression. Then he saw me and stopped in his tracks. His eyes widened in terror. Scott whipped around and started back to his truck. A man, very much the huge giant I'd seen in the family photos, stepped from the curb to the street.

Scott spoke to him and used hand gestures, glancing back to me in nervous distraction. I felt a tap on my back.

"Let's get out of here," Aubrey said.

"But Scott…" How could I leave him now? I wanted him to come with us.

"Later." She jogged across the lawn.

"Aubrey," the huge man I assumed was Mr. Cooper said, "Where the hell are you going?"

I went to Aubrey, naturally trying to be a shield for her. We wouldn't make it to my car without intersecting her father and brother.

Aubrey stopped dead in her tracks. "Dad." She whirled on me and clung to my arm in an affectionate hold. "This is my boyfriend. We're going on a date."

Dumbfounded, I looked at the girl. Then, I schooled myself and brought my eyes to the two men. In a different situation the shock on Scott's face would've been priceless. But here, now, I couldn't stand his hurt, confused expression. I cringed, hoping he'd go along.

My "girlfriend" pulled me along, trying to get to my car. I whispered, "Aubrey?"

"Sorry, I couldn't think of anything else," she whispered back.

"Excuse me, young lady," Mr. Cooper strode up to intercept. "Didn't I say no dating?"

The man looked angry as a hornet and a bit on the drunk side. What I wanted to know was how he got out of jail so fast.

In the spirit of a peaceful outcome I held up my free hand to greet the man. "Mr. Cooper, let me explain."

He stepped up the curb, making short work of a straight path to me wearing a daddy death glare. The kind of look that warned of shotgun weddings.

Mr. Cooper's fist came out and made a wide swing. *Whoa!* Reflexes made me duck under his arm and jump back. This man did not know how to fight. His mass must have proven enough for other altercations.

"Dad!" Scott jumped on the larger man. "Stop it! What are you doing?"

"Brother!" Aubrey yelled.

Mr. Cooper yanked Scott over his shoulder and threw his son flat on his back. Scott wheezed out a breath and stayed on the ground. Shit. His ribs hadn't healed yet.

Aubrey ran past her father towards a figure walking up behind us. "Kai!" She scrambled towards him.

Mr. Cooper whipped around, giving me the chance to kneel over Scott. "Are you alright?"

He struggled for breath. "Go."

"Not unless you come with us."

"Mr. Cooper," Kai's strong, monotone voice rang out. "I see you did not heed my warning."

Aubrey ran to Kai and hid behind him as if he were home base. Good. At least she was protected.

"Aubrey, come here." Mr. Cooper walked towards Kai and his daughter.

"Are you out on bail, Mr. Cooper?" Kai stood firm. He wasn't just a wrestling champion. He also competed in a nasty form of Krav Maga. At least way back when. I wasn't worried for Kai, even as Mr. Cooper approached him.

"I imagine it would not look good to the judge if you assaulted me on a public sidewalk."

Mr. Cooper jerked to a stop. "And I'll tell him you were attempting to kidnap my daughter."

"Up," Scott whispered, holding out his hand.

I helped him stand.

"Now get the hell out of here," Scott hissed. "What are you thinking?"

Being reprimanded by an eighteen-year-old—again—was annoying.

"Come on." I tried to pull him along with me.

Scott yanked out of my grip. "What the hell is going on?" he fumed. Scott's eyes were turning into burning hot coals. He glanced over at Aubrey.

"We're getting out of here. All of us." I willed him to come with me. To run over to my Porsche and make our escape.

"Aubrey, in the house!" Mr. Cooper stood five feet from Kai.

Good choice. I knew how lethal Kai could be. I feared for Scott's father if Kai had reason to lay hands on him.

"No!" Aubrey found her courage and stepped a foot out from behind Kai.

"Mori," Kai said. "It is time to go."

"No, it's not, you little punk." Mr. Cooper crossed his arms and widened his stance. "You're going to answer me. Who the hell are you?"

I held my hand out to Scott, hoping he'd take it and leave with me. Scott took a step back and shook his head.

"Come with us," I said. "I can take you and Aubrey to a safe place."

"What?" Scott fisted his hands. "I'm not leaving."

Mr. Cooper turned to us. "No one is going anywhere except the strangers on my lawn."

Kai took advantage of Mr. Cooper's attention being diverted and handed Aubrey a set of keys and pointed to his BMW down the street.

Mr. Cooper turned back just in time to see Aubrey beating feet.

"Aubrey!" he shouted. He started to go after her but was blocked by Kai. "Step aside, shrimp." Mr. Cooper pushed Kai back. Bad move.

Now within his right to protect himself, Kai pulled his rattlesnake move and had Mr. Cooper in a wrist lock, bent over and screaming before Aubrey was even down the street.

"Dad!" Scott took a step forward.

Kai flicked his dispassionate, hard eyes to Scott and my student stopped cold.

My Cowboy turned to me. "Make him let go." Scott's firm tone and expression warned me this was an unforgivable sin.

Before I could retort, Kai pushed Mr. Cooper forward, opposite of his fleeing daughter.

"You don't have to stay here," I whispered. "I can take you away from this."

His eyes widened in horror. It made me feel like a stalker.

"Scott, you know this guy?" Mr. Cooper slurred his words. His attention was all over the place, going from me to Kai to Scott.

My Cowboy looked me straight in the eye and said, "No. I don't know him at all."

Fractures penetrated my heart. My chest ached. Just as Itsuma predicted, Scott was lost to me. A wave of numb acceptance filled my senses. My sight dimmed and my muscles grew heavy. I blinked in rapid succession. Shock. This was shock.

That's when a familiar SUV pulled along the side of the curb. Itsuma's Judo team. Todd jumped out and held a phone to his ear, observing the "carnage" of the scene. The driver and backseat passenger stepped out with grim expressions on their faces. Oh god. Waunita. Was she okay? I should've taken her to the hospital. Hell, *I* might need one soon.

"Scott, come here." Todd waved the phone at him.

"No." Mr. Cooper turned and threw his chest out. "Who are you?"

"A friend from school," Scott replied and walked over to the Judo captain.

"What's this about?" Mr. Cooper tried his intimidating tactics on Todd, but the man looked like a drunkard trying to start a fight.

Todd ignored Mr. Cooper and held out his phone to Scott.

Scott bent over, picking his hat off the ground, and squared it on his head. Then he took the phone. "Hello?"

While my Cowboy was occupied, Mr. Cooper eyed up Kai. "If you don't get off my property right now, I have the right to forcibly remove all of you."

Kai stood his ground. "Mr. Cooper, as a child care investigator I find your activities suspicious and am calling for removal of your youngest two children from your household."

"You can't do that!" Mr. Cooper waved a wobbly fist in the air.

Kai went on. "I find it suspicious on the grounds of Tommy Cooper's injuries."

"He was injured playing baseball."

"True, the broken arm was from a blunt object, presumably a baseball bat; however, I find it strange he was not admitted to the hospital until ten-thirty."

"He didn't notice it until after dinner."

"So he was playing little league and did not notice till after the game?"

I wanted to shout, *you sorry fuck, who doesn't notice a broken bone until hours later?*

"That's right," Mr. Cooper said.

"Funny thing about that alibi, Mr. Cooper, is that three parents confirmed there was no game that night."

"You son-of a—" Mr. Cooper pulled back a fist.

Kai didn't move. Shit. Was he going to take a punch?

"Dad!" Scott threw the phone back to Todd and rushed his dad. "We can't afford you going back to jail, or a hospital."

"He has Aubrey," Mr. Cooper said.

"She'll be back." Scott grabbed his father's arm, and at the same time shied away as if protecting his own face. "She always comes back."

Mr. Cooper looked around. I think he finally noticed there were five of us and two of them. That is, if Scott fought against us. But his actions showed he'd take the blows rather than give any.

This sucked. I wanted to defend my actions. Tell Scott he was the most important thing. Tell him I loved him. I would protect him. Make him come with us. But all I received was a glare that stabbed daggers of death my way.

Todd shifted, posing as though he wouldn't hurt a fly. I knew better. "Mr. Reis, we should go."

"Okay." I nodded. Scott wasn't going to budge. He'd all but told me we were through.

Kai shifted, drawing Mr. Cooper's attention. It was a distraction tactic. Damn if I didn't know Kai as well as myself. He was giving me the chance to get to my car. I took it and gave Mr. Cooper a wide berth. Even as I did, Scott's father eyed me like he was going to make another move. I'd welcome the chance to hit the guy.

"Dad, don't be stupid." Scott stepped closer to his father. "After you just posted bail, the cops would question you, not these guys."

Plus, he had faith that Aubrey would return. Fat chance. Not if I had anything to do with it.

"This isn't over." Mr. Cooper turned around and stormed to his front door.

I took a step towards Scott. He brushed me off and turned without a backwards glance. This was the last I'd see of that cute ass. I stared at the door until a hand slipped into mine and tugged me away. Numb and mindless with inner turmoil, I followed.

Chapter 13

The shopping spree I'd planned for Aubrey was subdued compared to the hope I'd felt before seeing Scott. I waited for her to pick out bed sheets on the second floor of Target. Kai had left Aubrey in my care while he got back to work. Which left me staring at Aubrey while she tried finding the cheapest, most hideous excuse for a comforter I'd ever seen.

"Really?" I gawked. "You're going to make Tommy sleep on grandma's pink-and-green quilt?" God, I wouldn't pay five dollars for that.

"He likes this kind of stuff."

I raised my eyebrows and grabbed the clear plastic holder. "Just because he likes men doesn't make him a girl." I shoved the comforter back on the shelf. "That's just cruel."

"Well then, how about this one?" Aubrey pulled out a red-and-white polka dot comforter.

I rubbed my neck and sighed. "I'm not buying that."

"But it's for me."

"Okay." I dropped my hand to my side and tried to grin at her, but couldn't. I felt like a stroke victim trying to smile through my loss. Scott's harsh dismissal of me affected me more than I could convey.

"Hey, are you alright?"

"No." I looked up towards the ceiling and rolled my eyes to keep the emotion inside. But too much saltwater filled my lids and one droplet finally escaped. Aubrey dropped the comforter and wrapped amazingly strong arms around my waist. Her small frame allowed me to hug her in an equally firm hold. I buried my face in her long hair, hiding the fact that there was too much dust in the air.

"You're very brave," she said.

My soggy laugh finally overcame the despair. "Thank you, but you're the gallant one."

"Ha!" She pulled back and offered me a tissue from her purse. "Hiding behind the social worker is really awe-inspiring."

Blowing the last of my embarrassing moment away, I picked up the polka dot comforter and put it in our cart. "Leaving your family for a new life when you're just fourteen is brave."

Aubrey fiddled with her hands. "I'm not leaving my family, just one of them in particular."

She seemed to have hope Scott would still come with them, eventually. Aubrey went to the solid-colored bed comforters and picked out a grey queen size. "Is this safe for Tommy?"

I nodded.

She put the plastic package in our cart. "So, I couldn't hear, but I take it things didn't go well with Scott."

"No," I whispered.

"Then he's stupid." Aubrey pulled the basket and grabbed a fourth covering. "He's always so stubborn, but if Itsuma could bring him around then I'm sure you can too."

"Thanks for the vote of confidence." I smiled. Her faith was my only hope, and I latched onto that notion.

Shopping with the sister I wished I'd had calmed me into the here and now. I focused on the task of feeding and sheltering the three I could save. We bought provisions and regrouped at the house.

When we returned, daylight was on its last legs. Itsuma was playing some game on his phone with his feet up on the marble coffee table. Waunita watched Tommy play in the back yard from the kitchen table. They were safe. Happy. It had to be enough. Even if Scott never wanted to see me again, at least I could give him the satisfaction of knowing his family was secure. At least he'd know after he contacted them with the disposable cell phones I bought.

"Hey." I picked Itsuma's feet off the coffee table and deposited them on the floor. He lived to irk me.

"What's up?" The Japanese Prince flashed his winning smile. What I wouldn't do to straddle his lap and let him fuck my tension away.

"Go help Aubrey bring in the supplies."

He got up, pulled me in and gazed down at me. Eye to eye, Itsuma's gaze filled with concern. He said nothing but he leaned in and said more with a kiss than any words.

Before I could clear my head, he headed out the front door. It took me a moment to recover.

I wasn't the only one who'd lost Scott. I was so far into my own thoughts I'd forgotten I had a partner in all this. Itsuma was with me all the way. He'd gone along with my scheme knowing we'd lose our third. Was it worth it? Time would tell.

Waunita sat in the wood chair of the kitchen table watching her son monkeying around on the jungle gym. Even with his arm immobile, Tommy swung on the bars with one hand.

"Ah, to be young again." I pulled up a chair and reclined my sore ass on the seat. "He doesn't let the cast get in the way."

Waunita gazed at Tommy with a content smile on her face. "Yeah, he's always been the resilient one."

Aubrey and Itsuma put away the food as Waunita and I enjoyed the scenery. Of course Scott's sister and Itsuma flirted. Which still got under my skin. Aubrey brought in a Verizon bag and handed it to me. She and Itsuma agreed to set up the beds and left us. The peaceful silence that lingered faded with the sunset.

"I met your husband while we were out."

Waunita stiffened but remained quiet.

"Actually, I wasn't formally introduced. It was more like a Mexican standoff."

"I'm surprised you're still in one piece."

"Scott was also there." I paused, wondering if I could have said anything different to him, or maybe if I'd got him alone, would he have come with me? "He opted to stay with his dad."

"I'm not surprised." Waunita's blissful expression turned sour at my news. She closed her eyes like she was praying for her firstborn, and I took a moment to join her.

"Maybe you can convince him to stay here." I pulled out the cell phone I'd bought for her and turned it on. Dancing lights and a song played as the phone powered up.

She shook her head. "I'll never see him again."

"Don't say that."

"Don't you see?" She turned to me. "His only wish is to protect us. I know my son. He'll stay with his father."

I laid the phone down next to her. "You never know. You'll be able to bribe him with fancy technology."

She looked at the phone.

"Please use this wisely," I said. "I bought four. One for each of you. It's to let each of you keep in contact. Don't call him. Not yet."

She looked at me and pulled back, as if she expected me to start demanding things. "Four? You're optimistic."

"Yeah." The events of the day tumbled down and I suddenly felt exhausted. "Can we continue a plan of action tomorrow? I have to take Itsuma home and I need to grade papers."

She gave me a warm grin. "You really are a teacher."

"But of course." I returned her smile. I'd teach until the school board told me to get the hell out.

"Okay." She took the phone, holding it like a lifeline. "I know what to do."

I stood up. "This time is different. You have support. My number is already programmed in. Just let me know if you need anything."

Tommy finally noticed me and came running across the yard.

She nodded. "We'll stay here. But I will not leech off you. We'll pay rent. I'll pay you for the food."

"Wait until this blows over…"

The small boy opened the sliding glass door and crashed into me. "Mr. Mori, this place is amazing!"

"Yeah? Think you can stay a while?"

He nodded emphatically.

"That means no school tomorrow."

Tommy widened his eyes. "That's okay. Sis told me I might not see everyone again."

Wow. Aubrey was right on track. "You'll make new friends." I patted his thin, bony back. "I'll come back tomorrow."

"You're not staying?" Puppy dog eyes assailed me. Saying goodbye was tough.

"I'll be back tomorrow."

He sighed with all the disappointment a nine-year-old could muster. Adorable.

"I guess," he said.

"Thank you." I tussled his tawny hair.

Aubrey came bouncing into the kitchen with Itsuma trailing behind her. "What do you want for dinner?"

"Itsuma and I are going home," I said.

She glared with incredulous accusation.

"Ugh. I'm taking him home to retrieve his car."

"I didn't say anything." Aubrey rolled her eyes. Typical teenager style.

I smiled. "You thought it."

"Thank you." Aubrey stepped over to me and gave me another of her amazing hugs.

Itsuma and I left the somewhat happy family hoping they would do as I said and stay out of reach and contact with Mr. Cooper. When Itsuma and I passed the community gate he leaned his arm against the car door and twisted towards me. "Aubrey said you saw her dad."

"Yep." I didn't want to hash it out with him, but Itsuma was Itsuma. He wouldn't let me rest. It didn't matter if it was sex, studies or life, he'd gnaw me raw. But that was what I loved about him.

"How did that go?"

"I'm still here."

He grunted. "She also said you spoke with Scott."

"Yep." I got on the freeway and changed gears on my Boxster.

"I called him," he said. "I tried to plead your case."

"Was that you on Todd's phone?"

"Yeah."

"Good thing your friends were there."

"She also said Kai was there." His tone was light.

Ah, here we go. "Yes. You should be thankful. I might have been in the hospital after Aubrey's attempt at deflection."

"Eh?"

I gave him a sideways glance. "She told her father I was her boyfriend."

He stared at my profile for a split second before he started laughing so hard he was still wiping his eyes when I pulled off at our exit.

"Yeah, yeah," I said. "It was all she could think of."

"So…" He brushed his palms off on his jeans. "Kai Akiyama was there."

"Yes."

"Your high school *friend*."

"Yes."

"The guy you didn't sleep with."

"Itsuma, I'm exhausted. Can we wait till tomorrow to continue this?"

"No. Is he the guy who owed you the favor?"

"Yes."

"Does he have anything to do with what Aubrey was talking about?"

"About what?"

"About you going to the hospital seven years ago."

"That's in the past." I pulled onto my home street, where Itsuma's car was waiting.

"Answer. Yes or no," Itsuma insisted.

"Yes! Alright! Yes! Okay? My first time taking it up the ass did not go as planned. Would you like to know more fucked-up, embarrassing shit I've done?" I was so angry my hands shook. My emotional guard was depleted. "Or are you just obsessed with the legion of men that I posed as a cum bucket for? How about the fact that I have to have a colonoscopy every year even though I'm only twenty-three?"

I stopped there because Itsuma looked both angry and horrified. Perfect. This was why I'd never had a steady boyfriend. I scared them shitless and chased them off. I shut down. My insides were numb. I'd already lost Scott, but if Itsuma didn't want anything to do with me, I was sure to just slide back to my old precocious ways. One-night stands. Fucking strangers. Lust without love. Maybe a real relationship just wasn't in the cards for me.

We pulled into my garage and I heaved my aching body from the low driver's seat.

"Sensei?"

"You should go." I faced my back to him. I couldn't look at Itsuma right now. "I have a lot to catch up on."

"No," he whispered. His gentle rebuff was out of character. It made me turn and look at him. I'd seen Itsuma's haughty look, his triumphant look, his imp look, I'd seen him plenty angry and even his sexy orgasm face, but I'd never seen Itsuma sad—until now.

"You shouldn't be alone right now." His face seemed to age. Itsuma's mischievousness was nowhere to be found.

I hid my face in my palms. "Itsuma, I'm sorry. I didn't mean to snap at you."

While I stood there, trying to wipe the exhaustion away, Itsuma lifted me into his arms, princess style.

"What the—Itsuma!" I clung to him as he cradled me and went into the house from the garage.

"I was afraid you'd meet up with Mr. Cooper." He held me close and walked us over to the couch. "You keep doing crazy shit. I don't know if you're insane or have it in for yourself, but for the rest of the day can we just be?"

"I don't feel up to playing."

"Me neither."

He kept me close and sat down on the couch, settling me into his lap. His embrace felt warm. Not just in temperature. Inside I felt this contentment. Itsuma was a sparkling diamond. A dichotomy of studious learner by day and wicked seducer by night. The ultimate tempter. An intelligent bad boy with heart. I wanted him to hold me. I'd never felt this safe before. Being surrounded by Itsuma helped heal the slice across my heart.

"Scott and I had always been childhood friends." Itsuma stroked my hair. "I was already trying to mend my screw-up with him when he admitted to his family he was homosexual. After the crap went down with the lawsuit, whatever relationship we had fell apart."

"You seemed like good friends to me."

He pulled me closer and chuckled. "Good enough to slam me against the lockers and warn me away from you."

"What do you mean?"

"You know that day you took my iPod away?"

"Yeah."

"That afternoon he tried to tell me to stop fucking around with you."

"So, this whole thing started as what? A pissing contest?"

Itsuma chuckled. His rumbling chest tickled the fine hairs along my face. "He liked you. It irked me enough to take a closer look at Sensei."

"What did you discover?"

"Don't think I like you because of Scott. I like you despite Scott."

"You love him?"

Itsuma nodded. "I do. With him it runs deep."

"And me?" My voice small. Was I just a fling?

"Sensei…" he whispered in my ear. "I don't ever want to let you go." Itsuma squeezed me tight. "If I were a different person, I'd have played by the rules, saved myself for you and come back after university. But I'm not that person. I'm not as patient as Scott. And I know a good thing when I see it. I'm not willing to let it slip through my fingers."

"You don't think you'll be coming back, do you?"

"I… don't know."

"You're following what your parents want for you."

"I owe them that."

"Because of the past?" It seemed as though our lives ran on parallel paths.

"They're just looking out for me."

"It's your life." This time I sighed and snuggled into his chest. "You're going to have to make decisions for yourself one day."

Itsuma sighed and rested his chin on the crown of my head. We didn't speak. Staying in our cuddle position, I fell fast asleep in his arms.

Chapter 14

The morning after was a waking nightmare. All through the night I'd woken up, looking in the darkness, feeling around my bed for a warm body, only to discover reality was worse.

In my dreams, all I saw was Scott sneering at me, repeating the same line. *I don't know him at all.* My Cowboy turned, then I saw Itsuma's backside as I watched him board a plane. I tried to stop him, call out, tell him to wait, but the scenes repeated over and over.

When I woke up, neither Itsuma nor Scott was with me. I'd been put to bed with my underwear on, but there was no sign of my lovers.

I wanted nothing to do with school. I went anyway.

All through first period my throat constricted and I was constantly reaching for my bottled water. When the bell for homeroom went off, neither Scott nor Itsuma attended. I checked them on the roster as present anyway. Their no-show dropped my mood to utter despair.

"Mori? Hello?" Movement caught my attention. I looked up, and up, into Mr. Goyas's concerned face. "Hey, you don't look so well."

"I'm fine." Just a little heartbreak. Nothing to see here. I couldn't even muster up a smile.

"You don't look fine," Mr. Goyas growled.

"What's it to you?"

His face turned an angry red and his eyes narrowed. "If you weren't in a room full of students," he whispered. "I'd slap your mouth so hard…"

I looked around. I didn't remember giving out a test, but all my students' heads were down as they worked on an open book quiz.

"Now that I have your attention, you're wanted in the office."

"You're my stand-in?"

"I'm supposed to be." He looked over the classroom. "But I don't know if I can let you go up there alone."

Crap. Was I in trouble? Had Principal Ellis come to his senses and decided to toss me out? "I'll be fine."

"Damn it, Mori," he whispered. "I told you to leave it."

I stood up and gave him the challenging glare I wanted to give to Mr. Cooper. "Well, I'm sorry if I don't play it safe."

We stared at each other, both of us boiling in testosterone. Mr. Goyas turned to the students. "Hey. You batch. Stay here."

"What are you doing?"

Most of the students looked up. Some responded, "Yes, Mr. Goyas."

He was the shop teacher. Everyone knew Mr. Goyas. They also knew not to piss off the teacher that gave easy grades and could make sharp metal objects. He grabbed my arm and pulled me out of the room.

"Do you have your keys?"

I nodded.

He took my arm, hauled me into the hall and pushed the door closed.

"Let go of me," I said through gritted teeth.

Mr. Goyas eyed me and released his grip. "You're not as wispy as I thought. There's muscle under that billowy shirt."

I scoffed. "I was on the wrestling team."

"You were a string bean then. You filled out."

Humph. Before Itsuma and Scott I'd have been all over Mr. Goyas and his praise. But now his compliments didn't move me as much.

"You don't have to go with me." I started walking out the long hallway towards the main offices. "Won't you get in trouble for leaving the students by themselves?"

"Maybe I like to live more dangerously than you think." Mr. Goyas kept walking alongside me.

The campus was deserted. There weren't many who attended summer classes. "So why am I being called?"

He shrugged. "Beats me. It's not for the principal. He's out today."

We turned the corner and there, at Betty's counter, stood Mr. Cooper.

An array of things crossed my mind. *Oh crap. Oh, good. I can beat the crap out of him. Wait, no I can't. I'm a teacher. Not on school grounds. Why is he here?*

"You!" Mr. Cooper stampeded towards me.

"Shit," Mr. Goyas uttered under his breath. He stepped slightly forward in front of me.

"You little faggot…"

"Hey!" Mr. Goyas shouted.

It was enough to break Mr. Cooper's laser focus on me.

"This is a school," my fellow teacher said. "His sexual orientation has nothing to do with school business."

"Where's my son, faggot?"

I wanted to rip his head off. "I don't know."

"Bullshit, he was with me yesterday afternoon, but he wasn't at the house this morning. He probably slipped over to sleep with you."

I saw Betty pick up the phone. She hit numbers on the push-button dial.

"I haven't seen him since yesterday afternoon."

"You're lying." Mr. Cooper went to grab for me.

Mr. Goyas was faster. He took hold of Mr. Cooper's wrist and twisted. "Don't touch him, you fine-right bastard."

"Fuck you," Mr. Cooper spat. "Get off me."

It was like two grizzly bears roaring at each other. I was *not* going to get in the middle of that. A small guy like me, I'd be destroyed.

"Hey, do you want to go back to jail?" I pointed at Betty. Who knew if she was calling the police or not, but it was a good bluff.

"Where's my son?"

What the hell? What about the rest of his family? Did he not care about his daughter? She was seen with me too.

"He was absent from first period and third period," Betty said, hanging up the phone. "Just as I told you. He's not at school."

"Then he's at this guy's house." Mr. Cooper pointed at me.

"No. He's not." I shook my head. "He's extremely loyal to his family, so why the hell would he leave you?" Unless he escaped to the refuge house, where his mom and siblings were. I could only hope.

Sirens sounded and Mr. Cooper ripped away from Mr. Goyas and bolted.

"Hey, asshole!" Mr. Goyas yelled out. "Don't come here again! Ellis isn't going to cover for you anymore."

The shop teacher was shaking and flushed. I just stared at him. He turned to the front counter. "Betty, why'd you call the police? Ellis is going to be pissed."

"I didn't call the police," she rasped. "I called Mike."

"Who?"

"My boyfriend. He is a cop, though, so technically I did call the police."

I gave Betty a once-over. This high school administrative assistant with a cop? I'd never have guessed.

"Go on, you two. I'll tell Mike. We'll take care of it."

"Thanks, Betty."

She smiled at me. "'Bout time that kid had a savior."

♂♂♂

The meet-and-greet with Mr. Cooper left me with too much adrenaline in my system. As we walked back to our classrooms, I pulled out my cell phone with trembling hands and powered it on. No messages. No texts.

I dialed Itsuma, hoping he was ditching school and not avoiding me. I wanted to warn him Mr. Cooper might decide to harass him just for shits and giggles. But I got his voicemail.

Call me, I texted.

I had enough time to call one more person before I got back to class. Waunita might know where Scott was. I dialed, but her phone went straight to voicemail.

Damn. I stood by my classroom door.

"Will you be okay?" Mr. Goyas loomed over me.

"Not until I find Scott." I raked a hand through my hair.

The phone rang in my hand. I answered. "Hello?"

"Mori?" Scott's sister was on the other end. She sounded upset.

"Aubrey," I sighed in relief. "Are you okay? I was starting to worry."

"Yes, I'm fine." But she didn't sound fine.

"Have you heard from Itsuma?"

"Not lately."

"I'm not sure if he came to school today." I kept my eyes peeled for any sign of Mr. Cooper.

"Ah, okay." Her voice trembled.

"Aubrey, what's wrong?"

She inhaled with a shaky breath. This was not good. I leaned my back against the lockers. Mr. Goyas watched me with interest.

"Well, Scott is in the hospital."

"What?"

"Itsuma found him this morning lying in the living room." Aubrey's voice cracked over the phone. "He brought him to the hospital, and now I think Itsuma is going to kill my dad."

I didn't blame him. If I'd known, I would have swung at Mr. Cooper even if it meant getting crushed.

"Scott's in surgery right now." Aubrey started crying.

The floor shook beneath me. I couldn't stay standing. My knees buckled. "Surgery?"

"Internal bleeding. They caught it in time, just. He had to go right away."

I covered my face with my knees. I wasn't sure when I'd slid down, but the tile floor seeped its cold hardness through my slacks. "He'll be okay?" I was in shock, numb confusion overtaking my logic.

"The doctors say he'll make it, but I'm worried for Itsuma, and my dad."

"Your dad is fine. I just saw him."

"Where are you?"

"School."

"He came to your school?"

"Yeah. He left in a hurry. He was looking for Scott."

She huffed. "Dumbass probably walked over him to get to the bar."

"Did Scott say anything?"

"No. Itsuma found him unconscious, but Scott was wearing the same clothes he wore yesterday."

"Your father said he was with him yesterday afternoon, then he was gone this morning. Oh god, what have I done? Aubrey…"

"Don't even think this is your fault. None of us think that," she said. "You don't know him like we do."

But I couldn't help but think it was all my fault. "I'll leave right now." My voice was starting to fail me. I looked up to Mr. Goyas. He might be able to fill in for me.

"No! Don't come. There's really nothing you could do anyway."

"Are you sure?" I wanted to be there when he got out of surgery.

"Please, don't come. It's… please don't come."

I was shocked. Her plea made me feel even worse. I might screw everything up more if I went. But I had to see him.

"Okay. I understand."

"Please don't think you're not welcome. It's just…"

"No, I got it." I shielded my face by pretending to rub my temples. "Aubrey, thank you for calling."

"Just let me know if you see Itsuma," she said.

"I will." I hung up.

In the silence, the reality of what I'd done kicked me in the gut.

"Well?" Mr. Goyas crouched down.

"Scott is in the hospital. He's in surgery. But he'll be okay."

"Jesus…" The old bear of a teacher went pale.

"I have to get back to class." Dumbfounded, despite what I said, I didn't move to get off the tile floor.

"Mori, are you sure?"

I nodded. "I have to."

If I went to see Scott right now that would be a dead giveaway that he meant more to me than just as a student. Plus, I had kids to teach. Principal Ellis warned me. I'd never felt so impotent. I blinked up at Mr. Goyas and raised my hand. He took hold and yanked me up easy as picking up a box of cereal.

"Thank you," I said.

Mr. Goyas clasped my shoulders. His meaty palms kept me from sinking to the floor again.

I straightened, trying to regain myself. "Please don't say anything."

"Mori, you're in shock."

"I'll be okay." I gently pushed him away and stood on my own. "I just need to get back to class."

"I can cover for you."

"You have another class."

"Mori…"

"Please! I have to pretend everything is fine, or…"

Mr. Goyas gaped at me. He shut his mouth. Then opened it to ask a question, then pressed his lips together and nodded. He opened and closed his fists. I could tell he wanted to know, but in this case, knowing was a detriment.

"If you need anything…"

I nodded. "You're right down the hall. Thank you." I got my classroom key out and opened the door. The chatter quickly died. A stack of papers lay neatly on my desk. Such good kids.

The bell rang and I sat in my chair staring off at the chalkboard at the back wall. The kids didn't move at first. Then, slowly they filtered out like ghosts, and my next class trickled in.

The hours seemed to travel backwards, making it impossible to hold onto my sanity. Every class had a pop quiz. I couldn't handle talking or answering questions. I just wanted to get to Scott.

Surgery. Fuck. I left him there. Just left him to die. How could I be so stupid? I should have kidnapped him. Gagged him, knocked him out in the middle of the night and taken him to the other house. Stupid.

Itsuma must have lost it when he found him. Poor kid. Finding his lover broken on the floor must have been a horror all its own. I was to blame.

Finally, the last bell set us all free. I grabbed my bag, shut off the lights, waited for everyone to get out and locked the doors. I daresay I was one of the first ones in a car and out of the parking lot.

County hospital was fifteen minutes away. When I got there the antiseptic smell sent a shock to my senses, making this circumstance very real.

The nurses' station at the front gave me his room number and a visitor badge. I ambled like a slow-moving zombie, terrified of what I would see.

I rounded the last corner and went straight into room two-thirty-two. There was Scott, lying under the covers of a hospital bed. He had a cast on his right arm and one on his left leg. A tube ran up his nose. New bruises lay over his old ones.

And there, sitting in a chair beside Scott, was Mr. Cooper. His head was bowed in a remorseful pose.

You better be praying for forgiveness, you sick fuck. I wanted to pummel him. The empty, helpless feelings I'd suffered through all day flipped to anger. My jaw clenched. Every one of my muscles bunched. I was ready to throw him out the window.

He looked up. Streaks of dried tears and his flushed cheeks gave me pause.

"You again," he growled.

Good. I'd take his anger. Maybe I could settle some unfinished business.

"You have a lot of gall being here," I threw back.

"You're the one with nerve." He stood up.

I was ready to throw down if he was. "You're the one sending your own family to the emergency room."

He whipped around the bed. My hand balled into a fist. No thought, no strategy. I'd deliver a clear and simple beating.

"Dad," Scott whispered.

Mr. Cooper froze.

"Dad, I need to talk to Mr. Reis alone, okay?"

Mr. Cooper made an about-face and stepped closer to his son. "You sure?"

Scott shifted closer to the edge of the bed. He grimaced, but there was relief and affection in that pained expression.

His father lowered down and Scott whispered in his ear. I couldn't hear what he said. Mr. Cooper pulled back and nodded. Scott's father patted his son's cheek. Probably the only place the kid wasn't bruised.

I still wanted to pummel the guy, but my mood flattened. Their touching moment had me sulking. I wanted to run over to Scott and hug him, but I wouldn't dare. Busting his father up in front of him was not something I wanted Scott to see. So Mr. Cooper had a pass—this time.

My new nemesis stood and gave me a cool browbeating. I returned his gaze.

"I'll be back in twenty minutes." He ignored me and walked out the door.

Good riddance. When he was out of the room I rushed to Scott's side. He looked at me with his one good eye. The expression chilled my heart. This was not going to be a fun conversation.

"You missed the rodeo today," he said.

Oh, god, I should have ditched school and come straight here. No, that would have looked too suspicious. It was enough that Mr. Goyas, Principal Ellis and Betty knew about my affections for the boy. I didn't need to leave an easy paper trail for it too. Still, I would have tossed it all if I'd known he was awake.

"Aubrey told me about your surgery." I wanted to take his hand, but it was in a cast.

"Oh, that…" Scott raised a listless, left-handed - thumbs-up. "Piece of cake."

I wanted to smash a window. This brave kid deserved more—something better from his family and his lover.

"The real entertainment was my sister screaming over my body, telling her dad to go die."

I snorted. *Go Aubrey.*

"But what really threw me off the bull was my mother." Scott's accusing glare dropped my stomach down to the morgue.

I drew breath. *Crap. Please tell me she didn't cave.*

"It was eerie, really," he said. "I've never been afraid of mom before."

"Did she yell?"

"No." His eyes glazed over. The kid looked shell-shocked. "She didn't yell at all. She just stood there, looking at him. Her eyes… I never want to see those eyes again." He turned his head to me. "I'll never forget those eyes."

I set my fingertips on his shoulder. Anything to comfort him.

"She was like the angel of judgment. Dad couldn't keep it together. I've never seen him cry." His frightened eyes bore into mine. "Then she said three words."

Three? As in those three? "What did she say?"

He swallowed. "She said 'we are done'. Then she looked right through him. He was there one moment and the next, for her, he wasn't. He was a ghost. Dead. No matter what he did she wouldn't acknowledge him. Afterward she turned to me and said she'd visit every day until the doctors said it was okay to take me home. She'd come for me to live in the new place." He shook his head. "She didn't say 'I'm done', she didn't say 'we're done', she really meant it."

"Scott, maybe that's for the best."

He grimaced. "Mr. Reis, you taught me kindness and understanding is the route to happiness. I know you did all that you did to help me, but…" He looked down at himself.

Yeah. He'd taken the brunt of my cockamamie scheme. I shielded my eyes with a hand. There was dust in the air. "I really fucked up, didn't I?"

"Mr. Reis," Scott whispered. "I know you love me, but this isn't the way to help me."

My breath stuttered. All the stress of the day came to a head. I couldn't retort, even if he were wrong.

"We have to heal as a family," he said. "A whole family. Otherwise there's no point."

"I'm sorry," I choked out.

"There's a lot I have to repair in this family, so for now, I don't want to see you."

There it was. My heart torn out, on the ground. I would have flat-lined if I were hooked up to an EKG. Scott was so calm. His tone so—adult.

"But, not forever?" My words crackled, trying to get around the lump in my throat.

Scott looked away.

Please god, don't let this be the end. I shouldn't be seeing him other than as a student, but not seeing him at all? The shock of his words sent my mind into a tailspin.

"Please leave."

After a moment, I stepped back, memorizing his state. The outcome I'd wrought. Without another word, I obeyed his request and left the room.

Chapter 15

Itsuma returned to class the next day. He was the same as always, coming in like he owned the air we all breathed.

The bell rang and everyone sat down. Just another day. I tried telling that to myself as I *silently* checked off names for roll call. I'd finally learned all my student's names and faces.

"Hey, Sensei, aren't you going to take roll?"

I looked up at Itsuma. *Where the fuck have you been all yesterday and all last night?* I must have called him five times. He hadn't returned my texts either. "I know everyone by name now, so it's done."

The announcement speakers went on and gave the news for the day. Itsuma eyed me. After the bell rang, he left the room without looking back. I couldn't help but think he blamed me, just a little, for Scott's predicament. He wasn't wrong. I would fix it. Somehow.

♂♂♂

Mr. Goyas strolled in after third period ended. Usually this was my free time to grade papers or go for a long lunch. But today, I sat in my chair thinking over my life choices.

"Do you ever have a class?" My voice came out harsher than intended.

"Yeah. I just have good kids."

"Sorry."

"How is Scott?"

"I don't want to talk about it." I washed my face with a hand.

"He alive?"

"For the most part."

Silence.

"Ellis wants you," he said.

"Great," I muttered. "Thanks, I'll be up in a minute."

"Mori, for what it's worth, I never wanted the kid hurt." He sighed. "Naw, forget it." He turned his back to me.

"Say it," I demanded.

Mr. Goyas turned back. "What I said, about that boy, about something about him…"

"Yeah." I glared at the shop teacher.

He snorted and shook his head. "Don't take that tone of face with me, boy."

"Why not?"

"I was going to say I think I figured it out."

"What's that?"

Mr. Goyas narrowed his eyes. "Well, it's not about him being gay; otherwise, I wouldn't hang with you so much."

He knew about me? A brick dropped from my throat to my stomach. Mr. Goyas was sure to hear the *ker-thunk* when it splashed down. Still, I kept my face stony.

"It's the fact that he always backs the wrong side," Mr. Goyas said. "Awww, hell, what do I know." He shrugged. "Anyway, Ellis wants you." He turned and slipped out the door.

I sat there, frozen. He knew. Did he know I'd had a raging crush on him during high school? What a fantastic week I was having. I started for the main offices thinking about my hot-for-teacher school years. Should I tell him I didn't have such lust for him now? Or should I just let him have an ego? Or did he know I had liked him?

I walked into Principal Ellis's office without paying attention and closed the door. When I looked up, I stopped short.

Mr. Cooper stood behind Principal Ellis's chair, arms crossed, a big smirk on his face.

Principal Ellis, on the other hand, steepled his fingers and looked up at me beyond his white, fluffy, intimidating eyebrows.

"Yeah, you're in for it now—" Mr. Cooper's sentence was halted by Principals Ellis's hand.

"Thank you for coming, Mr. Reis. Please have a seat."

I folded my arms and widened my stance.

Principal Ellis sighed. "Please, this is a discussion, not a ring or a mat. Please sit." Ellis turned his head towards Mr. Cooper. "Both of you."

I stared at Scott's dad. Principal Ellis simply waited us out.

If this turned into an altercation, I could kiss my professor job goodbye. On the other hand, beating his ass was very tempting. He and his son could be in the same hospital room. The thought disturbed me, not because of how my mind jumped to violence, but because his father would spend more time with Scott than me. This jealousy thing was a pain in the ass.

I pulled up a chair, moved it over five feet and sat. *Go ahead, you big, lumbering tree, attack me while I'm sitting down. I'd love that.*

Mr. Cooper sidled up to the chair, pushed it out with a foot and sat. He was so heavy the seat groaned at his weight. The man had muscle. I hated to admit it, but he was gorgeous. If that was how Scott would fill out, I had no complaints. But he wasn't Scott. He was the bastard that put his son in the hospital. I hoped his wife made good on her promise. She didn't need him. No one needed a shithead like him.

"Thank you, gentlemen," Ellis said. "Now, for the matter at hand." He looked at Scott's dad. "Mr. Cooper has a grievance with you, Mr. Reis, about his son. Please, Mr. Cooper, would you elaborate?"

The big lumbering ass-wipe pointed at me. "That son of a bitch is fucking my son."

I went to open my mouth, but Principal Ellis jumped in first. "That's a strong accusation. What proof do you have?"

"Scott told me."

Principal Ellis brought the weight of his piercing eyes to Mr. Cooper. "He specifically said he was having an affair with Mr. Reis?"

"I know he is." Mr. Cooper leaned forward.

"I'll ask again," Principal Ellis said. "Your son specifically named Mr. Reis?"

His question seemed to chill Mr. Cooper's hotheaded attitude. "I know he is."

Principal Ellis bored his intense gaze into Scott's father. "Tom, that is a serious allegation. One that I'm not inclined to jump to because of your son's proclivities. You have no proof. No confession. I'm not accusing a teacher of this school only to find him innocent after his career has been ruined. Allegation does not cut it. On the other hand, you have a record. There are files in the system about your… actions." Principal Ellis eyed Mr. Cooper. "You don't have a sparkling reputation in this town."

"He's a faggot," Mr. Cooper interjected.

"Which makes what you're doing right now look like a hate crime."

Mr. Cooper tsked. "So you're just going to let this go?"

"May I remind you that Scott is eighteen. He is of legal age."

"He's a student of this school."

"He has technically graduated."

"So, that's it?"

"I will investigate. But the reality is that Mr. Reis is only temporary. I'm not blacklisting him for a drunk ex-mayor." Principal Ellis clamped his lips together. I could tell he wanted to say more, and might have if I weren't in the room.

"Go home, Mr. Cooper." Principal Ellis gritted his teeth. "Get your life back together."

"Great, he gets a pass."

Principal Ellis stood up and leaned over his desk toward Mr. Cooper. "Tom, everyone has a past." The words hung in the air. "Yours isn't sunshine and unicorns."

Mr. Cooper said nothing. With the eyes of death Ellis dished out I'd have frozen to stone. It was like staring into the eyes of benign justice. Unmoving. Unwavering. Full of scorn and judgment. I wanted to confess all my sins, and I was not even the recipient of the stare-down.

Mr. Cooper stared back nonplused, like a righteous man who knew god was on his side. Maybe I deserved to be tossed out of this school on my ear. It still didn't make it okay that Scott got beat to shit by his own father.

Finally, I saw Mr. Cooper flinch. "Fine, I'll go." He looked at me. "But I'm not done with you, you son of-a bitch."

I narrowed my eyes. "Try it."

"You'd like it too much." Scott's father matched my challenging glare.

"Mr. Cooper," Principal Ellis said. "You have worn out your welcome."

Tom got up out of his chair and walked out of the office. The door slammed when he closed it behind him.

My hackles went down a little. Now was my turn with the good Principal Ellis. The man didn't say a word. He folded his hands and evaluated me. I knew this game. Kai had taught me how to play it well. The *who would blink first* game. I wasn't going to bend on the fact that trying to get a student away from an abusive parent wasn't a bad thing. Perhaps the way I got involved was not the best way to handle the situation, but something had to be done. No one would convince me otherwise. Not even Scott.

The oppression in Principal Ellis's glare pinned me to my seat. It took everything I had to keep my eyes up. If I didn't know better, I'd think he was working out a conversation in his head.

Beads of sweat dampened my cotton dress shirt. The man across from me stared without blinking. I was not able to do the same, but I kept my line of sight on Principal Ellis.

Then he sighed. "Your father would be disappointed."

"I'm not my father." And I don't need his approval.

"No, you're not. You're more like your mother."

What was that supposed to mean? "Why did you defend me?"

Principal Ellis stared at me. "I do not approve of either one of you. But in my position there is little I could do."

"You're the principal of the school. You can report me. You can report abuse."

"Ahhhh…" he lifted a finger to his lips. "Can I?"

"Yes!" I was getting frustrated. Technically, I should be in jail.

"I choose battles I can win."

"That's absurd."

"Really? Did you think it's easy to watch families implode? How long have you been teaching?"

"It doesn't matter."

"Mr. Reis, I've been teaching high school for forty years. I've been a principal for six. I have seen the sons and daughters of my high school classmates grow up. I have taught their grandchildren. I know the family history of this town. So tell me, when you report abuse, does it go away?"

"The abused don't get hurt anymore."

Principal Ellis shook his head. "Really? Is that what you think?"

"I…" Now I wasn't so sure.

"There needs to be a significant change in either or both parties for that to be true. Mostly it must be the person's own idea to change, but on occasion outside influences pressure the person to modify their behavior."

I frowned. "What are you getting at?"

"What I'm getting at is that you don't see the whole picture. By denying Tom his form of *justice* he'll have to look at this situation in a new way. He'll possibly question his actions. Perhaps he'll stop blaming other people for his mistakes. For his responsibilities. Do you understand now?"

"I guess."

"Do you also understand that both Scott and Itsuma are of legal age and have already graduated—thanks to No Child Left Behind."

"Why are they taking classes?"

"I insisted Scott remain for summer session. Itsuma joined him." Principal Ellis gazed at me like a timeless, wise dragon. He knew Scott should have been held back. He also gave me the impression he knew about the three of us.

"Scott's a smart kid. He would have been fine."

Principal Ellis's predatory smile was more frightening than his scorn. "Well, I did know you were coming to teach."

"What does that mean?"

"You have a certain way of creating waves."

I wasn't sure if I should be offended or not.

"Go." He dismissed me with the flip of a hand. "As far as I'm concerned, you've done nothing all that impressive enough to bring unwanted attention to my school."

"I disagree…" I mumbled under my breath.

"Oh, and Mori, fighting is prohibited on school grounds."

"I know that," I snarled.

"I'm sure you do." A sparkle lit in his eyes. "However, your time is your own."

Did I just get permission to beat the snot out of Mr. Cooper? I looked at Principal Ellis. This whole situation could have gone devastatingly wrong. The more I thought, the more Principal Ellis became someone I did not want to piss off.

"Thanks." my tone carried grudging respect. When I walked out I made sure to shut the door quietly.

Mr. Goyas was there talking to Betty. He saw me and snapped up to my side. I walked back to my classroom with the shop teacher on my heels.

"You okay?"

"Just peachy." That was the strangest conversation I'd ever had. Lots to think about. "Don't worry, I still have a job."

"That's good."

The shop teacher dropped me off at my room, closed the doors and left me to my own devices.

chapter 16

Angst from Scott's request to stay away, Itsuma's nonplussed attitude, Mr. Goyas's understanding, Principal Ellis's words, Mr. Cooper's appearance... these circumstances clogged my head. It was like a bad dream. Like reliving a car accident. My mind went over it again and again. Helpless, angry and spoiling for a fight, I used my energy to teach until the day's end.

When the last bell rang, I sat at my desk, gazing with my chin resting in my palm, absorbing today's events. As I sat, I listened to scuffling sneakers against tile floors, metal lockers opening and shutting, kids hollering out, their voices echoing off the walls.

Twenty minutes later the sounds died down and I was left with a stack of papers on my desk. One kid left me his iPad, saying he didn't have time to print out his homework. *Seriously, when is the public school system going to reach the internet age? These kids should just email me their papers.*

I pulled a report from the top, sighed, and started in on grading. Right now, I'd do anything for any distraction from my dismal life. I heard a snick—the sound of a door closing. The air pressure in my classroom tightened in my eardrums.

Mr. Cooper stood at the back of my class. His stance didn't encourage discussion. That was okay; I wasn't into talking either. *Tread carefully, Mori. Principal Ellis warned you.*

"I told you we weren't finished." Mr. Cooper stared from across student desks.

"I guess we aren't."

We stared at each other. I knew what that mean look he flashed at me meant. I measured my opponent. He might be big, but he wasn't ready for what I'd dish out. If I ever saw him outside the school, he'd get a chance to find out what a trained wrestler could do.

He prowled between the desks. I stood and waited for him to approach, measuring his movements, searching for weakness. His gait was even and steady. As big as Mr. Cooper was, he didn't lumber. The man seemed agile. Nothing there to exploit. Mr. Cooper struck me as the boxing type. I had a tough body and experience, but matches and real fights were different animals. This could get ugly.

Scott's father got closer as I waited. He was past all the chairs and now five feet away. Only my desk stood between us. The door handle jiggled. My attention went off to the side. Itsuma's pissed off face filled the window. Then I saw stars.

Damn. I'd taken my eyes off Mr. Cooper. Huge mistake. My jaw hurt. At least I wasn't knocked out. He must have wanted me awake for a pounding. His fist was going to leave one hell of a bruise. Scott endured a pummeling at these hands.

A huge mass came forward. I had enough time to block. I regained my whereabouts and kept my anger in check. I stuck to the rule of *when in doubt, make space*.

I used a push technique Itsuma showed me. It worked. My training helped me dodge another swing.

"Come here, you chicken shit." Mr. Cooper advanced.

Crap. This was a no-good situation. This guy was way faster than his size let on. With the doors locked there wasn't much of an escape. Turning my back to him would get me caught, so I dodged.

"Hey, asshole!" Itsuma crouched on the open ledge of a window. Resourceful kid. Another reason why I loved him.

Mr. Cooper swung his back to me. That was the opening I needed. I leaped onto his back, wrapped my arm around his neck and squeezed. Chokeholds didn't always mean you had to deny your opponent breath. Pressure at the right angle would make him pass out in three to five seconds. To make sure I wouldn't do permanent damage I wrapped my legs around his waist so I could hold on.

Scott's father rushed backwards and knocked into my desk. The man was so tall my legs didn't even touch the surface. He rolled back, using his weight to slam me against my desk. Smart move. Too bad I was already used to that type of defense.

"Don't worry so much," I whispered in his ear. "I'm not into married men."

He was getting weaker. His fists pounded my arm. Then he was out. His body slumped. Unfortunately, I was now trapped between a bear of a man and my hardwood desk.

Itsuma climbed into the room, watching with a serves-you-right face.

"Itsuma, don't."

He stopped and narrowed his eyes at me.

Caught under this boulder of a man, I could barely breathe. "Don't touch him."

Itsuma's scowl turned to livid anger, but he obeyed for once.

"Help," I gasped.

"You sure?" Itsuma crossed his arms. "You said not to touch him."

"It… suma…" I heaved.

He tsked, took Mr. Cooper's arms and lifted.

I scrambled out from under the man. "Thank you," I sighed.

Mr. Cooper's arms dropped with a bang. That would hurt later. But not as bad as the headache he would have when he woke up. We had a few minutes.

"Sensei?" Itsuma rushed over, wrapping me in his arms. "Are you okay?"

"Yes." My touch-deprived senses responded to his affection and I pulled him into my body. I buried my face in his shoulder and breathed in. The smell of Japanese Prince was my favorite right now.

"I saw Scott's truck in the parking lot." Itsuma started trembling. "I thought maybe he was doing something stupid."

"I don't think Scott's going anywhere." Not with two casts.

"You don't know Scott. He'll be out of the hospital today or tomorrow unless they drug him."

"Have you seen him lately?"

"No. Not since yesterday morning."

"He's got two casts. One on his arm, one on his leg. He's not just going to pick himself up and leave."

Itsuma cast a death glare at Mr. Cooper.

I let go of his embrace and stepped back. "Help me take him to his truck."

"Scott's truck. He paid for it with his own money."

"Just help me with this lug."

"Why?"

So obstinate. "Because I want to leave and I don't want him in the classroom."

"Fine. I'll drag him to the hall."

I sighed and rubbed my forehead. "Good enough. He'll be up soon."

Together we hauled Mr. Cooper across the classroom floor and left him leaned against the lockers. I took my bag and papers, turned off the lights and locked the doors. Time to go. He was due to wake up, and I'd been warned not to fight at school. The fucker was probably trying to get me booted. *Nice try, asshole.*

Before I left I checked his pulse. His heartbeat was strong. I wasn't worried. The only reason I had any concern was because this man was important to Scott. That was all the respect I could muster.

Itsuma stared at him while I locked my classroom doors.

"Hey, come on," I said, walking down the hall.

Itsuma turned and followed me. When we got to my car he set his hip against my driver's side door and crossed his arms. I had a full load in one hand, keys in the other.

"Itsuma…" I looked around. "Please don't do this. You promised not to do this."

His jaw muscles worked, clenching and grinding. "Fine."

He backed away with his hands up. "I just wanted to make sure you got to your car safe."

My lips compressed. "Thank you."

"You're welcome." But of course, in Itsuma style, it sounded more like *fuck off*.

I got in my car and drove. My chest felt hollowed out.

♂♂♂

I hadn't expected Itsuma to come for tutoring, but here he was, dower and glaring at me on my front porch.

"Can I come in?"

"I don't know, can you?" I turned and walked back to the kitchen, leaving the door open.

"Ha-ha."

"I'll be with you in a minute. Go sit."

He didn't. Itsuma leaned against the kitchen-living room column watching me cook. "What are we having?"

"Spaghetti and meatballs."

The rice cooker chimed in completion of steamed rice, and I sighed.

"Do you often have rice with your Italian?"

"I've been distracted," I snapped. "I was going to have chicken and rice." But there wasn't any chicken. In my befuddled state, I'd forgotten.

His cool eyes watched me stir noodles. I concentrated on the swirling water.

"Want some rice?" I said.

Itsuma chuckled. "Sure."

I stopped stirring the pasta and turned to the rice cooker. Fetching two bowls, I spooned long, white grains. Itsuma's front pressed against my back. He felt so good my ass automatically leaned out, trying to feel for the hardness between his legs. *Bad Sensei.*

One arm wrapped over my chest. His other hand tilted my chin up.

"Itsuma," I sighed.

"Sensei, I'm pissed."

I froze. He wanted to sling my ass for a completely different reason than I thought.

"I'm pissed at you. I'm pissed at Scott, at his dad, at Aubrey for calling me, at Scott's mom for not calling me…"

I swallowed.

"But I'm pissed at myself most of all. Want to know why?"

I didn't move, didn't speak.

Itsuma pulled me in closer. "Because I fucking knew this was how it was going down."

I wanted to apologize, but really, did it matter?

"And now I fucking can't have either one of you. You fucking moron." He let me go and pushed off, letting me feel how much he'd like to pound my ass with his cock. Our session would be angry fucking at this point.

"I wasn't going to have sex with you till graduation anyway." I sounded childish and pathetic. I didn't care. If I looked like a five-year-old pouting in the corner, so be it.

"No."

I turned around. His deep, dark eyes brooding. "What do you mean, no?"

"You're mine. You're Scott's. Do you understand?"

"Spell it out for me." I knew I was being petulant, but my ego needed to hear it.

"Don't. Fuck. Other. Men."

My heart leaped. "How many times must I tell you? I didn't sleep with him."

"The thought was there."

"Argh, Itsuma." I was exasperated.

"Next time you pull that shit, I'm going to walk into homeroom, slam you over your desk, pull your pants down and fuck you up the ass in front of the entire class until you scream out my name." Itsuma raised his voice with every syllable. "And then I'm going to piss all over you so everyone can smell that—You. Are. Mine."

He even deadpanned the last part. The tension of the day—all of it made me crack. Slow and steady, we started laughing. It began easy, then spread into manic, uncontrolled relief.

"Really?" I cackled. "Why not shit on me while you're at it?"

Itsuma laughed so hard water leaked from his eyes. "Don't think I won't do it."

"I know." Streams of tears rolled down my face. "That's why I'm laughing."

I didn't have time to blink. Itsuma's lips clashed into mine. Our tears mixed together. The shared laughter died off, converting into lust. His tongue went further down my throat. Damn, he was going to choke me with that thing.

I relaxed into his desperate attempt to maintain control. My hands felt his body up and down, sneaking down his jeans and climbing up under his shirt. I clawed his back, desperate for him to grind that glorious cock against me. I wanted him. Needed him. *Yes, please forgive me. Take me away. Fuck me into oblivion.*

As I relaxed under his powerful direction he clung to me as much as I did him. Soothed by his desire, I started rubbing myself along his front. Itsuma pulled back. He pushed my shoulders and regained his breath.

"No," he said. "You don't get off that easy."

"What! Oh, come on. You've got me hard as a steel pipe." But deep within my soul I wanted the punishment. Deserved it. "You're going to tease me into insanity."

He lifted his head. Hair covered one eye, but what I could see was the madness of a man denying himself what he craved more than life. This punishment wasn't just for me. It was also for his pleasure when he finally took me.

I lifted my head towards the ceiling and let my frustration out with a groan. "Ahhh!"

My middle bucked in disgruntled agony. *Fuck this forced abstinence.* Itsuma rushed in and sucked my neck below my ear. At first the sensation was pleasant. Then I felt teeth. He dug in like I was dinner.

"Ouch! That hurts!" I pushed him off and felt the area, expecting to find blood.

"That's just in case you decide to end your castigation with anyone other than us," Itsuma said.

"That hurt."

"Good. It'll last the weekend."

"You marked me?"

He held up a thumb and forefinger in front of my face. "I am this close to making it a tattoo."

I rubbed the sore. Itsuma smiled in satisfaction.

"Put a ring on it," I muttered.

He narrowed his eyes. Yeah, that's right, after graduation you won't be here. Now I was pissed. I pushed past him to the boiling water on the stove.

"Get your own damn rice." I was out of there and eating my food in the dining room before the heat made the kitchen explode.

Itsuma scooped up some rice and sat next to me. We ate in silence. I was still reeling from having a hard-on, knowing I wouldn't be getting any. This was bad. I had the guy I wanted knee to knee and was not allowed to touch. My frustration was unreal.

During our tutoring, Itsuma continued to tease, making my distraction issues worse. The moment he took his math book out of his satchel he placed a possessive hand over my thigh. I couldn't throw off his touch, and I couldn't ignore it either. When he asked questions, his fingers would inch closer to my throbbing cock. Was this my penance? Was it how I had to regain his trust?

I'd blown it in so many ways. The only thing I could do was show him my genuine sincerity and endure this atonement. It was the worst test of my life. After tasting Itsuma and Scott, the thought of not having them made me throb.

Itsuma chuckled at me each time I jolted at his movement. At one point, after struggling to answer his questions I looked him in the eye and said, "You're going to make me resent you."

Those dark pools of infinity pinned me to my seat. Guilt flooded my soul. I went back to concentrating on math. By the time Itsuma's curfew came around I was a panting, oozing mess.

"Sensei, you might want to take care of yourself." His gaze traveled down to my crotch.

These pants needed to go in the wash. I smiled in bemused surrender. Masturbation no longer satisfied me. "Maybe. This so-called teasing isn't enough to make me that desperate."

"Tough talk from a guy who moans and pants out my name every time I get inside him." Itsuma focused on my mouth and licked his lips.

My cock jumped. "Itsuma, I'm going to wait for you."

He looked up, a fleeting moment of vulnerability crossing his expression. "Are you into denial sex, Sensei?"

I lifted a hand to touch his face. Itsuma's expression soured and he leaned away. My hand fell to my side.

"I'll purge myself." Sorrow permeated every part of my soul. Every syllable of my words asked forgiveness.

"You think abstinence is going to make me forgive you? Make Scott forgive you?"

The blood drained away from my face. "You told him about Kai?"

"I told him your plan."

My jaw dropped. I was speechless. "W… wh… why?"

"Trust me, it's better he knows."

"He didn't…"

"And you don't need to use your body as leverage. You should have let us worry about it, not go to your old boyfriend for help."

"What do you know about it?"

"Plenty. I know about you being in the hospital. I know you and Kai went to school together. I know other teachers remember him and you."

"You talked to Mr. Goyas?"

"It doesn't take a brainiac to figure out Kai was the one to hurt you." Itsuma was up in my face, not giving me an inch. "And you went back to him."

"I didn't go back. I just… why are we fighting about this? It's done. I'm not going back to him. I have you and…" Or maybe I didn't have the two of them anymore. "I'll wait until you tell me we're through or you decide I'm worthy again."

"Just promise me one thing."

"What?"

"Don't do anything. Let me handle this. Stop trying to turn yourself in."

"I've done all the damage I can do."

"Short of walking into a police station."

A sweeping exhaustion overtook me. "I promise."

Itsuma collected me in his arms. The safest embrace in the world. "I still love you."

Every muscle in my body froze. "You love me?"

He squeezed me tighter. "I love you."

At that moment, everything was alright. I melted into Itsuma. "I love you too."

"I loved you first."

I snorted into his shirt. "Technically, Scott loved me first." I wanted to get his goat.

He didn't take the bait.

"Yeah." Itsuma released me. "Without him I might have never noticed you."

"Maybe."

He gave me a rare sad expression. "See you tomorrow?"

I nodded. "I'll be at school."

Itsuma turned and walked out. Once I was alone with my thoughts, I realized that was my first confession. I'd confessed before, but no one had ever said *I love you* back. And certainly the other party hadn't confessed first.

My phone rang as I was putting dishes away. I didn't recognize the number.

"Hello?"

There was silence on the other end, and the faint sound of breathing. In the background, I heard a muffled intercom and a woman paging doctor Radcliff, then a door rattling closed.

The roller coaster that doubled as my heart started climbing up.

"Scott?" I whispered.

Riding the lamb of hope, I pressed the phone into the side of my ear.

"I know I said I didn't want to talk to you, but I have to hear it from you." Scott's voice was a murmur.

I sank to my knees and rolled back on my ass. The cool refrigerator door caught my slide to the floor.

"Did you sleep with a man named Kai?"

I closed my eyes. I knew how it all sounded. "You heard the whole story from Itsuma, right?"

"So it's true?"

"What did he tell you?"

"That you fucked a guy." His voice grew angry. "That's what I heard."

I sat there, roiling in pain. He wouldn't understand. If I denied it, I'd sound like a liar. If I explained, it would sound like a lie. Scott was angry. Angry men did weird shit.

"You betrayed me."

"No!" I snapped. "Maybe I betrayed your wish, but I didn't betray you."

"As if there's a difference."

"Because there is! You can't just expect me to watch by the sidelines."

"It's none of your business."

"None of my business? Do you understand how painful it is just to sit there and watch the person you love get beat to death? Is that what you would do? Stay out of their business?"

"This is different. This is my family."

"And you're mine."

Silence and heavy breathing from both ends dragged on until I spoke again.

"I'm sorry that I'm crazy in love with you. So crazy that I'm going to do stupid, brainless, incredibly rash and shortsighted things. But I'm sure you wouldn't know anything about it, because you're the calm, rational, get-beat-to-shit type."

More silence. His uneven breathing broke my heart. I wanted to tell him I loved him, that I was sorry. That I'd tried other ways to get him loose from his father. But words would only crash the silence. Listening to his ragged breaths, knowing this emptiness was all we had left, I'd said what I wanted to say. The fact that he was still on the phone gave me hope that he understood what I was trying to tell him. My heart screamed *I love you* with every passing beat.

"I get it," Scott said. "It don't mean I like it." Then the phone chirped and the call was disconnected.

If I'd made my point, why did I feel so dismal?

A knock on the front door brought me to my feet. *Did Itsuma forget something?*

I padded to the little peephole. There, with his bland expression, stood Kai. Fantastic. I set my head on the wood. Just what I needed. I turned the knob and opened the door.

"Kai, I don't feel up for a visit." I stepped outside and shut the door behind me. It would be a mistake to let him inside.

"I wanted to check on you." Kai stared down at me. He hadn't moved when I stepped out, and our chests touched. He was close enough so that all he'd have to do was wrap his arms around me and I'd be encircled in his embrace.

"You are fine?" His eyes remained fixed on my neck where Itsuma had left a hickey. "You do not look fine."

"I don't need your sympathy."

He pressed me against my door. "I do not want to give you sympathy."

My cock responded, the little traitor. I blamed Itsuma for getting me riled up. "I don't want *that* either."

"We deserve another chance."

I pushed against his chest. "I couldn't do this at the hotel. What makes you think I can do this now?"

"You know I will wait for you. But I do not want you to forget me." Kai dipped his head. Shit. I turned my face, just in time, preventing our lips from colliding. The scrape of teeth and soothing of soft lips across my neck sent fire spiking through my body. A desperate whimper escaped my throat. Kai took it as encouragement and settled a hand on my hip. He knew what I liked, how to seduce me, and all my pleasure buttons. This would be a one-way train to my ruin. *Please, no.* I had to be true to Itsuma, Scott—to myself. But my body, weak to pleasure, froze in place. At this rate, he'd have me on my own front porch.

His thick cock pressed against me, working me over. I was falling under. A part of me enjoyed his attentions. The part gorging on nostalgia. At one time, when I loved the boy, now a man, this would have been what I craved from him. But I'd wanted this from him in the past. Kai pursuing me. Loving me with his hands, his mouth, his fat cock. But I'd let go of my past, and that's where Kai belonged.

My cock pressed against my sweat pants. A dark wet spot spread, exposing my desire. The tip of my hardness pressed between us.

I couldn't resist, and I didn't. "Kai?"

He pulled back and looked at me.

"I'm honored at your affection." My hand clutched the doorknob. "But you are not who I want." I turned the knob, and at the same time, I pushed Kai away.

By some miracle, he'd been off balance and stumbled back. I wobbled inside my house, closed and locked my door. *I did it, I resisted temptation.* God, my body felt like it was on fire. I shuffled to the kitchen and got a glass of water.

Fucking Kai. What was he thinking? But I was more desperate for Itsuma and Scott than ever before.

Chapter 17

They knew I was coming, but I knocked on the door of the new Cooper household. Itsuma answered in jeans, a shirt, and a purplish shiner on his left eye.

"What happened to you?" I'd wanted to ask since homeroom. He'd gotten it between the time he left last night and this morning.

He shrugged. "I underestimated an opponent."

My back stiffened. "Mr. Cooper?"

He shook his head. "You'd be the first one I'd call to help bury that body."

I was feeling more and more the same way.

"Oh, thank god." Aubrey stomped over. "Mori, will you talk some sense into my mother? She's being completely stupid."

"About?" I walked inside, breathing in Itsuma's scent. I was still reeling from his teasing and Kai's all-out attempt to get me in bed. I'd gone to sleep hard, woke up hard, and had bouts of sexual ache between erections all day. A simple touch could get me up. It took effort to calm down.

"About filing for a separation."

"Aubrey," Waunita called out. Her voice reverberated in the kitchen. "This is my decision."

"Are you for or against?" I asked the teenager in front of me.

"I'm for, she's against," Aubrey said.

"I've never known a child that wanted to have her parents divorced." I walked inside and headed for the kitchen.

Itsuma closed the door and followed us. He seemed subdued today.

"A separation is only a precursor to divorce, but you can reconcile. However, if she files for separation, then she gets child support, child custody and property division."

"You sound like a divorce lawyer."

"This is all important stuff."

"I'm not filing for divorce." Waunita smiled at me and gestured at the table chairs. I sat. Itsuma took a seat next to me. He was brooding.

"But if you got child support you wouldn't have to burden Mori so much." Aubrey waved a hand at me.

Waunita's eyebrows knitted together. Aubrey was using a sledgehammer against her mother's pride. Waunita came over with homemade cake. Itsuma and I both received a piece.

"Please, burden me." I took hold of Waunita's hand. "Burden me all you want."

Her tired, kind eyes softened as she smiled.

"Out of curiosity, is there any other reason why you want to stay married?"

"People think they can run away from their problems. But wherever you go, there you are."

"You're always with yourself." I nodded.

"It's the same when you marry." Waunita's accent started to thicken. "Everyone has their faults."

"But he's abusive," Aubrey cut in.

"He's still your father. You can't change that."

"It's not like someone trying to quit smoking."

"Ah…" Waunita lifted hand, palm out. "But is it? The first stage is admitting you have a problem."

"Well, it doesn't look like he's ever close to saying he has any problems." Aubrey pouted in her chair.

"My child, when you love someone, you don't give up on them."

I thought I was going to cry. That's exactly how I felt. I wasn't going to give up. My eyes flicked over to Itsuma. His nod was so slight I might have missed it.

"Mori!" a pubescent voice shouted. A tiny hand and arm wrapped around my side. Tommy plastered himself against me.

"Hi!" I blinked a few times and smiled.

Tommy looked up. A blush spread across his cheeks. Adorable. He hid his face in the crook of my chest and arm, his cast hand clutching my shirt.

"Tommy, get off Mr. Reis." Aubrey crossed her arms. "We're trying to have a discussion."

"I'm just saying hi," Tommy shot back.

"You're mauling our guest."

"It's his house."

"Both of you stop it." Waunita's word silenced the two.

"It's okay, Tommy." I petted his head. Poor kid didn't have a safe male figure to go to. I didn't mind if he felt the need to cling to me. Scott's family was also mine.

Tommy smiled up at me. The kid reminded me so much of Scott a pang shot through my heart. Back to the conversation. I turned to Waunita. "Just out of curiosity, why decide to stay married?"

"Where I'm from, divorce is not done."

"Mom, you're so weird. You can't divorce, but you can accept your son is a homosexual?"

I hoped this wasn't a case of self-sacrifice. "It's okay for you to find happiness."

"I am happy. My two youngest are here with me and my eldest will be coming home soon."

"See." Aubrey waved a dismissive hand. "She still has hope for that bastard."

"He is your father." Waunita cast an angry browbeating at her daughter.

Tommy squeezed his good arm around me, and I shielded him with my arms, as if it would protect him from their argument. "Hey guys, want to tone it down a notch?"

Aubrey swung her furious eyes to me. When her gaze landed on Tommy her expression softened. "I think we should go to family counseling."

I gave a weak smile and nodded. "Agreed. I have a few recommendations for that." Then I tapped the table to break the somber mood. "Now, what things do you need?"

♂♂♂

We went through all the items the Cooper family had to have. Food was taken care of. They had a way to communicate with the cell phones. Tommy and Aubrey would take a home schooling program. I gave them a few counselors' names and phone numbers that Waunita would call tomorrow. Besides that, nobody had to leave the house if they didn't want.

During the conversation, Aubrey sidled between me and Itsuma, fidgeting all the while. Finally, we settled everything, except nothing was said about Scott. Itsuma had been suspiciously quiet, and Aubrey couldn't sit still.

When Tommy went outside and Waunita went to the kitchen to prepare dinner, I turned to Scott's sister. "So, what have you been dying to say?"

Aubrey bit her lower lip. "I, umm, gave Scott the extra cell phone last night."

I stared back at her.

"I thought he might chuck it when I told him it was from you." Her knee bobbed up and down.

I looked at Itsuma. He stared back. Then I asked her, "Did he chuck it?"

"No." She looked at me expectantly and lowered her voice. "I was, ummm, the one that technically called you last night."

Itsuma perked up.

I narrowed my eyes at her. "Technically?"

"Yeah. Did he talk to you, or did he just hang up?"

"We talked."

"And?"

"We talked."

"Arrrgh! The two of you are so stupid in love. It's so frustrating."

My heart squeezed at her words.

"Get over yourselves," she said.

"Trying."

"Yeah, try harder."

That was the plan.

♂♂♂

"So, you were suspiciously quiet tonight." I opened my car door.

"You don't mind giving me a ride?" Itsuma stood by the passenger side of my Boxster. "I can call Todd. He'll give me a ride."

I narrowed my eyes and set my arms along the roof of my convertible. "Who are you, and where have you put my arrogant prince? You know, the one that barges in like he owns the place?"

Itsuma lifted the door handle and stepped into my car. His subdued manner unnerved me. But I had a feeling he too wanted to talk. Why else would he have set it up so I had to drive him home?

I slipped into my seat, started up my car and drove. It took till we were past the compound gate before Itsuma opened his mouth.

"I saw you and Kai yesterday."

My blood ran cold. "I didn't—"

"I know." He stopped me with a hand. "I saw. I'm not blaming you. I thought you tossing him out was cool."

The biggest sigh of relief rushed past my lips. "So, you're telling me that's where you got your shiner from?" The opponent he underestimated. I would've liked to have seen that fight. I imagined calm, collected waters against a raging fire.

"Yeah."

"And the subdued attitude?"

"I found out some stuff."

"What stuff?"

"Stuff."

Guess I wasn't allowed to know about this *stuff*.

"Did you know Kai has a portfolio of all the guys… no, never mind."

"Tell me."

Itsuma sighed. "He's got a file on all the guys you've ever been with."

Oh. That list was long. Greeeaaatt. That kind of anal was right up Kai's alley too. Itsuma must have seen that and been put off. Well, I couldn't change the past.

"Sensei, am I enough?"

I turned a hard right, parked my car along the curb and turned to Itsuma.

"Baby, whatever he said to you, don't let him get in your head."

Itsuma kept his focus on his hands. I didn't like this change in him.

"You unsteady me. You still think I'm a kid."

"I beg to differ."

"You don't take me seriously. That's why you didn't believe me when I said we were going out."

"Itsuma, you didn't give me a choice. There was no discussion. You decided on your own that I belonged to you and Scott. That whole deal in my classroom, I felt like I'd been clubbed over the head, then dragged to your lair and told I was now your wife."

Itsuma grimaced.

"Any other teacher would have you in jail."

"That's just proof you don't take me seriously."

"What did you expect? I don't know what to say anymore." I threw up my hands. "I love you. I want to be with you. I want to go out on dates with you. I want to spend days in bed with you. I'm even planning a future together with you and Scott. But I don't know if there's one to be had. I might be the only one thinking that way."

Itsuma looked to me with wide eyes and a defenseless expression. "Really?"

"Yes," I sighed. "We are going to get through this. Adults do that. I'm not perfect. You're not perfect. Scott's not perfect."

"What do you mean I'm not perfect?" Itsuma pulled back and gave me a mocking grin.

There he was—my arrogant Prince. I felt relieved. "I'm doing what you asked. I'm not doing anything. If that's not trusting you or taking you seriously, then I don't know what is."

Itsuma leaned back. "Okay. I get it. You're letting me handle things."

"Are we good?"

"Yeah." He nodded.

"Don't take what Kai said to heart." I put the car in drive again and went on our way.

Itsuma smiled. "I don't think Kai will be making any passes towards you any time soon."

I shook my head. "Do I want to know?"

"Nope."

Chapter 18

It was way too early on a Saturday morning to receive visitors. An insistent knock at the door roused me from sleep and I dragged my ass to the front of the house. Whoever it was would have to deal with a half-naked, sexually starved grump. I opened the door without much coherency, but the sight of Kai in his usual suit and tie woke me the hell up. It was as if I were recovering from a bucket of water dropping on my head.

"Hey." I crossed my arms and planted my feet in a defensive stance. "What are you doing here?"

Kai had a few bruises on his face and covered his eyes with shades. Itsuma had everything to do with his beaten face. Ha, ha. A smile curved my lips. "I see you've finally met your match."

"A few lucky blows is not my match." Kai frowned.

"Yeah, well I didn't see many headshots on him."

The man standing in front of me stood as straight as a rail. He was ruffled. The urge to jab at him more warred with the need to shut the door in his face.

"I am here to apologize."

No way would I make anything easy for him. "For?"

"The other night." He smoothed back his hair. "I was rude."

"That's normal for you. You don't know when to quit."

"I just wanted to let you know I will not be bothering you again."

Whoa. What had Itsuma said to get The Wall to move? "Apology accepted."

Kai turned and stopped. "Your boy is impressive."

"Yes, he is."

"Try to keep this one."

He didn't need to tell me. I was still figuring out how to do just that. "Thank you, Kai."

The Wall waved a hand as he walked back to his car. I could detect just a faint hint of a hobble in his stride. Impressive indeed. Maybe all this time Itsuma had been gentle with me.

I closed the door and slid down to the floor with my back against the entrance. What plan should I employ to get Scott and Itsuma back with me? The true answer—it was not up to me. They needed to decide if I was worthy of them. I could not force someone to accept my flaws. I would wait for Itsuma. I would wait for Scott.

Arms around my bent knees, I prayed for mercy. For forgiveness. For a miracle. How had I fallen in love with two students? The beginning of this year I'd resolved to try out a steady boyfriend. See if a steady guy in my life was what I wanted. Now I couldn't see myself with anyone but the Zuma-Scott combo.

Before all this, before them, I might have slept with some random guy to get rid of the frustration building in waiting for them. But ever since I met my Cowboy and my Prince, my weekends were spent alone, working, cleaning and thinking about those two. Well, now I'd have to be strong, suck it up, maybe plead for another chance. If putting up with Itsuma's punishment would get me together with them on the other side of this, I was all in.

♂♂♂

Even six days later, Itsuma still tormented me, and I was letting him. A part of me wallowed in guilt for what I'd done. I'd failed Scott, broken Itsuma's trust, and I felt like a hypocrite. And this was all compounded with the fact that I was so horny I was losing my mind. Masturbation proved fruitless.

Itsuma came over, night after night, but only to study. I felt like he was there to keep an eye on me. Make sure I didn't *do anything*. Whatever that anything was. Yet he wasn't making any advances. I wasn't going to make the first move, but I wasn't throwing off his touch either. He was still my student, and we still needed a grown-up conversation about our relationship. A resolution of some kind.

"Can we talk about it now?" I said.

His hand gripped my inner thigh. "About what?"

"About us."

"You sound like a girl."

I took in a breath to keep calm. "Real men have these conversations."

"Is that a manipulation technique, Sensei?" Itsuma looked up from the book he was reading.

"Are you avoiding the topic?"

Itsuma closed the book and stood up. "I should be going."

"No." I took his hand in both of mine. "Please. You leave in two months. Scott won't talk to me. I'm not allowed to go to the house. Please stay."

I'd been using Itsuma as a go-between for me and Waunita. Together we made sure the Cooper family had all they needed. I'd talked to Scott's mom, his sister, even Tommy on the phone, but I was told Scott did not want me there. Not yet. I tried calling him, but it always went to voicemail. At least Waunita had taken him home when he got out of the hospital.

His family gave me dribbles of information, and assured me he was with them and healing, but he'd given his ultimatum. Scott swore not to tell his dad the whereabouts of the new house; in exchange I wasn't allowed over there. I didn't dare challenge that for fear of him moving back in with his father.

Itsuma shoved the book aside and pulled me to my feet. "You're right, Sensei. Things are fucked up. But he's still pissed."

My shoulders slumped. "Have you explained to him I didn't sleep with Kai? This limbo is killing me. Don't you know anything?"

"Scott and I have been talking."

My head perked up. "He's talking to you?"

"Through his bedroom door. When I provoke him."

"Don't push too hard."

He shrugged. "That's the only way he'll listen."

Worry must have crossed my features.

"Trust me." Itsuma beamed a salacious smile. "I've done this before."

While I'd always considered the phrase *trust me* right up there with *watch this* and *hold my beer*, I put my faith in Itsuma.

"So, what have you got out of him?"

"He blames himself. Typical martyr. But he misses us."

"Yeah?"

Itsuma leered at my mouth. "Yeah. I noticed he got closer to the door when we were talking about you. He'll tell you it was because he didn't want me to yell so the whole house could hear, but I know better."

My heart started beating fast. I swallowed. All my focus was on Itsuma's lips. "Yeah?"

He grinned and dipped his head closer. I didn't move, trapped in my heady want. I should have pulled away, but I had no more reserve.

Itsuma closed even more distance between us. "I think I know how to get his goat."

"I don't remember them having any pets." I breathed steady and hard.

He smirked. Then I tasted the sweet waters of Itsuma's kiss. With my eyes closed, tentative, light touches sparked my desire into need. Itsuma was stripping me of my sweatshirt and pants, pushing me onto the dining room table. Hard and ready, I spread my legs so I could encircle his hips.

Itsuma whipped out his cell phone and the snapshot sound of a digital camera brought me back from my wanton state. "What are you doing?"

Itsuma used both thumbs on his phone, obviously texting. "This will make him respond. If he doesn't call in two minutes, I'll send a video."

"What?"

He set his phone aside and captured my mouth once more.

I pushed him back. "Itsuma?"

"Don't worry, I sent it via Threema. It's secure."

"I have no idea what that means."

Itsuma pushed in for another kiss, but I held him off. "Explain. Who did you send that to?"

His phone rang and Itsuma's smile was very Cheshire cat. "That would be Scott."

My stomach hit bottom. Itsuma grabbed his phone and hit a button. "That didn't take long."

"You sumbitch, what happened to waiting?" Scott sounded angry. Powerful. Not the soft-spoken Cowboy I knew.

"Sensei can't wait." Itsuma unzipped his pants. "He's too needy."

"Scott?" My voice was a mere squeak.

"Mr. Reis?" The gentle voice I'd known returned. "He's not hurting you, is he?"

Itsuma guided his shaft towards my hole and started poking enough to make me groan. He held the phone over my body, at his chest level. "Does he look like he's in pain?"

"He can see me?" I said.

"Oh yeah, he can see your gorgeousness all lit up in desire." Itsuma pushed in a little.

I gasped a yelp.

"Zuma!" Scott growled. "Stop!"

"Shit." Itsuma looked around. "Where's the lubricant?"

I pulled Itsuma in with my legs. As his cock breached the rim of my hole I hissed.

Scott's voice returned to his original coarseness. "Itsuma, I swear to god…"

"Sensei, are you alright?"

"Oh yes. Please, don't stop."

"But you're as tight as the first time."

"I only want you and Scott." My legs pulled him in tighter.

"Then we'll go slow." Itsuma's smile lit up his face.

"No!" I rose and gripped his shirt. "I mean… please don't hold back."

"Sensei…"

"Nothing less than everything you have is going to be good enough. Otherwise, you'll leave me wondering if this was a delusion. I want to feel it no matter if I'm sitting still, walking, awake or dreaming. Anything less is going to leave me unsatisfied."

Itsuma smirked. "We can't have that, then."

"Go ahead. Take me the way you want."

"Don't regret it later."

"I won't." Even if I did, I wouldn't tell him.

Scott's heavy breathing over the phone confirmed he was still on the line. I looked at what must be the camera lens and snaked a hand down to my stiff cock. As Itsuma pushed in I arched my back and stroked myself. I'd forgotten the sweet soreness Itsuma's cock delivered. Even when doing nothing he left me panting. My mouth watered, remembering the taste of his kiss. The pain and pleasure sent a wash of sensation clogging my brain. My eyes fluttered with the rolling spasms coursing through me. Lost to Itsuma's cock, I jolted with every millimeter that entered my ass.

"Sensei, you're sucking me in."

I looked down at our connection and we watched as that girth of his was taken in by my greedy hole. My bottom suckled him until he was balls deep. I lay my head back and groaned.

"Scott, fuck, I need that mouth of yours." The admission sent shivers through me.

Only a whimper over the phone replied.

"It's not fair," I panted. "I can't see you."

Itsuma grunted out. "Sensei, this is incredible." He pulled out halfway and again my body suctioned him back in. "Oh, shit, oh fuck, Sensei." Itsuma rolled his neck and pulled out, letting my ass suck him back in. This was the slowest I'd ever been made love to, and it was ecstasy.

"You seeing this, Coop?" Itsuma lowered the phone next to our connection. "We're going to train your slut-hole properly. Your ass'll suck cock just like Sensei."

More whimpers came across the line. Itsuma let his pole slide all the way in and his whole body tremored.

"You keep sucking me in, Sensei. It feels… it feels… I've never felt anything like this." His abs tightened and rippled. Itsuma threw his head back.

"Oh, Scott," I said. "You should be here to see this."

I took Itsuma's phone as he stood paralyzed and turned the camera around. On screen I could see Scott's naked chest as he pumped his dick in a state of perpetual bliss. Eyes half slit, mouth agape, panting and… fuck, he still had his Stetson hat on and cocked upward. In another box on the screen I could see Itsuma losing all his composure just from being inside me. This would do me in. I'd get addicted to this view. Both men in complete reverence to pleasure would make me lose my mind. I'd orgasm just by looking at this. Fuck, if this was recording… masturbation would be effective with this video.

"Hey…" Itsuma grabbed his phone back. "Mine."

"Look who's greedy now," I panted, and went back to stroking my own eager pole. Itsuma cast his gaze to the phone. Now I knew what he was watching, and it made me go insane. Seeing Scott like that again, wanting and sexy, pushed me into overdrive. His seductive gaze so fresh in my mind sent my cock aching. Wanting to stick my hot and heavy rod inside him made me all the more desperate. Even if he were just a voyeur, he was with us.

Now that I'd seen him watching I put on a show. Casting lustful gazes at the camera, letting my hair sprawl out around me, biting the tip of my finger to entertain my men brought out my inner tease. All the while, I stroked myself suggestively. Crap, I was so vainly into this.

Itsuma continued softly, pumping me. His tenderness clawed at my desperation. I wanted more, harder. I wanted to feel him. I'd said I didn't want to be able to walk normally, and I meant it. But he wasn't going faster or harder. He was a man trying to be taken seriously. Itsuma was making love to me.

In my realization, his face became a watery blur. I lifted my hand to his face. "Itsuma, I love you."

A vulnerable gaze flashed across his face. Then he smiled. "That's not going to work. You won't get what you want, Sensei."

"What do you think I want?"

He pumped me slow. "You want to use me to feed some self-punishment so you can feel better about your poor life choices."

"I wasn't saying it for forgiveness." I couldn't care less if he loved me back. My feelings were mine. Only I could deal with them. "It doesn't matter how you feel or how far away you are. I love you. The same goes for Scott. It doesn't matter if he holds a grudge. I love him too."

"Ahhhhngh!" Scott cried over the phone.

"Oh god!" I clawed at Itsuma's phone. "Let me see!"

My Prince pulled out, turned me on my stomach and topped me from behind. His thick cock nestled between my cheeks. But what really got me was the screen in front of me showing Scott completely lost to masturbation. He was still watching, and now I could see Itsuma above me in the smaller screen alongside Scott. Their faces were beautiful. My ass spasmed in delight.

"Please fill me up again," I said.

Scott twisted his body as he stroked himself. He looked close to coming. His face displayed a gorgeous blush that reached his ears. Those half-lidded green eyes sent my palm searching for my cock. Itsuma's thick head probed me as I reached down and took myself in hand.

"Fuck, there's no comparison to your mouth," I said into the phone.

Scott licked his lips between panting breaths. Sexy Cowboy. The tip of Itsuma's head breached my hole once again. I hollered and pushed my ass back.

"Mr…. Reis…" Scott opened his lust-filled eyes.

"Yes, good, yessss…" I hissed as cock pushed into my back channel. "It's good."

"Oh god, Sensei, you're sucking me in again."

"I want to see," Scott said.

Itsuma raised up, taking my beautiful view along with him.

"See? I'm not pushing. His ass is pulling me inside."

"Ohhh… fuck…" Scott moaned.

As my innards consumed Itsuma like a fine wine, I squeezed my inner muscles. "Don't take that camera away from me."

"Crap, Sensei, that's tight."

"Bring it here."

Itsuma's warmth once again covered my back and the gorgeous view of both my men returned.

"Itsuma, please, harder," I said.

My Prince made me hold the phone with both hands.

"Raise your ass, Sensei." Itsuma lifted my knee up onto the table and lifted me up until my tiptoes barely reached the floor. He kept me stable but remained slow with his cock. My plea didn't faze him.

"Let him see your ass and face on screen," Itsuma said.

I adjusted the camera and watched myself be taken. Half of Scott's face was covered by a pillow, but he was in total bliss. I recognized the sheets I'd picked out for him. Him being in the house I owned made me happy. He was safe.

"You wanna see me pound Sensei's ass, Coop?"

Scott gave out a whimpered mewl for confirmation. I thought my ass was going to melt. Itsuma's tight abs started working and his hips finally pumped. He pulled out and pushed in. He was still going slow. Damn, he wasn't giving me what I wanted. I wanted to lose my mind. Stop this endless ache in my ass and my cock. Be with him and Scott together, not being tortured by watching on a phone. If I could touch my Cowboy, feel him, be able to reach out to him, I'd give anything. But the amazing part was being able to watch Itsuma's body move while working me over *and* seeing Scott's reactions.

Itsuma sunk into me, and it felt as good as it looked. He was an amazing lover. His control matched my indiscipline.

"So, Sensei," Itsuma's fingers wrangled my hair into his fist. "This is the only cock allowed to tap your ass, got it?"

"Make me feel it," I said.

He gripped my hair tighter. "Oh, I will. But not in the way you want it." His hips nestled against mine and he shoved, pushing me into the table.

"Fuck," I cried out. "I already feel you in my heart."

"It's not enough," Itsuma growled.

"What more do you want, then?"

He shoved again, sending sparks down my spine. "Your body."

"You have it."

"We want your soul," Itsuma said.

Scott watched me with a painful sadness. I'd put that expression there.

"Then I'm yours," I panted.

Itsuma shoved inside me. "Not good enough! You agreed before and look what happened. I need to babysit your ass."

"I didn't agree," I said, trying to push my ass back into him.

He pulled back, preventing me from getting his cock inside me further.

"I said I understood. I didn't agree." My cock bobbed in frustration, trying to gain purchase on anything.

Itsuma pulled my head back and shoved with his hips. "Then do you agree now, Sensei?"

"Yes! Yes!" Just fuck me already.

"What do you agree to?"

Scott watched me closely, searching my face. He was more cognizant. This was important to them.

"I agree to be yours. I belong to both of you. I won't see other men. Only you two," I said. "I won't fuck other men."

"Not even for the sake of saving us?" Itsuma asked.

"I promise." I lay on my kitchen table as a feast for my boys. This was no time to mince words or be coy. No room for misunderstanding. I'd have to use words, lots of them, to convince these two I could be trusted. "I get it. I won't throw my body away. I won't disregard what my body means to you. You both have my heart. Before, my body was a tool for pleasure. Now I understand. I've hurt you both. I never felt more like an idiot before in my life. But, Itsuma, when you leave, you're going to leave with half my soul."

Silence.

"That's how I felt when…" Scott whispered. "When Itsuma told me what you did."

He didn't need to explain. What I'd intended to do with Kai had crushed him. Made him feel like our time was nothing. That was so far from how I felt about Scott. Only now did I realize my blindness.

"Hey." Itsuma shoved his cock in me. "Stop it, both of you, or you'll make me soft."

I looked at Scott on the screen and smiled. "By all means. Prince Itsuma, do fuck me until you're satisfied."

Itsuma started to pump. "I will, peasant."

I laughed.

Scott smirked.

Then Itsuma started to really move. All that angry energy fueled his hips. I held the phone so Scott and Itsuma could see my face and ass getting royally fucked.

I loved how ruthlessly he poured his cock into me. On camera Itsuma's inner porn star came out, sneering and slapping my ass. Every hand-spank strung me up and made me clench so hard I thought my hole was going to bite his dick off. There were going to be handprints after this. Even Scott grunted at each slap.

I writhed, trying to get Itsuma deeper. All the while my cock swung, hitting the edge of the table. My rod drooled all over the place. The table, the carpet, my inner thighs.

Itsuma took hold of my shoulders and shoved himself in at every stroke. My ass was giving him a hard time leaving.

"See?" I looked back at him. "We fit so well, even my body resists you leaving."

Itsuma smirked. "That's right, feel it."

Oh god. I swallowed the pool of lust in my mouth.

Scott started crying out again. He held the phone with what must have been his feet. He stroked himself two-handed. I had an underside view of his rod, with his face way above the up close and personal *important* part of him.

"You want to suck his dick?" Itsuma asked.

"How could I not?"

Two fingers slid into my mouth, and I began to suckle Itsuma's fingers as if they were Scott's cock. My tongue worked over the rough pads of deliciousness. I was in heaven. My ass was getting pounded. My mouth was full and my cock was being teased. The climbing orgasm blocked out all other sensations.

I watched the screen, listening to Scott's desperate grunts. My nose was buried in the monitor I held, pretending my Cowboy was right here with us. Itsuma was doing all he could to fulfill that fantasy. His fingers and his cock were going to meet inside my middle. Every time his balls slapped against my ass it sent my cock thrumming. Itsuma knew how to make my toes curl. *So close. So very close.*

As my stick hung low and circled the air, my mouth suckled the two fingers pressing my tongue down. Itsuma filled me. Scott decimated my control with his cries. My eyes feasted on his hand, deeply working over his hard pole.

My muscles clenched from ass to chest—a reaction to my oncoming climax. My cock wasn't getting any kind of purchase and swung in the wind.

"Shiiit, Uma..." I said, working around fingers. "Unfeee..." Speech didn't come out right with a tongue depressor.

"What's that, Sensei? Harder?" Itsuma squeezed my hips and went for a more punishing pace.

I groaned. It wasn't a complaint. I melted under the Prince's dominance. *Oh god. Please let me come. I'll be good. I swear.* I'd be crazy to give this up. To fuck it up. I wouldn't. Not ever again. Especially when Itsuma mastered me as he did now. He made me feel him right down to my core.

"Nuuu ri…" I said. *Scott, Scott, please suck me off.* One hand let go of the phone and I tried to snake my arm down between the table and my legs.

"No you don't, Sensei." Itsuma brought my hand back up.

I grabbed the phone with both hands again.

"You can come without that."

"Zuma…" Scott moaned. "Don't be vicious."

"I'm not." Itsuma pounded. "This is his penance. Sensei needs punishment or he'll feel guilty."

I groaned and pushed my ass up further. The twine like grapple-hold of guilt wrapped around my heart unfurled. Yes. Finally. He admitted to my need for discipline. I could handle any kind of retribution. If he admitted the torment being my atonement, we could move on. Eventually be together once more. The desperate wish of my heart.

I'd remained stoic in my wantonness until Scott's hand moved a bit more vigorously. He was more into my punishment than he let on. The view from Scott's end changed. Now his hat was off and he was laid flat. Pillows surrounded his head. From his face to his navel, Scott dominated the screen.

I tried watching his blissful face and his masturbating hand simultaneously. Both mesmerized me.

"Zuma… Mr. Reis…" Scott arched his back. "Ahh! Fuck!"

Streams of white spurted out his tip and covered his chest. His cum looked sticky and delicious. A spent Scott lay satisfied on his bed as we watched him from the screen. This was a magnificent sight after a long dry spell. So sexy. My ass melted, allowing Itsuma in deeper. Oh god. My sight went fuzzy. I grunted with every slap of his balls.

Scott gave the camera a lazy grin. "Your turn," he said.

"Nope." Itsuma took the phone. "If you want to see his *O* face, get your ass down here."

"What?" Scott's eyes bugged out. His lips quivered. A hand brushed back his blond hair.

"He'll hold out for forty minutes."

"You fucking bastar—"

Itsuma tapped the connection off and tossed the phone on the table.

I offered myself to my tormentor, apple in my mouth and all. "He's not in any condition to drive."

"I don't expect him to."

"I can't hold out that long."

"Don't worry," he whispered. "I'm not going to last that long either, but it might get Chicken-Little-Shit to stop pouting."

"Oh," I breathed.

"Sensei, bring your knee down." He pulled at my leg.

"It was all a show for him, wasn't it?"

"He has to remember what he's missing." Itsuma helped straighten out my leg. "Time will do that, but I'm speeding up the process."

Once my leg was down and my toes could touch the floor Itsuma gave me a reach around.

"Oh Christ, that's good." I bucked my hips, making myself the driver of a poke and hole. His hand was all I needed to bring my orgasm to fruition. "Let go, Itsuma, I'll come."

"No," he whispered. "Come."

Oh, this was going to blow both my heads off. Scott's exhausted face, Itsuma's whispers… my ass spasmed so hard I thought I was going to die. Tremors burned over my body. Each release became more intense than the last. I felt the cock inside me pulsate. Itsuma was coming with me. The thought intensified my pleasure. There wasn't anyone else who could make my orgasm last for minutes on end like this—except for Scott.

My knees grew weak and still my cock pumped. I wasn't even sure if fluid was still coming out. This orgasm wasn't letting go. Nor did I want it to. *Last for eternity. Keep me in this state. Let me always feel Itsuma up my ass and Scott wrapped around my dick.*

The crudeness didn't stop there. My slutty hole slurped up everything Itsuma gave. A butt plug was in order for the next week. Crap. I started sliding down. "My legs can't anymore."

"I've got ya." Itsuma pulled me with him and I splayed onto his lap on the floor.

We panted, catching our breath under my kitchen table.

"You think Scott will come?"

Itsuma sighed. "Maybe."

I reached for his hand and entwined our fingers. "Do you forgive me?" I couldn't look at him. His rejection might kill me.

"Angry make-up sex is fairly awesome."

I huffed. "Will you ever trust me again?"

Itsuma sighed—bigger this time. "I actually never did. But that's my problem. I think I can start now."

I leaned forward and detached from my lover. Big mistake. Jizz dribbled down my thighs. "Oiy!"

My Prince jumped up and went for the kitchen.

"Towel?" I asked.

Itsuma came back and handed me a kitchen towel.

Perfect. Now I sat on a wet folded square instead of wet-spot carpet. "I'll feel this tomorrow." I grinned.

"Good." Itsuma squatted in front of me, his cat-lidded gaze inscrutable. "I have to leave."

"Now?" I looked at the clock. Oh. Ten-thirty-five. *Holy crap. We were going at it for over an hour. Intense.* My elated afterglow dampened. I palmed my face, trying to wash away my disappointment. I swallowed the tiny voice begging *please stay with me tonight.* I wanted to be in his arms. To wrap my body around his. To lay my head on his chest and float in this euphoria before it completely faded.

"Hey." Itsuma reached up and pushed a lock of hair behind my ear. "Just because I have to live under my parents' rule doesn't make me a kid."

My eyes closed automatically to his touch. "But I can't look at you this way in school."

"Lecherous old man." He laughed and got up. Those wonderful privates dangled temptingly in my face. Before I could convince him otherwise, he got his clothes back on as I tried to mop myself up. I'd need another bath.

Itsuma bent down and gave me one more lascivious kiss. "Goodnight, Sensei."

"Oh, I will." My eyes could scarcely focus enough to see Itsuma walk out the door.

After he left I breathed in deep and let out a groaned sighed. Wow. That was an experience. The memory was now an all-time favorite. The fact that it was with lovers who I cared for would keep it in the top five greatest shaggings of all time.

A few bodily sighs later, I got up, wiped myself off the best I could and put on a pair of sweat pants.

Pounding at the door sent my heart racing. Scott? Maybe he wasn't as Chicken-Little as Itsuma thought. I went to the door and flung it open. My giddy smile turned to horror at the hulking form of Scott's father.

The man crowded the threshold and muscled his way through my home entrance. The anger in his eyes burned like two bright blue sparks.

"You took away my family," he growled.

I pushed the front door and it closed with an ominous click. My back tall and ready for this long-awaited showdown, I wasn't going to turn tail. "No, you lost them."

He'd come to finish what he'd started that day in the principal's office.

"You're going to tell me where I can find them."

A smile carved into my face. Knowing they were safe, that he'd tried to find them and couldn't, was worth the hurt I'd endure.

"It gives me great satisfaction to know you won't be beating on your wife and children. But hey, you can come here and try to beat it out of me anytime." Cool and collected, I raked my hand through my hair, flashing him flirty eyes.

Mr. Cooper flinched.

Doing my best to unnerve him more, I twirled my fingers around a strand of hair like some flirty trumpet.

"You fucker…" He grabbed for me in his brawling style.

Instinct took over. I knocked his arms out of the way and went straight for eyes, nose, throat and groin. Itsuma would be proud. Wrestling made me wily and fit. But there was one simple rule I could not ignore. Mr. Cooper was big. His weight advantage was not to be underestimated.

Scott's dad crouched, holding his face while gasping for air. I hadn't hit him hard enough to crush his trachea, but it had been enough to make him think twice.

"I tell you what," I said. "If you can get me to tap out I'll give you a phone number. But if I get you to tap out you'll join them in a family session."

"One of those shrinks? No thanks." He ducked and lunged towards me.

Dodging into my hallway, I kept going to the back of my house. The dojo was back there.

"I really don't want you destroying my living room." I stepped onto tatami mats. The room was a twenty-by-forty-foot training cage. I went to the middle and turned to face muscle and fury stepping into my sacred space.

"You should feel privileged," I said, channeling my inner Itsuma. "There aren't many who even know this is here."

Mr. Cooper eyed up the punching bag, the racks holding very non-decorative katana swords, the closet of practice body armor, gloves and a cabinet of wrestling trophies. But most of all the space to spar. There was room enough for two men to have an all-out match. A brawler was used to cramped quarters. Mr. Cooper would find no tables to throw, no chairs to break over backs or glass to cut my face off. He seemed to realize I just might know what I was doing when it came to fights.

He entered with reluctant steps. Then his focus locked on me. I turned so that my right foot stood before my left. Knees bent, hands at my sides, I waited.

Mr. Cooper raised his two fists in the classic position. Someone with an untrained eye might think I was defenseless with my hands down. If he knew anything he'd understand that my open stance was a taunt. A sign of mild disrespect. I probably looked weak in his eyes.

He swung a wide arc. An easy dodge. Mr. Cooper followed with a one-two punch. Again, I dodged. He kept swinging. I used as little energy as possible, away from his predictable movements. He was testing me.

"Just as I thought." He stepped away. "You're a coward."

Remaining calm, I moved us in a circle. "Riiight. I'm so willing to give you an address. See me quaking in my boots?"

Mr. Cooper pulled back. *Oh no you don't. You're not controlling the mat.* I moved in. He swung an uppercut. I turned my hip, feeling the wind of his fists, threw my other hand to block from the other side, and smacked his face with the back of my hand.

He jumped back, stunned.

I went back into fighting stance. "Like my version of a bitch slap?"

That got him.

Mr. Cooper lunged for me. Fists went flying. I blocked, blocked, blocked, blocked, knowing the bruises that would come in the morning.

He was fast, but sparring with Itsuma helped keep me quick. Good thing. This guy had speed.

"You're fast for an old man," I said.

He stumbled back, breathing harder than when we started. Mr. Cooper was losing his air. Admirably, he kept going. His uppercuts were the worst to deflect. Hard, heavy brick blocks were softer than his blows. He knew how to throw a punch, and all I was doing was defense. I'd be a turnip tomorrow, but it didn't matter. This was cathartic.

"Why don't you fight back, faggot?"

"Do you get it yet? You can't touch me. Not when I'm paying attention." I wanted him to know what it was like, having someone who could fight back. Who wouldn't back down or take his shit.

"Is that your excuse?"

"I'm not going to hit you." I used a body push to make space. "One day, you are going to be my father-in-law."

"That's disgusting." He came after me with open palms.

"Oh, you want to grapple?" I took his shirt, snaked my heel behind his leg and tapped the back of his knees with a one-two kick. As we fell, I shifted him backward. He went down on his left side and I followed him down, making sure I remained on top.

He pushed at my chin, turning my face. We landed in one of my favorite sex positions. Too bad this wasn't Itsuma.

"Get off me!" He yelled and thrashed.

"What a baby." I jumped up and stood back. He'd make me into an accordion if he got his hands on me.

Scott's father breathed so hard he sounded like he was having a heart attack. Still, he got back up. Keeping space between us, he stalled the fight, trying to catch his breath. *Oh no you don't.* I prowled around him, forcing him to circle. My opponent lumbered. Our fight wasn't at all graceful or epic. No long rounds of getting hit in the head several times. All either needed was one good strike and this would be over. I had to be the last man standing.

Mr. Cooper went after me again. His last push before he ran out of energy. His breath tumbled over me. It was faint, but I could smell the alcohol. He went for a swing, but, as any tired, untrained brawler, he was sloppy. He left himself open.

Rule one: Make sure your opponent can't tag you in the chin.

His wide swing let me dodge, then I cast a right hook. He went down. Out. Unconscious.

I checked his breathing. All okay. Fifteen minutes later a pool of saliva dampened my tatami mats and he groaned his wakefulness.

"Stay down or I'll knock you out again," I said. "And this time I'll call the cops to come take you away."

Mr. Cooper rubbed his eyes. "Hey, asshole, you didn't do anything funny to me, did ya?"

"You're not my type," I said. "And you still have your clothes on." Stupid, ignorant hillbilly. I poured sake in a shot glass. "Drink this." I handed him the thimbleful of rice wine.

"The hell is this?"

"Japanese beer."

He sniffed it, then threw the shot back.

"Good." I poured more sake in his glass. "Have another."

"I see what you're doing," he said.

"Oh? What am I doing? You think I'm trying to get you drunk to shag you? How many times do I have to explain? I'm not interested in you."

"No," he scoffed. "You're trying to make peace."

"Maybe," I said. I'd meant what I said about him being my future father-in- law.

"Well, it won't work." He downed the shot.

I tipped more sake in a shot glass without drawing attention to the fact. "Why do you think you're here?"

"I'm here because you know where my family is and I want them."

"How do you know I'm the one keeping your family away from you?"

"I just know."

"So you're going on an assumption?"

"Fuck off. Why else would they leave?" He downed the third shot of sake.

I gritted my teeth and poured another covert shot in his glass. "Maybe because they didn't want to get beat anymore."

He looked me in the eye.

I didn't flinch. "They are doing better without you."

"Bullshit."

"They miss you, but that's not the same as need."

"I don't have to listen to your rhetoric." He set his glass down and got up.

Sake is the best falling-down-drunk type of alcohol. The best truth serum, and it leaves mere mortals incapacitated. Mr. Cooper immediately slammed back down on his ass. "What the hell," he slurred.

"Yeah, rice wine does that." I took another shot. "You tend to step out of sober."

"You bastard." He flopped on his back. "You did this on purpose." He waved a drunken, shaky fist.

"Yeah, I did." I shifted my weight and smiled down at him. Fear dominated his eyes. "Oh, give it a rest, already." I set my bottle and shot glass down. I stood up, knowing full well what would happen. As soon as I stood and took a step, my feet stumbled over each other.

Mr. Cooper laughed. "Whas the matter, fairy, lost your wings?"

I laughed too. "Oh, I was never good enough to have wings." I fumbled my way towards the hall, leaning on the doorjamb for support. There was no doubt in my mind that he'd be spending the night in my dojo. I crashed into the closet drawers and pulled out a blanket. Effort and fortitude were my saving grace for waddling back to the dojo.

Mr. Cooper was out. I plunked the blanket on him and spread it over his body to the best of my inebriated ability.

Oh god, the spinning. I crawled on my hands and knees to my bedroom. The blinking light saying my phone was charging was stabbing my eyes. I climbed onto my bed and lay on top of my comforter, letting the world whirl. While the merry-go-round of life spun in one direction, I picked up my phone and dialed. It was late, so I was patient.

"Hello?" a familiar teenager answered.

"Aubrey?"

"Are you okay?"

"You were the first one on my list," I said.

"You sound drunk enough to be my dad," she soured.

"Drunk." I nodded. "You have a thing tomorrow?"

"You mean a meeting with the shrink? Yeah."

"Okay, that's good."

"Hey, are you okay?"

"Oh, yeah," I said. "How's Scott?"

"He's good."

"'Kay." I was fading fast. "Night."

"Goodnight." She hung up first and I let oblivion take me away.

Chapter 19

"Hey!" I poked the very large bear in my dojo. "Hey. Wake up." I had forty-five minutes to get him to the Cooper family session, then get to work. I'd already told Principal Ellis I needed a substitute for first class, but that didn't give me license to be late. "Come on, don't you want to see your family?"

A groan came from the bear.

"Get up. Take a shower at least."

That got his attention. He woke wild-eyed, looking around.

"Sleep well, sunshine?"

Blurry eyed and horrified, Mr. Cooper looked me up and down. "What the hell?"

"You came over last night, don't you remember?" I teased.

He shot up on his feet. "There's no way."

"Don't sound so hopeful." I stood.

"Fuck off."

"Whatever." I waved him off. "For the record, whiskey dick doesn't satisfy me. Neither does screwing the unconscious."

"Then why is my back killing me?"

S.N.McKibben
♂♂♂
282

I raised an eyebrow. *Exactly how would you know… never mind.* "Because you slept on tatami mats. I would not randomly pick you off the street and bring you home."

His face turned red. He actually looked ashamed. Maybe there was hope for him yet.

"Do you want to see your family or not?"

"Yes."

"Then take a shower. At least wash off the reek of alcohol."

"Don't tell me what to do."

"Aren't you on parole or something?" I turned my back on him and went down the hall. "If that's the case, get out of my house."

Really, after everything, after all his bullshit, I was losing my patience. Still, best to go with optimism. I went into the linen closet and grabbed two towels. Just in case he would deign to take a shower. He stood between the threshold of the dojo and the hallway. His form was mostly in shadow, so I couldn't make out his expression, but the cadence in his voice was… meek.

"I want to see them."

Totally vindicated, I shut the closet door. "Then take a shower and follow me to Dr. Kleck's office."

"A shrink?"

"That's right. You either attend with mediation or you can leave."

He scratched his neck stubble. "Fine. Where's the shower?"

"This way."

Mr. Cooper followed me and I pointed to the bathroom.

"Coffee?" I asked.

"Black." He lumbered into the bathroom and locked the door.

Well then, he *could be* a human being.

Ten minutes later we were headed out the door. Mr. Cooper sipped his Columbian coffee and remained suspicious of my every move. As if I had some disease.

"Don't get your hopes up. Dr. Kleck is expecting you and will hold you after the session so your family can leave first, without you. There are guards in the building, and they won't hesitate to throw you out. If you so much as raise your voice at them, you're gone."

He remained quiet, but the scowl said volumes. The ride there with him following me in Scott's truck made me miss my Cowboy. If I pushed out the world and all logic I could pretend my boyfriend was following me in his car. The mood changed when I watched Mr. Cooper park and called out a "Good luck."

"Fuck off."

Okay then. What was I expecting?

♂♂♂

My curiosity was overshadowed by my embarrassment, preventing me from calling Aubrey. Waunita, though kind and grateful, deflected my questions without making me feel jilted. All those years of convincing parents, teachers and authorities that her family was just fine made her a pro at deflecting me. So it was only Itsuma eating with me tonight.

My phone rang with an unidentified number. *Great. Another parent?* Without much enthusiasm, I answered, "Hello?"

I heard a gasp from the other end.

"Hello?" I said.

"Mr. Reis?" His soft timbre pulled the air out of my lungs.

"Scott?" A flood of his sexy faces over Itsuma's video feed shot through my mind. I was instantly hard. Oh shit. Talking to him over the phone was going to be distracting.

"Can we talk?" Scott's voice on the phone was a lifeline.

"Of course." Like I'd say no.

"Ah, I wanted to, uh, call and thank you," he said.

I closed my eyes and listened to every breath, every syllable, every subtle change in his tone. "Thank me? For what?"

"For getting my dad to the session… and last night," he whispered *last night* so faintly I'd have missed it if I weren't concentrating on his voice.

"I didn't do anything worth your thanks." Whatever got him to call me—I'd take it.

"Yes," Scott said, "you did."

Hell if I'd argue with him, and yet… "I just led him there. He made the choice to go."

Silence. *Shit. Just be grateful, Mori.* "You're welcome," I said.

After more of a pause, and shame telling me to leave it at that and hang up, Scott spoke again. "He wouldn't have come by himself. Whatever you said brought him there."

"Was it a good session?" Tongue tied by a kid. I bit my lower lip.

"Well," Scott's voice cracked. "We've got a long road, but there's hope. I think one day we'll be able to communicate without it becoming a yelling match."

"He yelled at you?" Defensive rage boiled in my blood.

"Uh, no."

Scott paused. I really wanted to know, but I was terrified of scaring him away.

"Actually, it was a lot of Aubrey screaming at him."

"I bet." A chuckle escaped my lips. "Dr. Kleck allowed that?"

"Yep. She said if he could sit there and listen to what his child had to say, then she'd let him come again."

"Wow." Not sure I approved of screaming matches, but I supposed that was cathartic. I listened and gave supporting grunts, all the while eating every morsel of Scott's attention.

"I was proud of Mom. She didn't fold," Scott went on.

I could see how he must have been just like Tommy at his age. Curious, sweet, affectionate. My ears soaked up his words, soothing my heart. Did this mean he forgave me? Or was it wishful thinking?

"He said you were different than he thought."

"Your father?" Our connection over the line was palpable and comforting. I cradled the phone as if I were holding Scott's blown glass heart. "Different how?"

"Ummm, he said you hit on him."

I let out a barked denial. "I did not!"

Scott murmured a chuckle. "He said you winked at him."

I groaned. "Seriously?"

"You are a bit of a flirt."

That I couldn't deny. "I only have eyes for you and Itsuma." My eyes flicked to my Prince. Itsuma gave a sideways glance—pretending to study.

Part of me held my breath. Scott could fling some very hateful facts in my face. He didn't so much as say what he thought, but I could feel the question of *why* in the silence on the other line. Defensive fear formed into a sphere of words.

"I'm sorry. You probably don't want to hear that," I said. "But I don't regret it." *Shut up, Mori.* "If that's what it takes to keep you safe, I'd…" *Shut up!* "I'd do anything."

I'd gotten away from myself. Silence and I had never really gotten along. "I love you," I said.

There was a gasp on the other end. *Really? Is he kidding me? Did I not tell him how I felt? Was that the first time I confessed? Damn. The kid had to know. How did this conversation go to shit so fast?*

"Please say something," I whispered. "Tell me you hate me. Tell me you can't forgive me. Say you don't care about me. But don't leave me in this black hole. It's like I'm in a sensory deprivation tank. I can't see. I can't feel. I hear nothing. My sense of touch is gone." Only Itsuma got through to me anymore. The only time I could relax was in Itsuma's arms.

"I love you," Scott whispered. "That's why it hurts so much."

"Please say we can get past this. I miss you. I'll do anything." Desperate. That was me.

"I don't want someone who will do anything for me, Mr. Reis. Have some pride." Scott's sadness poured forth.

"Not when it comes to you." My hand covered my eyes. Scott couldn't see me, but I felt more exposed talking to him like this than during our first night.

"So whenever I'm in trouble you're going to make a deal with the devil? A devil that would take what's mine?"

"If it keeps you safe."

"I don't want to be safe."

"And I don't want your life in jeopardy."

Another pause. This time the wind of heavy breathing muffled the connection.

"Then are you going to ask me to stop riding horses?"

"What? No!"

"Even though it's in the top five most dangerous sports?"

"Where is this coming from?"

"Can you understand my point of view?"

I'd painted him into a corner. Calling him wrong was not going to solve anything. "You can't stop me from worrying," I said. "And you can't stop me from wanting to help you when you need it."

"Sleeping with other men is going too far."

"If I told you I didn't sleep with him, would you believe me?" Trust worked both ways.

"It's what I want to believe."

"Scott, I do have pride. I wasn't able to sleep with him."

A sigh scratched through the phone. "I believe you."

I held my breath on my next question. "Then can I assume I still have a place by your side?" Shameless begging. I was down to bloody knees and pleading.

"I don't normally have phone sex with someone I don't care about." His voice was low and smoldering. "Maybe you do."

Good. Get it out. "You can yell at me, ya know."

"I don't want to be my father."

Agreed. But I said nothing. In fact, nothing was said for a brief minute. I expected this phone call to be short. Perhaps because we were talking we could sort this out. It gave me hope.

"So when can I see you again?"

"In a little while." Scott needed to let his anger seep out. "I'll call you later."

"Baby, I'm sorry."

He hung up.

My bubble of connection with Scott popped. I was back with Itsuma in my dining room. Thank goodness he was by my side.

He gave me a knowing smile. "Don't worry. He'll call again." He picked up his phone and started texting.

I flopped down on the chair and leaned over the dining room table. "Do you forgive me, at least?"

"No." But he wasn't serious. "It's going to take a lifetime of hard fucking before there is any forgiveness." He laughed.

There was a lot of phone tapping as his thumbs flew over his phone. The phone chimed and he cast a nasty glare at the screen. His lips tightened.

"Well, at least there'll be fucking." I tapped at the math book in front of him. "Solve that. Stop texting."

Itsuma put the phone down and pushed his notepad to me. "Solved it."

The kid never ceased to amaze me. While I was talking, he'd worked out the last equation.

"Good work," I said, looking over his paper.

He leaned back, unbuttoning his jeans. "Time for my reward, Sensei."

Chapter 20

One month later

I stood at the back of my empty classroom, nostalgic for the place where I met the two loves of my life. I walked slowly down the row of chairs where Itsuma and Scott sat. My fingertips caressed the linoleum wood as I walked past their chairs. There was where my Prince had almost taken me. There was the floor where he'd blown my mind.

Slipping behind my desk, I opened the naughty drawer. One of Itsuma's iPods and his broken earplugs sat inside. I picked up the four dangling pieces and let memories pass over me. Some aggravating, others tender. My actions were past regret. I accepted my fate. Given the choice, I wouldn't make a different decision. In the end, Scott *had* escaped. Not as safely as I liked, but alive.

"The end of a year is always sad." Mr. Goyas slipped into my classroom. "I never know why. It's not like I really want to start the new semester when it comes, but I'm sad to see it go."

"Yeah." I took the iPod and all the pieces and put them in my bag. The rest of the junk I tossed in the wastebasket.

"How's Scott?"

The ends of my lips curled. Despite what the teacher said, despite his gruff attitude, Mr. Goyas cared about all these kids. "He's fine. I talked to him yesterday."

Scott phoned me about once a day. Every other call, Itsuma rubbed me off and did his best to make me sound breathless while Scott and I talked. Itsuma used the chance to get to know my ass better. I was not complaining. Just observing. Sometimes my Cowboy would tell me to describe what he was doing. But I still hadn't met Scott face-to-face. Neither had Itsuma. We agreed that it was best to stay away because Mr. Cooper might break his agreement and follow one of us to the house.

"And?" Mr. Goyas asked.

My blood rushed north and south. I knew my face had to be beet red. My cock was remembering Itsuma's ministrations while talking to Scott last night. "Ah, he's okay." I tilted my head and let my hair fall in front of my face.

A deep rumbling chuckle came from Mr. Goyas. He stepped closer. A hand ruffled my hair.

"Damn it." I swatted at his paw. "I'm not a kid."

"Yeah, yeah." Mr. Goyas turned and waved a hand behind him. "Have fun with those college brats. Don't forget Principal Ellis wants to see you before you leave."

I had to laugh. Mr. Goyas's way of saying goodbye brought me out of my nostalgic memory. I would miss the bear of a teacher. I never asked him how long he'd known about me, nor had he said anything more about the subject. His watchful gaze was always felt, and our short flirtations weren't the same, but I'd gotten the sense I could be myself around him. After all, he'd defended me against Mr. Cooper. I owed him props.

After clearing out my desk I travelled down the long corridor to the principal's office. When I got there, I shut the door. Principal Ellis handed me amber liquid in a glass tumbler. I sniffed at the contents. It smelled like beer.

"Well, Mr. Reis," Principal Ellis said. "Congratulations on keeping your difficulties with the Cooper family under wraps." He lifted a glass to me.

Under wraps wasn't the right term, but if the principal was happy, that was a good thing.

"Thank you?" I clinked my glass with his. My eye wandered out his window.

Scott's last report indicated his dad was still working out some heavy topics in therapy. Apparently Mr. Cooper still blamed me for a number of things. Hence one of the reasons why we agreed I shouldn't go see Scott. He wanted to set ground rules for his father. I was one of those things.

"So you're off to assistant professordom?" Principal Ellis said.

"Yep." I hadn't forgotten that Principal Ellis and my father knew each other. My old man had spies everywhere.

"And do you have plans for the rest of summer?"

"I might visit Japan for a few weeks." I shrugged.

A rare smile graced Principal Ellis's face. "Any particular reason Japan?"

"I like Japan." I smiled. "Maybe this time I'll learn the language."

Principal Ellis tapped his lower lip with his index finger. "I'd always wondered what came first? Japan or Kai."

I froze. Damn. His name gave me pause to this day. That man would haunt me. But I wouldn't give Kai any more space in my head. Itsuma and Scott were *it* for me. Full stop. "How do you remember Kai?"

"He's a child services officer." Without skipping a beat, he said, "He was your best friend when you both attended here."

I stared at Principal Ellis. "You remember that?"

He downed the rest of his amber beer. "I keep tabs on *unusual* students. You, Kai, Itsuma, Scott, Arthur…" he whispered the last name. Who was Arthur?

One thing I noticed—the unusual students were all male. *I wonder.* "So what makes us unusual?"

Principal Ellis shot me his iron blue eyes. In that look, the answer became clear. I pulled back. "No way," I huffed. I so badly wanted to ask him straight out, *are you homosexual?*

"Well, Mr. Reis, stay out of trouble."

I could take a hint. His demeanor screamed keep your hands off my students. I understood him more. Too bad I couldn't commiserate with him. I set my glass down, nodded to Principal Ellis and walked away from my old high school for the second last time.

♂♂♂

When I got home, it was the same routine. Bath, prepare for the Prince, restock the couch pockets with lube and condoms. Hydrate.

I no longer had to mentally prepare. Itsuma was brutal, but he also knew my limits. Today he was late. Texting got no response. Same thing with calling. No result. He was leaving tomorrow. Maybe he wasn't one for goodbyes. That smart. Leaving without so much as a kiss. The later it got, the more I resigned myself to the notion that he wasn't coming. Well, if he wasn't going to come to me, I'd go to him.

At seven I grabbed my coat, my keys and wallet and Itsuma barged through my front door.

"You're late." Relief flooded my heart. He was here!

Half out of breath, Itsuma stood and stared at me. His hands were shaking.

"What's wrong?" I glanced over him to make sure he was alright. This lost little boy look was not the Itsuma I knew.

He leaned back, closed and locked the front door. His eyes shut. His Adam's apple bobbed. "I think I did something really crazy."

Welcome to the club. "What did you do?"

A wash of triumph splashed over his face. "I said no."

This could be really good or really bad. "To who?"

His Cheshire smile appeared. "My parents."

It took me a moment. "You told them you weren't going to Japan?"

"Yeah."

Shock and concern hit me first. "But your education?"

"It's not like I haven't followed Scott around for years. Why stop now?"

That wasn't what I'd meant when I told him he'd have to make his own choices. "It should be your decision."

Itsuma straightened and walked over to me. "It is. I want this. I choose you and Scott."

"Are you sure? This was your chance to be independent."

"If I can do whatever I want, then I can do it wherever I want. But you're here. You're planning your life here."

"I'm not a reason to be held down."

"You don't hold me down." He hugged me. "You set me free."

What could I do but hug him back? His words hit me hard. "What did you tell your parents?"

"I ripped the plane ticket in half and said I wasn't going."

"That must have gone over well."

He laughed. "Yeah, well, I'm paying the consequences now."

"Ohhh, what happened?"

"I'm looking for a place to live, for starters."

"Oh." I bit my lower lip. "You can stay here."

Itsuma bent down and kissed me on the lips. "Thank you, but you're right. There are some things I should do on my own. This—I have to do. It's my hole, I'll climb out of it."

There was a naughty retort in there, but pride spread from my toes to the smile on my face. He was right. A man needed to have his own living space for a while.

"Bottom line is you're not leaving."

He shook his head. "I'm not leaving."

"What are you going to do?"

"Figure it out as I go along."

I was happy, but also sad. T University was a good school. He'd been accepted. I almost opened my mouth to tell him I could help him through any college he wanted to go to, but thought better of it. He wanted to prove to himself he could make it. In the two months I'd known him, my perception of Itsuma had grown from self-centered prince to strong, responsible lover.

"Don't look so forlorn, Sensei."

"I was just thinking how much you've changed."

"I haven't changed that much." He bent down and slipped me another kiss.

My muscles melted. His hands reached down to cup my ass. I'd well-oiled myself for a goodbye and was ready for action. I deepened our kiss and moaned.

Itsuma pulled back. "I'd love to play, but I have to sell my car, find a place and get a job."

My sex-addled brain couldn't change gears. "What?"

Before I knew what was happening, Itsuma was stepping outside.

"I'll get back with you when I get settled."

"Itsuma?" Bereft, I stared at the closed front door. A pitiful whimper escaped my lips. Nothing like getting what I wanted and it turning out exactly the opposite of what I thought that something would be.

Chapter 21

One month later

Apprised of the lead professor's hatred of tardy people, I arrived early in the lecture hall where I'd meet him. A tap, tap, tap on the tile floor echoed off the short hallway and a man in a heavy trench coat carried a walking cane inside.

His frail body contrasted with his strong aura. He wasn't unattractive, but he looked like a converted goth. Hand cream had more color. Dr. Tennison was thin, pale and impeccably dressed. But those sunken cheeks and blue veins made him seem sickly.

"Good morning, Mr. Reis, my name is Dr. John Tennison."

I shook the hand of the professor for abstract continuity theory. "Very nice to meet you, sir."

"Likewise."

"We'll have to get used to each other. You're my first assistant."

"Oh really?" I smiled. "Dean Puzo said you'd had several." I'd been warned. Dr. Tennison had a reputation. Not a good one. But he was a genius in the fields of mathematics, chemistry and just about anything to do with biology. Rumor had it he was on the verge of curing fibromyalgia.

"I don't consider the namby-pambies sent my way as being any kind of assistants."

Oh great. Pompous much? Still, he had a certain charm.

"However," he said, "Chancellor Pierce assured me you'd last longer than a day."

"Then let's endeavor for a semester."

A tiny smile cracked his perfect face. "I should make you aware of my condition."

"Condition?" That was rather frightening.

"I have, only once, fainted in my lecture hall."

That piqued my interest.

"I have lupus. Most of the campus seems to know."

"Ah." I wiggled a finger in the air. "I'm to keep an eye on you."

"Certainly not. You are a proper assistant. I chose you from your interview. You were the least stupid."

"Thanks…" I gave an inward sigh. If I could deal with Itsuma's arrogance, then I could handle JT's pompous stature.

"I have one rule."

"Only one?" My teasing nature overtook my common sense. I should really get along with this guy.

He pursed his lips. "Don't be late."

"Right." That was something I'd been told was a deal breaker for Dr. Tennison. "Anything else?"

His real smile was awkward, as if he didn't use the muscles around his lips much. "We should make it up as we go along."

Students started pouring in and I took my place at the desk while Dr. Tennison wrote on the overhead projector.

I was scanning paperwork when I felt—him. The room filled with an electric energy undeniably Itsuma.

I looked up, and in walked my Prince. My heart skipped when Scott filed in right behind. Like an idiot, I stared with a slack jaw. Scott blushed and waved. Itsuma gave me an arrogant *sup* head-nod. I jerked my eyes down and pretended to read.

For the next half-hour, I snuck guilty glances over at my two lovers. Dr. Tennison went straight into material. He was the type that expected everyone to have their books bought before the first day. A few students shared their copy. Scott shared his book with a cute blonde next to him. She was doing her best to either embarrass him to death or, more likely, try to interest him. Itsuma didn't have a book, but he took notes and focused on Dr. Tennison with the same intensity he used to figure out abstract algebra. By the end of the session, I was—almost—used to them being there.

I expected them to approach me. To say hi. To make a scene. But all I got was a wink and an *I'll call ya later* hand signal from Itsuma. Scott craned his neck to see me till he tripped over his seatmate who'd shared his text book. He mumbled an apology. Adorable. I was right. College kids were more mature.

Epilogue

The four Coopers now *rented* the house I owned. Tommy swung from the monkey bars in the backyard. He'd just gotten the cast off his arm and was going wild with two free hands. Aubrey was upstairs working on her computer, writing an article. She was the youngest freelance PR person I'd ever known. Waunita was in the kitchen with Itsuma teaching him how to not burn water. And I was in the warmest lap ever, my arms wrapped around Scott, his hands gripping me tenderly. Gentle, yet strong.

Loved, safe and ours.

"How did it go with your dad?" Scott and his family had another session with Mr. Cooper at Dr. Kleck's office.

"I had to drag Aubrey in with us." Scott tightened his hold on me.

"That good, huh?" I leaned in closer, hoping to steal a kiss.

"It was pretty quiet."

"Meaning nobody said anything." Great. Now my Cowboy was getting the silent treatment.

"It's progress." He leaned in as if ready to catch my waiting lips.

"Well, I guess sitting in the same room is a step forward." I wanted to add *with nobody getting beat on*, but I didn't.

Scott's eyes twinkled. "So is sitting in the same chair."

It had been a while since we talked about what I now called the Exodus Debacle, but we were communicating and figuring out our relationship as we went.

"You and Itsuma are mine." I dipped lower so he could catch my falling lips.

Scott played coy and pulled back. "No, you and Itsuma are mine."

A shadow crept over the two of us. Itsuma crossed his arms and loomed above us. "You both have it wrong. Sensei and Scott are mine." He lowered to his knees.

Scott and I included him in our hug. We huddled in a tight circle with our foreheads leaned in together.

"Together forever." Itsuma squeezed, his hold pulling us tighter.

Scott's rare smile and laughter appeared. "Like the three musketeers."

I kissed each forehead, then whispered for only them to hear, "For as long as you want me."

The End

There will be more *Notice Me Senpai* stories. Care to find out whose book will be next? Updates given at: http://eepurl.com/bAfZR5

Thank you for reading *Seducing Sensei.* Reviews are a tremendous help for authors. If you enjoyed this book writing a review would be a huge boon.

About the Author

Will Write For Puppy Chow!

Slave to a 100 lbs. GSD (German Shepard) and a computer she calls "Dave", you'll often see her riding a 19 hand Shire nicknamed "Gunny" to the local coffee shop near the Santa Monica mountains. Stephanie reads for the love of words, and writes fiction about Dark Hearts and Heroes revolving around social taboos. When ever asked, she'll reply her whole life can be seen through a comic—sometimes twisted, sometimes funny, but always beautiful and its title is adventure. Come play!

http://www.snmckibben.com